Alibi for Murder
Lessons in Murder, Book 12

Edale Lane

Alibi for Murder, Lessons in Murder, Book 12

By Edale Lane

Published by Past and Prologue Press

All rights reserved. No portion of this book may be reproduced in any form without written permission from the publisher or author, except as permitted by U.S. copyright law.

Edited by Melodie Romeo

Cover art by Melodie Romeo

This book is a work of fiction, and all names, characters, places, and incidences are fictional or are used fictitiously. Any resemblance to actual people, places, or events is coincidental.

First Edition, 2025

Copyright © 2025 by Edale Lane

CONTENTS

Ackowlegements	1
1	3
2	9
3	17
4	23
5	30
6	37
7	44
8	50
9	57
10	63
11	70
12	78
13	85
14	92
15	99
16	106
17	113
18	120

19	128
20	137
21	145
22	151
23	158
24	164
25	171
26	177
27	184
28	195
More Books By Edale Lane	202
About the Author	205

ACKOWLEGEMENTS

I appreciate my readers more than you know. A few of you have volunteered as beta readers, who are such a vital part of my editing process, and I want to recognize those who worked on this book: Mark Gaylor, Roe Swierczewski, Marguerite Schaffron, Karen Fitz, Maryann Kafka, and Debbie Fahlman. I also wish to thank my exemplary proofreader, Dione Benson, and my Facebook Group members, who voted on the cover art. Thank you, readers, for you are the lifeblood of this series. I have zounds of ideas for more personal character development and mysteries to solve, and will continue to write them as long as you read them. The last thank you goes to my wonderful partner, Johanna White, who's been with me for every word. Your support and encouragement sustain me.

1

Thursday, October 31

Halloween was a nightmare for Lieutenant Detective Jenna Ferrari as she and Sergeant Detective Ron Owens sprinted, ducked, leaped behind cars, and fired off rounds at their frantic suspects while trying to avoid being shot. Their investigation had led them to the junkyard, littered with rusty old trucks and autos missing fenders, wheels, doors, and engine parts. Expecting to merely interview the owner and his cousin about the car theft ring and chopping operation, they hadn't worn armored vests.

Randi will kill me if I come home wearing a fresh bullet hole, Jenna thought as she ducked behind a wrecked, once-white Ford pickup to catch her breath.

"It's not worth it, Hank!" she yelled. "Drop your weapons and come out with your hands up."

Her entreat was met with a ricocheted gunshot off the hood of the truck. Sirens blared from a distance, their screech growing louder as they neared.

"Look, guys, you won't get out of here alive if you keep this up," warned Owens in a tough, gritty baritone. "Doing ten years is a hell of a lot better than bein' dead forever." The blocky former linebacker Army veteran whipped his Glock around the dented tailgate in a two-handed grip and squeezed off three rounds in the criminals' direction. Jenna's heart raced as she listened to the reports and the ping of bullets striking metal.

"I ain't goin' back to prison!" one bellowed. The sirens whirred louder and closer, reminding the detective backup was nearby. Several more shots showered their position, sending glass flying from the cab windows, and then the stomp of stampeding feet.

Gripping her handgun and squaring her jaw, Jenna rolled out from behind the chassis and aimed at the fleeing junkman in his gray coveralls splotched with oil and grease. "Stop!" she demanded, firing a warning round that blasted apart a hatchback's passenger side mirror inches from his body.

As if in slow motion, she watched the average-looking, tan-skinned fellow in his grime-covered coveralls pivot, the glint of metal catching the light as he aimed his gun. He probably wasn't such a good shot, and his momentum kept him in motion. This was the moment of truth when a decisive action on Jenna's part would determine who went home that day and who didn't. He wore a ragged cap to match the unshaven stubble on his terrified face. This wasn't an evil man. He'd killed no one she was aware of, and yet, if she didn't act in a fraction of a second, he could make her his first.

Jenna wasn't sure which of them fired first. She felt the wind off his bullet as it whizzed past her ear, ruffling her short, black hair; her shot thrust him backward to the weed-infested dirt between old wrecks, his arms and legs flailing as if trying desperately to grab hold of a wisp of air—anything to break his fall.

Owens backed her up with two more shots, and the second suspect stumbled to a stop, twirled his pistol out of firing position, and raised his hands over his head. Facing them with fear and trembling, he yelled, "Don't shoot! Call an ambulance!"

"Drop your gun, Charlie," Owens ordered.

He threw it down with such haste and disgust that one might have thought it was made of molten metal. Then he dropped to his knees beside his cousin.

Uniformed officers poured into the junkyard, and Jenna slowly lowered her weapon with a heavy heart. Holstering it, she jogged over an axle and muffler and around a stack of worn-out tires. *He could still be alive,* she hoped. *Stupid, stupid man!*

Jenna kicked the gun away from Hank's limp hand and crouched to check his pulse. Owens cuffed Charlie and hauled the quivering sack of bones to his feet.

"Oh God!" Charlie bemoaned with an agonizing cry. "Is he dead?"

Hank, bleeding from a solid chest wound, had no pulse. Jenna's training had drilled into her the proper procedure in such a situation—aim for full-body mass and bring the shooter down. She couldn't aim to injure, hoping that would do the trick; she couldn't take her chances on him being such a poor marksman he'd miss. She and Owens had tried to talk them down, given them warnings and chances to surrender. It's not like she wanted to kill the poor bastard.

"God dammit," Jenna muttered under her breath. Lifting her gaze to Charlie, she snapped, "Why'd you do that? Why did the two of you run and then open fire on police officers? This is your fault!"

"Walters promised nobody would get hurt," he wailed. "He said the police wouldn't find out, and, if you did, we were to hightail it and say nothing."

"But you had to pull guns and start shooting at us," Owens added in a tone angry enough to match Jenna's mood.

"We were scared," he lamented. "I had an awful time in prison before. I'd rather die than go back, but I wouldn't rather Hank die. Is he?"

Jenna gave a resolute nod. Officers Girard and Washington took charge of the sobbing prisoner.

"Come on, now," Washington said in a consolatory voice. "We'll get you a lawyer, take your statement, and maybe the DA's office can work out a deal for you. At least you're still in one piece."

Girard added, "Whoever told you crime pays, lied."

Jenna hadn't moved from Hank's motionless body, soaked in blood from a bullet she'd fired into him. "It was a good shoot," Owens stated in assurance. "He was firing right at your head, Ferrari. You did what you had to, so don't beat yourself up. I'd rather it be him than you."

"I'd rather he had come quietly like a sane person would've done," she sighed. Pushing to her feet, Jenna met Owens's gaze. "I know you're right, but I still feel like crap."

Pulling out her phone, Jenna tagged the coroner's office and RPD Internal Affairs. "I need to report an officer-involved shooting at Blueridge Scrap and Save Auto Salvage Yard." She shared the pertinent information and was instructed to report to Captain Myers.

Tucking her phone away, Jenna scanned the acre-wide scrapyard with its blue aluminum building and requisite tow truck. Several uniformed officers busied themselves searching for spent rounds, so ballistics would have something to play with. It was an easy, open-and-shut case since the idiots decided shooting their way out was a grand idea. She suspected Charlie would be despondent and afraid enough to provide the names of everyone else involved in the scheme. His public defender was sure to advise him to.

A screeching bird teased her gaze higher, and she surveyed the splendor of color from changing leaves that circled the valley in a bowl of brown, yellow, orange, and red with pockets of evergreen interspersed. Jenna tried to remember if she'd ever taken time to appreciate the mountains before Randi entered her life. But even nature's grandeur couldn't dislodge the lead ball of remorse weighing down her spirit. This wasn't the first time she'd had to shoot a criminal, nor the first time she'd killed one; still, the experience always made her feel like she'd failed. While her job required her to stop a person posing a lethal threat by any means necessary, her goal was always to arrest a live felon, not send a dead one back in the ME's van.

"I can help you with the report," Owens volunteered.

Jenna glanced back at Hank, lifeless on the ground between a busted-up Cadillac and what remained of an old, original Volkswagen Beetle. "Thanks. Why don't you head back and get started, and I'll bum a ride with Dr. Valentine. I need to stay with the body until he gets here to make sure nobody tampers with evidence or picks his pockets or something. They'll find gunpowder residue on his hands, and we both turned on our body cams, so everything with IA should run smoothly."

As much as she tried to make everything sound official and logical, Jenna only felt the hole ripped into the fabric of the Universe by a wasted life. *Hank, you could have done, been anything,* she thought. "My dad ran a junkyard for most of his life—an honest business, and he made decent money too. We weren't rolling in dough, but it paid the bills. Now he's partnered with my brother in an auto repair shop. He wouldn't have dreamed of turning it into a chop shop for stolen luxury and sports cars and would have decked anyone who proposed the idea. Dad's many things, but a thief isn't one of them." It surprised Jenna that she'd said that aloud.

"No shame in scrap metal reclamation and selling used parts," Owens agreed, "as long as they aren't stolen. Are you sure? I could stay here with you."

Jenna shook her head and rolled her neck as she sensed the building tension. "No need. What could happen with all these eager, beat cops surrounding me like a sea of white knights? I'll ride back with Dr. Valentine, give Captain Myers my report, tackle the Internal Affairs paperwork, and turn my gun into ballistics for them to test. I expect to have it back by tomorrow. Then it's home for a shower."

"Jenna." Stepping closer, her team member and friend laid a broad hand on her shoulder and caught her gaze. "There's nothing else you could have done. It was a good shoot."

"Yeah, I know. Why are criminals so stupid and reckless?" Jenna peered up into the rugged, square face of the man who perpetually wore gray suits and proved he'd always have her back. "Why do they run when they've nowhere to go? Why go from chop shop suspects to attempted murder on a police officer? Do they suffer from some gene deficiency? Did their mothers drop them on their heads when they were infants? I mean, they might think crime equals easy money, but this was so dumb."

Owens shrugged. "I'll take a stupid criminal any day. Just think of what a mess we'd be in if they were all brilliant masterminds with foolproof ways of never getting caught."

"I suppose. Thanks. I'll see you at the office."

Hours later, Jenna trailed into the criminal investigations office, completely drained. Jamison sat at her desk in a stylish beige shell over sleek, dark green slacks, and a ridiculous pointy witch hat atop her flowing strawberry-blonde tresses. Spinning toward the door, she flashed a brilliant smile and stellar green eyes at Jenna. In an instant, her cheerful look faded.

While Detective Trisha Jamison had earned her stripes with solid police work, her true talent lay in reading people. "Owens told me about the shootout," she offered empathetically. Dragging off the costume hat, she set it on her desk beside the paper Jack-o'-lantern and black cat. "I know I'd feel bad too, but you did what you had to, boss. It'll be all right after Randi hugs you up tonight."

The sharp, younger detective was right. Dr. Miranda McLeod, aka Jenna's wife, had a knack for making everything better.

Owens clicked his mouse, and the office printer hummed to life. "I finished my report and sent you a copy to revise from your point of view. It'll save you time."

"Thanks, Sergeant." Jenna shifted her gaze to Specialist Ethan Bauman's empty workstation. His paintings and geeky action figures were missing; so was he.

Jenna would never begrudge Bauman his happiness and, if in his position, she'd probably have made the same choice. Seeing his vacant spot only drove home the reality that he'd been more than an employee or a coworker; his empty chair held a friend-sized hole.

"Yeah, lucky son of a gun," Owens mentioned at her vacant stare. "I'd love to get paid twice my current salary to not get shot at," he laughed.

"The cushy IT job with that civilian security company in Asheville is just the icing," Jamison quipped, joy returning to her tone. "Moving in with Mario is the cake."

"Who'd have thought?" Owens hummed curiously.

Jenna replied, "Well, the heart wants what the heart wants. My heart wants to find somebody tolerable who can do what Bauman did—if such a person exists." Shifting her gaze to the wall over the coffee station, Jenna smiled at the mural Mario had painted of the four of them posed like superheroes hanging on the wall. She could almost feel Bauman's geeky energy lingering in the air and hear his voice over-explaining some technical garble that sounded like Greek to her ears. Another tech specialist, yes; another Ethan, never.

2

Randi sat on a towel on the bathroom floor, her head hung over the toilet, with Byron hovering nearby, displaying anxious concern. She'd known this would be part of it from the onset, but having Jenna's baby—well, Jenna's brother's baby, to be more exact—was worth it. Her eighty-pound German shepherd didn't seem so convinced.

While most women in their first trimester suffer from morning sickness, Randi's system had to be different; she got nauseous in the evening, right around dinnertime. While inconvenient in one regard, she counted it a blessing since she could happily function teaching her classes all day without embarrassing runs to the restroom or turning green in front of the students. But it interfered with her meal routine, and she often couldn't eat until eight or nine at night.

This, too, shall pass, Randi reminded herself. Immediately, her brain began spinning to attribute the famous quote properly. *Abraham Lincoln used it in a speech, but he wasn't the first. King Solomon? There's also a story about a Persian king asking his wise men to come up with a phrase that would be true regardless of the circumstances.* With her stomach churning uncomfortably, Randi surrendered, concluding with a sigh, *It's very old.*

When the door opened, Bryon leaped up from the cool tiles and raced down the hallway to greet Jenna. Bandit, the frequently aloof tuxedo cat, when he wasn't begging for cheese or in a rare affectionate mood, seemed more disturbed than Byron over her stomach distress, keeping his distance while unpleasantries persisted. She detected the thud of his pads over the carpet as he jogged from his hiding place to find a human who might be in good enough repair to fill his bowl.

Jenna didn't sing out a greeting, but Randi knew the sound of her footsteps and the dog didn't bark. Instead, his tail pounded against a wall somewhere, echoing down the hall, through the open bedroom door, to reach her ears in the ensuite.

"Honey, where are you?" There was Jenna's voice, only lacking its usual emotion. She'd been as excited as Randi when the test strip came back positive, and, when she wasn't bouncing with energy, happy to be home, she was spitting mad about something at work. This lackluster tone worried Randi; she suspected something was amiss with her wife, with her day.

"Where do you think?" came her weak reply. "What's wrong?"

Jenna peered at her from the doorway with a pitying expression before moving out of view to change out of her work clothes. "Sweetie, I want to be in there holding your hair back and blotting a wet rag on your face, but I just can't. I know it's ridiculous, what with all the blood and death I work around, but that's the one thing I can't do. If I come in there to help, we'd both be throwing up."

"I know, sweetheart," Randi responded with empathy. "It's OK. That's what hair ties are for." Randi flushed, pushed up, and turned on the water in the sink to wash her face and rinse her mouth. "It will probably only be for a few more weeks. What happened with you today?"

Boots clunked to the floor, and Randi caught sight of Bandit hopping onto the bed to nest in the covers. "I'll tell you later when you're feeling better."

"I'm sorry I wasn't able to make dinner." Randi truly was. She loved cooking and eating; at the moment, she could do neither.

"I think I can heat up a can of soup," Jenna answered. "Could you manage downing some chicken noodle?"

"You mean those cans with all the extra salt and preservatives?" Randi bemoaned. But beggars couldn't be choosers. A few nitrates wouldn't kill her. "I suppose. Thank you."

Although Jenna met her with a pitying look when Randi exited the bathroom, seeing her wife half-naked in a black bra, revealing an abundance of delectable cleavage, and matching tight, low-rise boxer briefs squeezed over the most enticingly round, pinchable butt God ever bestowed upon a woman, color returned to Randi's cheeks. Jenna's short, black hair, tousled from undressing, framed a kind, intelligent face.

"I'm sorry you have to go through all this sickness," Jenna apologized. She reached for a T-shirt. "Do you think you're done in there for a few minutes?"

Randi smiled, leaning on the doorframe, soaking in the spectacular view. "I feel much better, thank you. Do you want to shower before tackling the daunting task of heating soup from a can?"

"Hey!" Jenna threw the T-shirt at Randi with a sarcastic smirk. "After the day I've had, I deserve a hot shower."

Stepping out of the doorway, Randi tossed the shirt back at Jenna. "Steam away, but don't be sorry about me getting the full pregnancy experience. I wouldn't have it any other way. I just hope I don't gain a hundred pounds that I'll never be able to lose."

By then, Jenna had crossed the room. She touched Randi's arm and kissed her cheek. "I'm confident that you won't. You've managed to feed me without me blowing up like an elephant—although I've noticed a few extra happy pounds clinging to my butt."

Curving her hand around the flesh in question, Randi raised a discerning brow. "Feels perfect to me."

The doorbell rang, Bandit flew off the bed, and Byron ran to the front of the house, barking out an alarm at full volume. "Who the hell could that be?" Jenna frowned, clinging to the wadded T-shirt as if it could protect her from being surprised.

Randi brushed a kiss on her forehead. "Trick-or-treaters, sweetie. It's Halloween, remember? I'll get it. I put a bowl of candy by the front door. You shower, make dinner, and then tell me about today. I'll take care of the kiddies."

"Sounds like a plan." While Jenna commandeered the bathroom, Randi went to answer the door.

"Hush, Byron!" she scolded. "It's just children who want candy, not an axe murderer."

The big dog whined, took one step from in front of the door to let her squeeze by, and peered up with a forlorn expression as if to ask, "Are you sure? I should stay here and protect you."

"Trick or treat!" A trio of a clown, a witch, and Bluey bounced at the door, holding out plastic shopping bags already half-filled with candy. Either a young mother or someone's older sister stood a few feet behind the kids, wearing normal clothes and an amused smile.

"Well, my goodness!" Randi exclaimed, relieved she wasn't about to hurl on them. "I don't want a trick, so I'd better give you all a treat."

She held out the bowl, expecting them to each select a piece, when three hands plunged in, retracting fistfuls. "Thanks!" the little witch exclaimed. "I won't have to turn you into a toad."

Randi pretended to shiver. "A toad? Oh, not a toad, please—all those warts!"

The kids' chaperone laughed. "They love coming to your house every year," she admitted. "You always have decorations and the front porch light on. Thank you."

"Well, I enjoy seeing all the cool costumes," Randi replied. "Come back next year."

"We will!" called Bluey as they hopped down the driveway to head to the next house.

"See ya." The presumed adult waved, pivoted, and trailed after the children. "Stay away from the road!"

Randi lingered at the door, a smile gracing her lips, as she pictured taking her little boy or girl out in a cute costume to collect candy on Halloween. They would only go to people's houses they knew to ensure no tricks or tainted candy. It was ridiculous how risky every little pleasure had become in this generation. You just couldn't trust anybody, and that was sad. Maybe Jenna would get off work early enough to make the rounds with them. It would be fun if they all had a costume—like she and Jenna could be Tweedle Dee and Tweedle Dum while their daughter dressed as Alice or their son as the White Rabbit. No, no! They could dress as Mandalorians, and their child would wear a baby Yoda costume! *What was the little guy's name?* she pondered. *It's not baby Yoda—that's just what everyone calls him.*

Hearing loud chatter and clomping feet, Randi glanced up to spot another group coming and smiled. Byron sprang into alert mode. "Sit," she commanded. He obeyed with a whine and licked his chops. "Be good, Byron. Halloween only comes once a year."

By nine o'clock, Randi felt completely normal, besides being exhausted for no reason. Her school day hadn't been taxing, nor had running to the door to pass out candy all night. She knew it was the wonderful changes taking place in her body that caused the fatigue.

Stretching out on the couch, she lay her head on Jenna's shoulder and snuggled in while they watched TV. Jenna had popped the tab on her second beer by then. "Are you ready to tell me what happened?" Randi asked.

Jenna gulped through half her can, set it down, and wrapped an arm around Randi. Resting her head atop Randi's, she lowered the volume with the remote control before dropping it on the cushion beside her. "You make me feel human—like I'm not a robot or a monster or a piece of some giant machine that makes the world go. And I don't like to worry you with unpleasant talk of work, but I know you'll be mad at me if I don't tell you, and heaven forbid you find out on some social media video."

Jenna's fingers circled the skin on Randi's arms lightly, and Randi waited, pleasured by Jenna's touch.

"There was a shootout today at that junkyard off Highway 460," she confessed. Randi shot up in alarm, staring at Jenna anxiously, searching for the truth in her blue eyes. "Relax," Jenna chided, pulling her back to her protectively. "I'm all right ... just not the other guy."

"You shot someone?" Randi asked tenderly.

"Yeah, and he didn't make it."

Randi sat up and twisted on the sofa to envelop Jenna in her arms. "I know you hate it when that happens, but, when they shoot at you, they leave you no choice. Are you OK?"

"I will be," Jenna promised. "I was asking Owens why criminals have to be so dumb."

"Most people appear dumb next to you," Randi reasoned. "Especially criminals. Still, you should talk to Dr. Grayson tomorrow, even if the department doesn't require you to."

"Jamison said I just need you to hug me up and I'll be fine," Jenna relayed. Pulling back, she smiled at Randi, peering into her eyes. "I think she's right."

Their lips met in an affirming kiss, a gentle connection brimming with compassion, condolence, and understanding. "I'll hold you all night, my love, and would drive away all your demons if I could," Randi avowed. "You should still tell Dr. Grayson."

"I suppose."

Randi brushed Jenna's lips with hers before settling back into her embrace. "But you closed the case?"

"We arrested the dead guy's partner, and, after his cousin was killed, he's eager to flip on the dude who hired them to doctor the stolen cars. We'll have to haul in the operation's boss and gather more evidence, but just routine stuff. I haven't forgotten about your prenatal appointment on Monday and will make it a priority to be there. This pregnancy is for both of us, even if you're doing all the hard parts."

"Oh, there'll be plenty of hard parts for you when the kid's older and we have to say 'No' to something he or she wants to do."

Jenna snickered. "Hard for you, maybe. I have no problem putting my foot down with a firm, 'No.'"

"Yeah, yeah, you say that now," Randi teased. "Just wait. And I can't recall a time you've put your foot down and said 'no' to me."

"Hey, that's different! Your special requests, while sometimes unconventional, always end up entertaining me. It's not like you're going to want to watch an R-rated movie when you're eight or say you're spending the night at a friend's house so you can both sneak off to a graveyard to say some creepy words out of a fake spell book. You don't beg to stay up past your bedtime or have sweets before dinner or any of those crazy kids' things. I can certainly say 'no' to stuff like that without blinking."

"That's my tough cop!" Randi chimed with a grin. "Remember that when our precious little one peers at you with sad eyes and their bottom lip quivers like they're about to cry."

Veering slightly off topic, Jenna asked, "Are they doing an ultrasound? Will we find out if it's a boy or a girl? Do you even want to know before it's born?"

Randi's fingers found the front of Jenna's robe and dipped inside to connect with her warm skin. "I don't know. Do you?" When Jenna didn't answer, Randi launched into pro and con mode. "It's fun to wait and be surprised—well, sort of. It'll either be a boy or a girl, so fifty-fifty. Back in the old days, friends would take bets and grandmothers would share ways they could predict the baby's sex. But if we knew, we could start decorating the nursery, buying clothes, and picking out names. We could say 'he' or 'she' instead of 'they' or 'it' when referring to the baby. Then again, we could just go with gender-neutral clothes, names, and décor, unfettered by society's norms. What do you think?"

"I think it will be hard enough on the kid having two moms instead of a traditional family, especially the way the current climate is leaning," Jenna mused with a touch of concern. "We don't want to give it some hippie name or paint rainbows and unicorns everywhere."

"Conservative is good," Randi agreed. "Besides being a progressive lesbian, I'm quite traditional. As to which room to convert into a nursery—"

"The home gym," Jenna decisively declared. "We can move it into the garage and give it a makeover. There'll still be room for my motorcycle, and I don't have to keep my car in there. If yours can be out in the weather, so can mine, and, no, you aren't giving up your office. Especially with your plan of taking the next school year off for your sabbatical, you'll need your office for research, writing academic papers, and whatever else you're supposed to use your time off for. I love the workout room you created for me—for us—but Junior comes first."

"OK." Randi had been thinking along the same lines but hadn't wanted to assume. She was happy Jenna was adamant about it. "Gym equipment, floor mat, inspirational posters, and bamboo trees move to the garage. We have lots of time, though. We don't have to do it this weekend."

"No, but I don't want to wait too long," Jenna said. "I'm excited about helping decorate the baby's room. I didn't think I'd be so into it, but the more tangible it becomes, the more I realize I *really* want this child. He, she, they'll be *ours*. I'm still terrified of everything that could go wrong, but I've been trained to handle it. I'll tell you the truth; if I'd just shot and killed someone who was trying to hurt our child, I wouldn't be heavy-hearted and conflicted over it one bit. It's just that this guy—and he wasn't all that bad either—was so stupid. You don't point a gun at an armed police officer unless you want to die. Maybe that was it, but I don't think so. He just panicked. I hate that I had to kill him."

"I know, sweetie," Randi comforted, expanding her heart energy to encompass Jenna in its magnetic vibrations. "I know and God knows, and, even though there's nothing to forgive, you're forgiven all the same. Everything will be all right."

3

Friday, November 1st

Back home as a kid, Jenna would have attended a special All Saints' Day mass to commemorate the souls of everyone of note who had passed, including any family members she might have known. One year, her private Catholic school in Paris, Kentucky, had packed up all the kids on buses and driven to the cemetery—where the school's founder, Father Francis, was buried—so they could pray to him for guidance. Other years, they'd spent the day researching various saints and listening to stories about their lives, sacrificial acts, or miracles they'd supposedly performed. Today, she, Owens, ADA Altman, Charlie Sullivan, and his idealistic public defender, Kyle Konrad, sat together in an interview room, ironing out all the details of the auto theft ring and Charlie's deal.

Back in the bullpen, she typed her report while Jamison and Owens, along with two squad cars for backup, went to arrest Holden and Kassy Cole. Jamison had secured a search warrant based on Charlie's testimony and, with any luck, the miserable case would be closed before supper, and she could enjoy her weekend with the wife she adored.

No skating, rock climbing, or other activities where she could fall, Jenna mused, *and wine tastings are out, even though it's the right time of year for them. We could go to the movies. Randi loves buttery popcorn.*

Her thoughts were interrupted when CSI Destiny Wilcox strolled into her office carrying a gun in a plastic bag. "Lieutenant Ferrari, I thought you'd want this back," she said, setting the package on Jenna's desk. A soft smile shone from her warm, earthy face. "Ballistics is done with it, and Captain Myers said you're all clear."

"Thanks," Jenna answered. She stared at the police-issued pistol she carried like an office clerk would a pen.

"You should take it downstairs to the indoor range and obliterate a target sheet." The astute suggestion emanated from the doorway, not from the woman who leaned on Jenna's desk. Recognizing the timbre of her voice, Jenna swiveled her chair to meet Dr. Jane Grayson's gaze. The psychiatrist was stunning, as always, decked out in monochrome shades of white, black, and gray that mirrored her hair color. Her heels and solid ebony pencil skirt accentuated her shapely legs and hips while the pattern of her blouse and blazer's cut reminded Jenna of her professional capacity as the department shrink. No matter how in love with Randi she was, Jenna could never look at Dr. Grayson without a proper amount of appreciation for the older woman's timeless beauty.

"Dr. Grayson," Jenna acknowledged, rising from her seat for no apparent reason. "I meant to come see you."

"Jane," she said, wagging a finger, a barely contained smile pursing on her lips. "When are you going to call me Jane?"

"Old habits die hard," Jenna confessed.

"They do, but only if you tarry in forming new ones." With graceful strides, the woman who'd helped put Jenna back together almost two years ago sashayed into the cop office as easily as if attending an afternoon cotillion.

"That's good advice. I need to get back on the horse that threw me before fear settles in. Wilcox, anything else relevant I should know?"

"The uniforms and CSIs recovered bags of slugs and shell casings from the junkyard, but probably not all of them," she reported. "I expect Sergeant Detective Owens will call on us soon to collect evidence from the Coles' residence. Too bad we won't be able to recover all the stolen cars since some were already modified and sold out of state, but we recovered a few that are still in mostly original condition in the garage at the Scrap and Save."

"Good, thanks, good work," Jenna praised. "Give me the makes and models and I'll contact the owners."

"Will do." Destiny's mouth curved. "Go shoot that gun first, though. See you later. Dr. Grayson," she acknowledged as she passed the psychiatrist.

Jenna picked up the gun, unzipped the plastic bag, and clipped the holster onto her belt. "I was going to come see you," she declared again sheepishly.

"Any issues with flashbacks?" Dr. Grayson asked.

"No, not like that," Jenna answered, shaking her head. "I just don't like taking a life, especially when it was just stupidity."

"Thank the gods for that," her therapist replied with relief. "It's when an officer doesn't get a pain in the gut after shooting a suspect that I start to worry. Your response is healthy, Jenna. Just don't let it drown you. I heard you and Randi are trying to have a baby."

"Boy, news travels fast!" Jenna stopped beside Dr. Grayson—Jane. No. The older, elite Columbia graduate would always be Dr. Grayson to her. *I don't remember mentioning it, so how could she hear anything? I swear, if psychics were real, she'd be one.*

"It does." The woman's green eyes twinkled at Jenna from behind her designer glasses, while her angular face filled with amusement. "Congratulations will be forthcoming, I presume."

"Thanks," Jenna answered bashfully. "We're excited about it—terrified, but excited."

Dr. Grayson laughed. "And that's normal too. Jenna, you and Randi will be wonderful parents. I doubt I'll ever see your child outside of social functions, and you'd better invite me to the shower."

Jenna's face and mind went completely blank. "Shower? Another one?"

Laughing, Dr. Grayson brushed lint from the shoulder of Jenna's pin-striped button-up shirt. "Yes, another one. Randi needs a baby shower a few weeks before her due date."

"Well, we have to be pregnant first," she replied. Although Randi was one hundred percent positive that she was, she didn't want to make it official yet. "Anything else I should know?"

"I doubt I can tell you something that your professor wife hasn't already researched. Just relax and don't stress too much. Tell me how you feel after the shooting range."

"Will do."

Jenna agreed it was productive therapy to handle her gun and shoot off the rounds this soon after the incident. She knew she had acted in accordance with police policy, rules, and procedures, but being reminded and affirmed by others helped. Feeling thirsty, Jenna stopped by vending on her way back to the criminal investigations office, presuming it would still be empty. *I need to talk to Captain Myers about a replacement for Bauman,* she thought. Suddenly, his voice filled her ears with an uncharacteristic urgency.

"Ferrari, a call just came in," he declared.

Seeing the tension in his neck, the grave expression that hardened his authoritative face, and the slight quiver in his hand on the door handle, every nerve in Jenna's body shot to attention. When her drink bottle thunked to the bottom of the machine, she didn't move to retrieve it. She knew her captain, and this was his "all-hands-on-deck emergency" cue.

"Judge Lester Hamden was just shot and killed outside his residence. Call in your team," he directed. "Everything else goes on hold. Chief Clarkson will meet us there. I already tagged Dr. Valentine."

Stunned, Jenna blinked and absently reached for her Diet Coke. "Judge Hamden? Shot? But he's running for Congress," she said, retrieving her drink. Her brain wasn't ready to process this information. "The election is next Tuesday. I already voted for him early in case I couldn't make it to the polls on the fifth."

"Yeah, me too. Hurry up and pull it together, Ferrari. The news is about to break, and we'll be neck-deep in reporters. Mayor Tackett tagged me to lead the investigation, and I need my best detective operating on all cylinders."

"Yes, sir," she responded crisply. "It's just a shock, is all. You can count on us, sir, but I need a tech specialist to replace Bauman."

"I'm assigning the boy wonder out of cyber crimes to you, along with two uniformed officers of your choice dedicated to this investigation alone."

"Murphy and Stone," Jenna quickly answered. "Stone is seasoned, and Murphy is as sharp as a whip."

"They're yours. Let's get moving," he ordered. "Patrol cars are already on the scene, and they've spotted no sign of a suspect."

"Right." Following on Myers's heels, Jenna hurried to her car while she tagged Jamison.

"Jamison, where are you and Owens?"

"At the Cole's residence. They aren't home, but—"

"Pass it to Girard and Campbell," she clipped as she slid behind the wheel. "I'm sending you an address. You and Owens get there fast, lights and sirens, run every traffic signal. Someone just murdered Judge Hamden."

Jenna clicked off the call and texted the judge's address to her partner. Willing her hands not to shake, Jenna popped the blue light she kept for emergencies onto the roof of her Honda and peeled out of the parking lot. She understood exactly what was at stake and the scrutiny the department would be under. If the election was over and Hamden had won, the Feds would be taking over this case. As it was, he was still a Roanoke County judge—chief circuit court judge of Virginia District 23, to be exact. She'd testified in his courtroom on numerous occasions, and, while they weren't on a first-name basis, she respected Lester as a man and a judge. This was going to be a rough ride, with no time for sentiment to get in the way. Everything would have to be handled by the book with no screw-ups. With the election only days away, the entire country would hear about this and be watching Roanoke—watching her.

Poor Judge Hamden's family, she thought as she weaved around traffic, tiny light and siren whirring. Hardening her jaw, Jenna swore she'd find who did this and make them pay. *Now that half-baked Congressman Cochran will keep his seat for another term by default. I'll bet he goes on TV, making a big deal of how tragic it is and that his opponent's killer must be brought to justice.* She ground her teeth and held back tears. They would have to wait. She had a job to do.

4

Jenna pulled up to the curb behind the ME's wagon a few minutes before five o'clock, the sun streaming in at a steep angle from the west. Other squad cars and official vehicles lined the street with a small army of uniforms, keeping curious neighbors at a generous distance. Detective Jamison and Officer Murphy stood across the street, consoling a woman with long, dark hair and two teenage boys, distraught and beset by tears.

The judge's wife and sons, no doubt. Though Jenna hadn't met them, she'd once seen a family photo in his chambers. *There's an older daughter too*, she recalled. They would have to wait.

Jenna glanced around as she walked toward Captain Myers, Dr. Valentine, and the victim, who still lay where he had fallen. According to the timeline, he couldn't have been dead for more than half an hour. Owens had his notepad out, talking to a chubby, middle-aged woman with short, curly hair dyed in Mardi Gras colors. *A witness, I hope.*

"Good, you're here," Myers acknowledged gravely. "Detective Jamison took some photos, but then Judge Hamden's family arrived home, and I sent her to handle them. We've got officers searching the area for a suspect and canvassing the neighbors. Hopefully, somebody saw something. Owens is with the 911 caller now. I tagged Hendrix, the tech guy, and he's back at the office scrounging for any traffic cam photos that might show a suspicious vehicle entering or leaving the neighborhood. No traffic cameras in here, naturally."

The neighborhood, while not filled with ostentatious mansions, possessed a quiet, affluent atmosphere, boasting a low crime rate, making it statistically one of the safest places to live in greater Roanoke. The houses projected a classic charm with large, manicured yards, attached garages, and pleasant shade trees. If Jenna remembered correctly, it was the same area where Jamison's parents lived, with a country club close enough to drive to in a golf cart.

"I haven't moved the body," Dr. Valentine reported, "only took a liver temp and made a cursory examination of the point of entry. Judge Hamden was shot in the back at medium range with a large-caliber weapon. I'll need to turn him over to determine if it was a through-and-through or if we have a bullet."

"Only one gunshot wound?" Jenna asked. She knelt beside the body of a man shy of fifty, fit, with neat brown hair, under six feet tall, wearing a lightweight, wool-blend, navy blue suit and black shoes, lying face down in freshly cut grass. A breeze floated several autumn leaves from the chestnut oak that sprawled between the driveway and front door of the stately, columned ranch-style house.

"That's correct," Dr. Valentine stated. "Our shooter must possess some skill."

"The witness reported hearing only one shot," the captain confirmed.

Jenna looked at Myers's official SUV parked at the curb, judging the distance from the road to the body. "Could have been a slow drive by, but let's go over this lawn with a fine-toothed comb for a shell casing or footprints." She patted his back pocket, detecting a wallet, while Myers called for an officer to get a metal detector. With as many people as had tromped through by now, Jenna suspected there wouldn't be any usable footprints.

The victim's wallet was stuffed with debit and credit cards, along with a hundred and twenty dollars in cash. This wasn't a robbery. It was exactly what it looked like—an assassination.

"What are you thinking?" Captain Myers asked.

Pushing up to her feet, Jenna met his gaze. "He was shot in the back, not up close, so the killer is a coward," she began. "But it also comes across as impersonal. There are no signs of a struggle, no messages left at the scene to speak to motive, and it's doubtful Judge Hamden even saw who shot him. It wasn't about punishment, as he wasn't kidnapped and tortured, and it wasn't a robbery. This was an execution, and professionally done, judging by the lack of evidence and witnesses."

"You think an enemy put out a hit on him?" Chief Joe Clarkson stepped up beside the captain, pinning Jenna with a disturbed expression. Compared to Myers and Valentine, the sixty-three-year-old leader of the force appeared downright short, although such was not the case compared to Jenna's diminutive height. A stocky man with close-cropped gray hair and a clean-shaven square jaw, Clarkson ran a tight ship. Under his leadership, the department had seen an increase in minority representation, including women and persons of color. He had instituted vital upgrades such as body camera usage, embracing advances in technology, and ensuring every officer was equipped with bulletproof vests.

"I can't say after a brief assessment of the scene," Jenna admitted, "but I'm sure a judge and candidate for Congress would have made some enemies. We'll find out who they are, follow every lead, and give this investigation our full attention until the killer is apprehended and we've amassed a mountain of evidence against him or her."

The chief nodded. "Dr. Valentine, let's get him out of here. The vultures are circling."

The noise Jenna heard from down the street, the shouts of questions, and the bustle of feet, could only mean the media had arrived.

"Will do," the tall, black-haired ME affirmed in his New England accent. "I'll have everything I can give you as soon as possible, but it would seem the shot to his back, probably compromising his heart based on its location, is the preliminary cause of death. I will treat him with the professional courtesy he deserves, Chief."

"I appreciate that," Clarkson replied. Turning to Captain Myers, he instructed, "Find the son of a bitch who killed Les. He wasn't just a respected judge; he was also a friend. I'll give my condolences to his family and then tackle the reporters. Get me an update once the scene has been properly inspected and cleared."

"Yes, sir," Myers responded. As the chief crossed the street to the grieving widow and children, Myers pivoted to Jenna. "I want everything you find, every witness statement, each tiny shred of evidence you uncover copied to me immediately. I'll be dropping in your office regularly as well. Chief Clarkson wants me hands on on this one. Whatever you need, you've got. Understand?"

For an instant, Jenna's spirits brightened. "Can we get one of those rapid DNA forensic testing machines?" She gave him a hopeful look. "The one our lab has takes twenty-four hours, but there are new ones on the market that can render suspect identification analysis in as fast as two hours. I believe that would be extremely beneficial to the department."

Jenna had been dropping hints and voicing wishes about a new machine since her visit to Kentucky last year, when she learned that Lexington's criminal investigations lab had the advanced equipment. Captain Myers narrowed his eyes at her. "We need a suspect and some DNA evidence before that will matter." Twisting his lips, he grumbled, "It's expensive."

"I know," Jenna muttered, her inspired moment deflated. "But when every minute counts—"

"I'll make some calls," Myers ceded, "but no promises. Now, do your thing."

"Captain, Lieutenant," Dr. Valentine said as two attendants saw to the body. "There's no exit wound in the judge's chest, so I should have a slug for ballistics to analyze."

"At least that's something," Jenna sighed.

She took a last look at the gurney with a black body bag holding what remained of a man she admired. *I hope Randi's right, and he's in a better place now,* she thought. *Either way, I'll discover who did this and lock them up forever.*

Jenna slowly wandered around the yard, weaving in and out of uniformed officers, one with a metal detector as they searched the lawn, picturing where Hamden had been standing, approximating where the killer would have to have been. Her best guess at this point was somewhere near or on the sidewalk. *Was he on foot? In a vehicle?* She frowned at the captain's SUV and squatted down to peer under it.

"Did you drop something, Lieutenant?"

Not needing to look up at the familiar voice, Jenna pictured the Boy Scout patrol officer with his cute dimples and sandy blond hair. "No."

Officer Matt Murphy wasn't a rookie anymore, but, even when he had been, she'd found him eager, honest, and capable. "Murphy, can you get under there and look for anything probative? A fresh oil drop, a shell casing, a piece of bubble gum or cigarette butt? Our shooter might have been where Captain Myers's SUV is parked."

"Sure thing." In a flash, the lean young man ducked under the chassis, scooting around on his belly like a writhing snake, inspecting the asphalt with the scrutiny one might employ when seeking buried treasure. "So far, I don't see anything, but we'll need to move the vehicle in case a clue rests under the tires."

"Thanks, Murphy."

"Hey, Ferrari." Owens ambled up to her. "The witness, Mrs. Maureen Galileo, retired schoolteacher, is the Hamdens' next-door neighbor. She heard the shot, at first thinking a car or motorcycle backfired. But when her little dog wouldn't stop barking, she stepped outside to look around and spotted the judge lying on the ground. She immediately phoned 911, then ran over to see if he needed help, if there was something she could do," he reported. "Upon seeing all the blood and that he wasn't moving, she stayed back and swears she didn't touch anything. According to both Mrs. Galileo and the responding officers, they were here within five minutes of the call."

"Did she see or hear a person?" Jenna asked urgently.

Owens's face drooped even more until he resembled a basset hound. "No, nobody. Just the bang."

"How many minutes between hearing the shot and stepping outside?"

"Maybe one, two tops. She said her dog alerts her to everyone who goes by, especially strangers," Owens conveyed.

"Did the dog start barking before or after the shot?" Without waiting for Owens to answer, Jenna trotted over to where the woman stood, wearing a sweater that in no way matched her colorful spray of curls.

"Mrs. Galileo, I'm Lieutenant Detective Ferrari. I know Sergeant Detective Owens already took your statement, but I need clarification. Did your dog begin to bark before or after the shot was fired?"

"After." The studious woman in her wire-rimmed glasses stood about Jenna's height and fixed her with a look of certainty. "Tilly doesn't miss a thing that happens on our street. That's curious, isn't it?" she asked, cocking her head. "If a stranger had walked past our house on the way to the Hamdens', she would have sounded the alarm, but I'm sure she only started barking after we heard the shot. I didn't think it was a gun," she added in dismay. "There's never been a shooting in the fifteen years we've lived here. My husband and I—he's a plastic surgeon," the woman added with pride, "have always had peace of mind knowing it's a safe neighborhood. But now ...."

She shook her head and hugged herself. "Lester was such a nice man. Tim and I volunteered with his campaign. It would have been quite the thing to tell our friends that we lived next door to a U.S. congressman. I feel positively awful for his kids. I taught his daughter, Anna, when she was in seventh grade—lovely girl, so kind and well-behaved. She's in college now, I think."

Normally, Jenna welcomed rambling witnesses because they revealed much more than they knew, but she needed to find this shooter pronto. "Back to Tilly," Jenna steered the woman. "How long after you heard the shot before you went outside to check?"

"Oh, it mustn't have been but a minute or two," Mrs. Galileo mused. "She was very insistent that something was amiss. Sweet little girl—Tilly must have sensed the nice man next door needed help. I still can't wrap my mind around it; somebody *murdered* Lester, right here on his front lawn. I won't be able to sleep for a week." A tear formed in the corner of her eye, and she dabbed at it. "Poor Amanda and the boys."

That reminded Jenna that now was the best time to talk to them. Even though she trusted Jamison to comfort, console, and ask all the right questions, she needed to speak with them, give them her card, and make sure they had somewhere to go where they'd feel safe. She didn't believe they were in danger, but precautions must be taken anyway.

"Thank you, Mrs. Galileo," Jenna said and handed her a card. "If you think of anything else, please call me."

Owens followed her across the street. "I was going to answer your question, but then you ran off," he grumbled. "You harangue me into taking the sergeant's test, then when I get the promotion you—"

"That's not it, Ron," she cut him off. "We have to work fast and can't miss a step. The world is watching, and it's my butt on the line."

"I thought Captain Myers is in charge of the case."

"He is," Jenna confirmed. "But we're the ones who have to solve it. You know he hasn't been in the field for years, and, while he was an outstanding detective in his day, riding a desk is bound to have smoothed out his edge. Please don't take anything I say or do personally."

"Of course not." Owens jammed his hands into his pockets as they approached Jamison and the judge's family.

Unmasked grief filled Amanda Hamden's narrow, tan face, and red, moist eyes. "Mrs. Hamden, Lieutenant Detective Ferrari and Sergeant Detective Owens. We're so sorry for your loss."

5

"Is there someone we can call for you?" Jenna asked.

"Detective Jamison already called my sister," the bereaved widow replied. "She should be here soon."

A reporter broke through the line and rushed toward them. "Mrs. Hamden, your husband has just been murdered. How do you feel at this moment?"

A second was right behind, this one a woman, thrusting forward a microphone with a local newsroom's call letters. "Who do you think did it? Will you run for the congress seat in his stead?"

"Get these reporters out of here!" Jenna snapped, venom practically dripping from the hard line of her mouth.

Owens extended his arms at his sides and shoveled them away, unafraid to make physical contact. "You were ordered to stay behind the tape," he snarled. "I've a mind to arrest you for interfering with a police investigation, not to mention the rabid insensitivity you just showed. Officer Stone!" he bellowed.

In an instant, the sturdy veteran officer, her blonde hair tied back in a tail under her cap, joined him, grabbing the male reporter by his arm. "Sorry, Sergeant. I'm not sure how they got over here, but I can put them in a squad car if you want."

"What?" The picture-perfect female journalist, in her pencil skirt and high heels, balked, a horrified expression consuming her camera-ready face. "We're just trying to find out what happened."

"A man was killed," Owens declared. "There's nothing else to report until we've had time to investigate."

As they moved out of earshot, Jenna shook her head. "Mrs. Hamden, I am so sorry about that. Would you like to go inside your house? Even if you're spending the night with your sister, you and the boys will need to get a few things."

Amanda shot a tentative glance at the house. The coroner's van was gone, and only a few officers still combed the front yard.

Jamison gently took her elbow. "We'll walk in with you. You should sit down and have a glass of water while you wait for your sister to arrive."

"It's OK, Mom," the older teenager consoled. "The police already looked inside and nobody's there."

"Exactly." The words fell from her lips with dismal finality. "Your father isn't there, and he never will be again."

The younger teen snuggled under her armpit opposite Jamison, his arm encircling her waist. The lad stood only a little shorter than his mother. "Let's go inside, where those cringey reporters can't bother us. Aunt Marta will be here soon."

Amanda nodded, and the detectives and boys escorted her inside. She collapsed on the living room couch, and the two boys—the older, a youthful copy of his father with lighter brown hair, narrow nose, and strong jawline, and the younger, tanner boy, whose black hair hung around a sweet face—flanked her, bestowing and receiving hugs.

"I'll get you glasses of water from the kitchen," Jamison offered, handing Jenna notes from her initial conversation with the family.

"Thank you," Jenna replied, taking a seat opposite the sofa. Glancing over the pad, she started with, "So, you two fine young men are Caleb and Joshua." She recognized them as Biblical names, though couldn't recall their stories. Randi would know.

"I'm Josh," answered the taller, more filled-out son. "That's Caleb."

The less mature-looking teen lifted his gaze to meet hers, teary shock and fear glistening in his chestnut brown eyes. "What happens now? Is the killer going to come after us too?"

"I don't believe so," Jenna rushed to answer, leaning forward, putting herself closer to the frightened boy. "But we aren't taking any chances. A police car with two officers will follow you to your aunt's house and keep watch outside all night long, just to be sure. OK?"

He sniffed and nodded.

"Thank you," Amanda responded. "You and Detective Jamison have been so kind."

Jamison returned with three glasses of water and set them on a glass-top coffee table. "We haven't done anything, really," she admitted and sat in the chair between the couch and Jenna's. "But we will, I assure you. Is there anything else I can get you? Anyone else I should call?"

"Reverend Hayburn," suggested Joshua. "He's our pastor—Christ United Methodist Church."

"Aunt Marta will call him," Amanda said, and pressed a kiss to Joshua's cheek. "Thanks for thinking of him. Now we're the ones in need of prayer. It feels ... different. This is the kind of thing that happens to other people, you know?"

Jenna nodded. "I know. Mrs. Hamden, Joshua, Caleb, may I ask you a few questions? I know this is a terrible time for it, with all you have to process, but the sooner we catch who hurt Judge Hamden, the better it will be for everyone."

Caleb wiped his eyes and sniffed. "I don't know how I can help, but I want to," he stated resolutely.

"Me too," agreed his older brother.

"I told Detective Jamison I don't know who would want to kill Les," Amanda said wearily. "He was a good man."

"I concur." Jenna met her eyes. "But even good men can make enemies. For now, tell me where you all were this afternoon and why you arrived home when you did?"

"We had cross-country practice after school," Joshua answered. "Baseball is our main sport, but it's in the spring, so I've been doing cross-country in the fall to stay in shape. This is Caleb's first year. The junior high gets to participate with the high school for some noncontact sports, like swimming and track and stuff. We were done at four thirty, and Mom picked us up. We stopped for a drink on the way home, but when we got here ..." His head fell, and he reached for his glass of water.

"Dad's a judge," Caleb informed Jenna with authority, as if she hadn't a clue who his father was. "There could be lots of criminals who are mad at him because he sent them to jail or made them pay a big fine."

"And we'll be looking at all of them," Jamison assured the lad. "Is this the usual time Judge Hamden returns from court on a Friday—around four-thirty?"

"If he isn't going to play golf or pickleball," replied Amanda. "Les has a big rally tomorrow, so he was coming straight home to get ready for it. His opponent, Congressman Cochran, had already scheduled his rally for this afternoon, and Les didn't want to have his at the same time, fearing Cochran would get more media coverage if they were. And he believed undecided voters would be more likely to attend his rally if it were on a different day, especially if they wanted to check out each candidate in person. Then tomorrow night he was to speak at a rally in Lexington, and the big last event was set for Monday night in Harrisonburg. We debated whether to return to Lynchburg, but Les said it would go for Cochran no matter what, so no point."

Jenna wondered where the two candidates stood in the polls, as she paid as little attention to politics as possible, but didn't think this was the time to ask. Joshua seemed to think otherwise.

"They were neck and neck in the race," he informed her. "It was anybody's seat to win. They thought this Green Party woman, or the Libertarian fellow, might turn out to be spoilers, but the polls from this week showed my dad with a slight lead. Is that why somebody killed him—they didn't want him to win the election?" It was another valid motive.

"Josh, we will pursue every motive and suspect until we find the right one," Jenna assured him. "Aside from all the police cars and commotion, did you notice anything different or out of place? Why did Judge Hamden park in the driveway and walk toward the front door instead of in the garage?"

"All the campaign stuff is in the garage," Caleb answered. "There isn't room for a car in there."

"You know Les," Amanda explained with a nostalgic aspect. "Anywhere to save money and be more efficient. He didn't want to rent a storage space, so all the leftover yard signs, swag boxes, and campaign pamphlets ended up in our garage. We joked they would be worth a lot of money once he was elected president." The instant of cheer faded from her countenance, replaced by gloom and despair. "I've never loved another man."

Suddenly, her eyes rounded, and she shot straight in alarm. "We haven't called Anna! Oh, God, how will I tell her? She'll want to drive home from college, but she won't be in any shape to drive. What if she's in danger?"

Jenna recognized rising panic when she saw it, but Jamison beat her to action. In a flash, her partner was on her knees in front of Amanda, taking her hands, soothing and coaxing. "It's all right, Mrs. Hamden. I'm sure Anna is fine. If you give us all her contact information, we'll see what we can do. I know this is hard, probably the hardest ever, and you don't want your daughter to drive while overly emotional."

"She's a freshman at Duke," the mother replied, seeming to calm a smidgen. "In Durham, North Carolina. She's started an undergrad degree in biochemistry. I'm a nurse, and Anna teased she wants to one-up me and become a doctor. She's going to be devastated! Her dad was the center of her universe."

"I'm sure all four of you will need to lean on each other in the coming weeks," Jamison said, rubbing Amanda's hands between hers. "You are lucky to have each other. Often, when we give notifications, the loved one has nobody. I can tell you're a strong family, and you'll get through this together."

Easing her hands from Jamison's, the widow wrapped an arm around each son, pulling them close. "We are, and we will."

When a knock sounded at the door, a Hispanic woman resembling Amanda rushed in with an older, compassionate-looking man whose dark suit contrasted with his warm ivory complexion. Jenna stood and Jamison followed. Placing a card on the coffee table, Jenna said, "Call me if you think of anything, need anything, or if you see anything suspicious. I'll make sure a patrol car follows you to your sister's. And Mrs. Hamden, for what it's worth, I knew your husband, and he was a good man. We'll do our best to bring his killer to justice."

"Thank you, and I will," she answered as fresh tears streamed down her cheeks. Jenna and Jamison left them to be comforted by Marta and Reverend Hayburn.

Outside, Jenna caught sight of Owens talking to one of the uniform officers and Matt Murphy up in the oak tree. Light radiated from behind the Blue Ridge, the sun now out of view. In another half hour, they would need spotlights if the search wasn't complete.

Owens shuffled over to her, bit his bottom lip, and shook his head. "They interviewed every person on both sides of the street. A couple of folks said they heard the car backfire or somebody setting off a firecracker, but not a single one saw a person or a strange vehicle around the time of the shooting. Murphy's convinced it was a Ninja assassin."

"Ninja," Jenna muttered and rolled her eyes. "But assassin, for sure. Any casing found?"

"Nada. But revolvers don't leave casings, or, if the shooter was in a vehicle, it could have kicked back into the car. We didn't find a single piece of physical evidence—not a shell casing, scuff mark, gun, cigarette butt, scrap of trash, or even a gum wrapper. If there were any hairs or fibers in the yard, they blew away. Wilcox might find something on Hamden's clothes."

"Maybe, but there were no signs of a struggle, and Dr. Valentine said the shot came from a short distance, not up close. Still, the lab will test for gunshot residue, DNA, and any substance that might have transferred to the judge's clothing, and the doc will get us the bullet. Let's head back to the office and start compiling a list of every person who had a beef with Hamden going back twenty years—criminals he tried when he was with the DA's office who might have been recently released, upcoming trials on his docket, political enemies, personal enemies, any threats made against him. We'll need his phone, computer, and tablet. If he received threatening emails, he might have hidden them from his family so they wouldn't worry. We'll get that new tech kid on his financials. I hope you weren't counting on making it to your kid's football game tonight. Oh, that reminds me!" Jenna pulled out her phone.

"Well," he answered sheepishly, "I kind of was. I'll call the missus too. She'll understand."

While Jenna texted Randi, Murphy shimmied down from the tree. "I wanted to get a good overall look at the area. From up there, I spotted all the smashed-down patches of grass. You know, we should take a sample of these grass clippings. If we do get a suspect, and he walked through that fresh-cut lawn, some will be on his shoes, and we might get a match."

Jenna's finger stilled on the keypad, and her mouth gaped. "You're brilliant, Murphy. Bag some grass and bring it back to the lab."

6

"Have a good weekend!" called Chelsea, a yellow belt in Randi's beginner's karate class. "And I hope you feel better soon."

"Yeah, me too. Thanks, and stay out of trouble." She managed a wink at the lanky seventh-grader, despite her nausea. Although Chelsea had found herself in the heart of a murder investigation a little over a month ago, she seemed to have returned to her chipper, eager self, skipping out the door with her friend as if nothing had happened. *Kids*, Randi thought. *They're so resilient.* The uncomfortable feeling roiling in her gut, reminding her of why she'd been dealing with bouts of sickness, brought a smile to her face.

"Are you staying for black belts tonight?" asked Kenji Moro, the sensei's son. The young man, about ten years her junior, showed off his fit physique and a top-of-the-line robotic arm in a black tank top and white gi pants while sweat poured from his shaggy ebony hairline. Randi tossed him a towel from her gym bag on the bench.

"Not tonight. I've got this upset stomach."

Randi and Jenna had agreed not to tell anyone she was expecting yet. She couldn't imagine the pain of informing them all she'd lost the baby if there were any early complications. It was better to wait until she'd been to the doctor, had her ultrasound, and was confident everything was all right first. Even though Randi didn't think of herself as old, her obstetrician had warned of increased risks of a later-in-life pregnancy.

"Take it easy then," he said, empathy filling his freshly wiped face. "We'll miss you."

"Thanks."

Kenji returned the towel and jogged over to where the other black belts congregated. Randi took a sip of water, contemplating whether to change clothes or wait until she got home. Spotting her phone in her bag, she pulled it out and browsed her messages. She'd been checking them all day after yesterday's shootout, and Jenna hadn't even thought to text letting her know she was fine. It was silly for Randi to worry; unfortunately, the knowledge didn't stop her from doing it.

Relief at a note from Jenna brought a smile to Randi's face.

'Don't wait up. I might be all night. Judge Hamden was murdered this afternoon. It will probably be on the news by the time you see this.' It was followed by a second note. *'Take care of my sweetheart and our baby. I love you.'*

Randi froze. For an instant, she even forgot to breathe. The news hit her in the chest like a pile-driver—hard, fast, and unexpected. The hardwood floor, inspirational posters, and sounds of karate practice faded into a distant blur as the spacious gym seemed to close in around her. Randi didn't know Judge Hamden personally, had never spoken to him, but he was a respected public figure whose picture frequently appeared in the newspaper or on TV. He was the kind of guy you felt like you knew because you'd heard so much about him, like a celebrity in a way. His campaign supported most of the issues that mattered to Randi, and she had hoped he'd win the election and represent the sixth district. Now ...

"Randi, you look pale. You should sit down." Sensei Yoshito Moro placed steadying hands on her upper arms and guided her to sit on the bench beside her gym bag. "Kenji said you have an upset stomach, only now I fear you will faint."

Steady on the bench, Randi peered up at her karate master and swallowed. "Judge Hamden, who's running for Congress, was just murdered. I need a minute, is all—nothing to worry about."

"Nothing to worry about?" voiced another black belt as a group of adult students gathered around Randi. "That's terrible news. I can't believe it."

"I read he had a big trial coming up next week," Kenji said, "and it's the election too."

Noah Williams, a young man who was also in Randi's Shakespeare class, lowered himself onto the bench beside her, a surreal expression overtaking his cool, smoky quartz face, genuine sadness dulling the luster from his sensitive twilight eyes. "I know him." The words dropped like tears from his thick lips. "He made all the difference in my life, and Anna, his daughter—we were in school together. I was a senior when she was a sophomore. Such a kind-hearted girl."

Randi pulled herself out of shock, regarding Noah with a blend of interest and sympathy. "You knew him?"

"Yeah, and I could have been royally screwed, except Judge Hamden didn't throw the book at me. Folks in the neighborhood are always going on about how the system is rigged against young Black men, and we can't ever get a break, especially from a white cop or judge. Usually, that's true. In my first semester of college, I got invited to this party, and all my friends were excited to go. I didn't drink in high school because I was focused on staying out of trouble and earning a scholarship—which, thankfully, I did. So, when people kept putting drinks in my hand, I didn't know how much was too much or what I should say no to. Before I knew it, my head was spinning, and the ground wouldn't stay still. That's when I decided I should go home, only I shouldn't have been driving. You know eighteen-year-olds—there's nothing they can't do, so I figured I could drive home just fine if I concentrated.

"The next thing I knew, I'd hit one of those big, blue mailboxes, and there were lights and sirens," he said with a short laugh, shaking his head. "I got busted for a DUI and destruction of federal property. Did you know damaging a mailbox, even by accident, was a crime?"

Noah raked a hand over his curly fuzz of coal hair. "When I went to court, everyone said I didn't stand a chance—they'd lock me up for two years or take away my license and slap me with a fine so big I'd have to drop out of school and get a job to pay for it. I can tell you—I was scared. My whole future, how my life would go from that point forward, was on the line, and my parents were so disappointed. My stepdad said he wasn't about to bail me out, and I was on my own. But then Judge Hamden walked into the courtroom, wearing his black robe and looking regal, and everybody stood up. He listened to the arresting officer's report, and my public defender pleaded my case. Then he looked straight at me, his intense gaze boring right into my scared-ass soul."

Randi noticed when Noah's countenance brightened with the memory. "He said, 'Son, do you understand how serious driving while intoxicated is? Do you realize if you'd hit a pedestrian, instead of a mailbox, you'd be up on manslaughter charges or worse?' I hung my head, saying, 'Yes, sir.' Then I explained I hadn't ever really consumed alcohol before and didn't know what it felt like to be drunk, and I was so sorry, and could he please go easy on me so I wouldn't lose my chance at a college education?"

Noah sighed as a tear trickled down his face. "I don't know if Anna had ever mentioned me at home or if he knew I was in college on scholarship or anything at all about me, but he struck his gavel and assigned me community service with a stern warning that I not appear in his court as the accused again. I loved that man."

Randi reached an arm around Noah. He laid his head on her shoulder and sobbed.

On her drive home, Randi called Jenna, hoping she wasn't interrupting. "Hey, sweetie. Can I bring a few pizzas by the office and drop them off for you and the gang?"

"You are my hero!" Jenna gushed.

Randi heard voices calling, "Meat lovers," and "Supreme," in the background.

"What? Nobody wants pineapple?" Randi quipped.

"Save the unwinnable debate for another time." Jenna's voice sounded tired and frustrated. "We appreciate you supplying food. This is a mega top priority case, as you can imagine."

"You'll still need to sleep to stay sharp," Randi advised. "Jamison?" she yelled into the phone. "Make everyone go home by midnight, you hear?"

"I hear!" sounded Trish's chirp from a distance.

"You nearly busted my eardrum," Jenna complained. "If we accomplish enough by then, but we might have to take turns on the couch. The mayor, the chief—everyone is anxious for results. I'm waiting on the autopsy now and then ballistics. Murphy and Stone are out chasing down leads so thin they're practically invisible, and this new boy wonder is supposedly digging into Hamden's financials, but I've yet to meet the kid. Captain Myers said he's assigned him to the team, but I guess he's still hanging out over at cyber crimes. Bring pizzas. I love you."

"I love you too," Randi echoed and turned into their favorite pizzeria to pick up pies.

***

Jenna had just gotten off the phone when a skinny kid in white kicks, baggy black pants, and a bright blue Dr. Who TARDIS T-shirt strolled in. Jenna frowned. "Are you lost?"

He stopped and stared at her, big obsidian eyes blinking from his youthful, taupe face. "Is this the criminal investigations office?" Well, at least his voice had dropped. He looked twelve.

"You've got it," Owens confirmed as he swiveled his chair toward the visitor, regarding him with a dubious expression. "Where are the pizzas?"

"I don't have pizzas," he answered, confidence returning to brighten his face. "I have Judge Hamden's bank accounts, credit card statements, retirement portfolio, and a list of every property he ever owned." Thrusting out a hand, he grinned at Jenna. "I'm Tyrelle Hendrix, your electronics and internet specialist, but everyone calls me Tyr."

"Tyr?" Jenna figured that when Captain Myers had called him the boy wonder, he'd be young, but this was ridiculous. *When did I get old?* she wondered.

"Yeah, like the Norse god of justice, war, and heroic endeavors." He beamed, and Jenna shook his hand.

"Welcome!" Jamison called, leaving her desk to rush over and hug him. *A hug?* Jenna wanted to roll her eyes.

"I'm sorry to ask, but are you out of high school yet?" Owens inquired before Jenna could pose the same astonished question.

"Yep! Graduated Carnegie Mellon University in December and shot through the police academy." He rocked on his toes with gleeful satisfaction. "Chief Clarkson sent me straight to the dungeon—uh, the cyber crimes computer lab."

"But why?" Jenna was dumbfounded. "I've heard of Carnegie Mellon, the only university more prestigious for computer science than MIT. Why aren't you making a jillion dollars writing code somewhere?"

Tyr stuffed his hands into two of the four, six, or eight pockets that sprouted from his cargo pants and blushed. "My dad's a sergeant with the Salem Police Department, and I've always wanted to make him proud. I couldn't play sports growing up and barely passed the PT to get on the force, but at least, if I'm helping him fight crime with my brain, he can be proud of that."

"I'm sure he's massively proud of you, Tyr," Jamison said with enough enthusiasm to match the kid's.

"So, how old are you?" Jenna had to know and didn't have the energy to look it up in his file.

"Twenty—twenty-one in a few weeks. Dad's going to take me out for a beer."

Twenty years old with a degree from Carnegie Mellon, Jenna thought. *At least he's not twelve, even if he looks it.*

"Congrats," Jenna said, morphing back into serious cop mode. "Give us what you've got on Hamden. Oh, and that's your station." She pointed to Bauman's empty quarters. "I need you where I can find you and pick that big brain of yours without having to descend to 'The Dungeon.'"

"Wow, my own station!" Tyr bounced, shuffled, and danced his way to Bauman's old spot, gazing at it like it was a hot belly dancer. "I'll take good care of it."

"The files?" Jenna prodded.

"Already in your inbox," he said as he slid into the swivel chair and adjusted the height down a few inches.

Jenna checked her email and opened the files—plural. He had done thorough work, she had to admit. "Everything seems to be in order," she voiced to the team. "No outstanding debts, no irregular deposits or withdrawals, reasonable savings account ... looks like he lived within his means, gave his ten percent to the church and then some, paying for his daughter's college, mortgage paid off, minimal credit card balances. There's nothing here to suggest money as a motive. What about his life insurance policy?"

Tyr whipped his chair around like it was a ride at the fair. "He used to have a five-hundred-thousand-dollar policy but bumped it to a million after he threw his hat in the ring. Considering the campaign expenses, I think a mill is reasonable."

"Yeah, a million dollars isn't what it used to be," Owens commented. "Now they say it takes a million dollars over twenty years to raise a kid—if you care for 'em properly and all. Crazy times!"

The idea of raising a child costing her and Randi a million dollars smacked Jenna in the gut. *What are we getting into? Am I crazy? Why didn't Randi tell me this part? Oh, she knows—I can guarantee she knows and conveniently left it out. What else didn't she tell me? We're screwed.*

Just then, Randi waltzed in with two extra-large pizzas and a jug of iced tea. "Dinner is served!" she declared with a grin.

I'll get you later, Jenna brooded, then smiled politely. "Thanks, honey. Meet our new tech specialist, Tyr Hendrix." *Million-dollar baby on my salary? Absurd!* And yet, her heart fluttered with the anticipation of seeing the ultrasound, of feeling the first kick, of holding their infant in her arms. *Maybe it'll be worth it.*

7

"Boss?" Jamison called in a soft, hesitant voice. She peered at Jenna over her shoulder from her desk, looking like she'd lost her last wind. "It's a quarter to midnight. Randi's right about sleep, I think."

Owens yawned and rubbed a broad hand down his face before shaking himself as if to stay awake. "We've pulled longer nights but—"

"All right," Jenna grumbled. She glanced at Hendrix, who looked as chipper as a rooster at dawn. It really wasn't fair. "Bring what you've got and gather around the table. We'll compare notes, make a plan for tomorrow, and catch a few winks."

"Excellent!" Jamison brightened, shuffled some papers into a folder, picked up the pumps she'd discarded at some point, and made her way to the table. Owens pushed out of his seat with considerable effort while the toothpick kid hip-hopped his way across the room, earbuds protruding from his ears, singing under his breath. Halfway to the table, he beeped—or rather, something on him beeped.

Jenna eyed him with concern. "Is that the alarm that warns your carriage is about to turn back into a pumpkin and your ..." she waved her hand at him, "rags are about to turn more raggedy?"

Tyr laughed and pulled a protein bar from one of the array of pockets. "No, Lieutenant. It's my blood sugar monitor saying I'm low and need a snack." He shot a bony arm into the air and pushed back the sleeve of his oversized T-shirt, revealing a stick-on glucose monitoring device. "If my glucose goes high, it automatically pumps a dose of insulin. If it goes low, the app on my phone beeps to let me know to eat something. A sight better than it used to be, with the blood tests four times a day and constantly adjusting medication levels. Science has come a long way, and now type 1 diabetics can enjoy normal lives, mostly. No football or hockey for me and my pump, but anything else is up for grabs." He grinned, plopped into a chair, and chomped off a bite of his energy bar.

"That's super," Jamison responded as she glided in across from him. "I have a grandmother with type 2 diabetes, and we're always worried about her taking her medication properly. She tends to forget or be obstinate about it." Trisha rolled her eyes. "Maybe we could get her one of those."

"I'm sure they sell similar systems for type 2 patients, although they can get pricy," he grimaced. "And it's vital that a type 1 diabetic gets their injection on time—not that it isn't important for everyone, just—"

"No worries," Jamison smiled. "I know what you mean."

Owens had already claimed the spot next to Jamison, so Jenna sat beside the newbie and called the meeting to order. "Owens, what do you have from the 'criminals who hated Hamden' hypothesis?"

With his elbows propped on the tabletop, Owens flipped open a brown folder. "There were plenty, but most are currently behind bars. However, I came across a couple who deserve scrutiny." He pushed a page across the table to her.

"Carter Mintz, age thirty-six, was just released from prison after serving twelve of a fifteen-year sentence for arson in a string of properties destroyed, some occupied at the time of the blazes. It was the last case Hamden tried as District Attorney before being elected to the bench, and it gave him massive publicity."

Jenna studied the image of an angry-looking White male with stringy brown hair and wiry muscles. His file listed him as five-foot-ten, weighing a hundred and fifty pounds.

"He was released from prison a week ago," Owens concluded.

"Then he's on parole, and we don't need a warrant to search his house," Jenna stated. "He could have wanted payback, and twelve years gives him plenty of time to plan. And I want his case file, everything, including interview recordings.

Then I want him in an interview room. I'll tag Murphy and Stone to make an unannounced search of his property and vehicle nice and early in the morning. Who else?"

"Lukas Monk, the guy whose trial is on his docket for next week." Owens flipped around a sheet on Monk, an African American male, forty-two, with two priors from grand theft auto and armed robbery. Going by the photo, he was covered in tattoos and a much more substantial man than the slender Mintz. Still, a gun makes a great equalizer.

"They completed jury selection, and Monk's attorney is kicking up a fuss about jury representation, claiming Hamden is a racist, a White elitist who won't give him a fair trial, blah, blah. Anyway, it looks like Monk would prefer a different judge to try his case."

"That gives him motive, and, with Hamden out of the picture, he'll either get Judge Williams, who's Black, or Judge Stroud, a woman. He might see either as more sympathetic."

"Especially since it would be his third strike," Owens confirmed. "At forty-two, he could end up spending the rest of his life behind bars. Jamison, we will need a warrant to search his place since this has nothing to do with the case he's being tried for."

Jamison frowned. "On a Sunday? Then again, I suspect every judge in the district wants to catch whoever did this. I mean, what if it wasn't just Hamden? What if the perpetrator targets all the judges?"

Alarm shot Jenna back into full wakefulness. "We need to get security details on them starting tonight." She madly sent off a text to Captain Myers. "Who else?"

Owens squirmed and placed another sheet in front of her. "Diego Guerrero." He shook his head. "Twenty-three years old. Judge Hamden sent him to the Onion on a first-degree murder charge. He and his lawyer tried to argue for manslaughter because it wasn't premeditated. Guerrero was robbing the house when the homeowner came home and surprised him. He whacked him in the head, he fell and hit the corner of his fireplace, and, between the two head wounds, he died in the hospital. Guerrero pleaded that he didn't mean to kill the guy, but, because he died during the commission of a felony, it's automatically first-degree murder."

"But if he's in prison," Jamison questioned.

"Not anymore. Two weeks ago, he was stabbed and killed in a prison brawl. A young fellow like that is bound to have people who'll be spitting mad at the judge for sending him to the roughest prison in the state. I'm sorting through them now—parents, brother, girlfriend. According to this, the girlfriend, Camila Diaz, had his baby shortly after he went in."

"Man, that's tough," Hendrix said, his face displaying compassion. "I wonder why the judge sent a young guy like Guerrero to the Onion?"

Owens glanced across at him, catching his eye. "He had a prior, and, according to the records, he acted out in court, cursed at the judge, and threw a fit at the jury when the verdict came back. It's still sad, and it's still a motive for his relatives. Those are my top picks right now."

Jenna nodded. "We'll see about arranging interviews for his family, but let's start with the girlfriend. Losing her baby's father could have triggered her the most." *Losing Randi could sure trigger me, even if I'd have the restraint not to murder a judge.*

"Jamison, what did you discover from the political angle?"

"OK, there were plenty of clubs, groups, and organizations that both supported and opposed Judge Hamden's campaign, but two stand out. Remember the Purity Fellowship Church that protests everything—the one our suspect Lennox used to be the pastor of before they kicked him out for employing prostitutes?"

"Yes." Jenna's face screwed into a scowl as she recalled the case of the murdered drag queen. Lennox hadn't done it, but he'd turned out to be an even bigger hypocrite than they had thought. She got a throbbing in her temple every time the "Christian" church's name came up.

"They have a new pastor, Rod Heckle, and the group is just as vocal against anyone who deviates from their idea of holiness as ever. Mr. Heckle has led a 'heckling' campaign—sorry, but I couldn't resist the pun—against Judge Hamden, declaring him to be a 'vile liberal,' and a 'queer-loving baby-killer' because he supports equal rights and is pro-choice. Heckle has been a guest on several conservative podcasts, arguing how Judge Hamden's stance on the issues will contribute to the downfall of America. Once again, we'll have to consider this organization's leader and followers, since, even if Heckle doesn't own a gun, I'm certain many of his congregation members do."

"Yeah, yeah," Jenna muttered, wishing she could stay as far away as possible from the Purity Fellowship crowd. "Who else?"

"Another adamant critic of Hamden is Patti Madden, head of the local PETA chapter. She claims the judge wasn't liberal enough and a puppet of big pharma and the cosmetics industry. Three months ago, she was arrested and charged with vandalizing a local chemical company because supposedly their research harms animals. Judge Hamden ruled against her in favor of the company whose windows were broken and walls graffitied."

"I've got stuff on her," Hendrix spoke up and opened his folder, "and some of the others. I didn't know if I should say anything or wait to be called on."

"Speak, Hendrix," Jenna said. "We're a team and value everyone's input."

He nodded, looking relieved. "I've only accessed emails on his official court address so far, and there were plenty of praises and complaints. As to the latter, there are several raging letters from Camila Diaz, who hopes Hamden rots in hell for sending her boyfriend to be murdered, claiming he's as culpable as the inmate with the shiv. Nothing from Mintz, but 'concerns' from Monk and his attorney, along with requests for him to recuse himself from the upcoming trial. There's a steady stream going back to the day Hamden announced his candidacy from Reverend Heckle, but none of them reach the measure of outrage expressed by the PETA lady, Madden. She threatens to carry out chemical testing on him to see how he likes it and says he's a complete fraud and no more of a progressive than Cochran ... and lots of expletives. But here's the kicker."

Jenna, her attention riveted, twisted in her chair to face him.

"I started out working on the traffic cameras, but, without knowing who to look for, it didn't help much. I mean, what makes a car suspicious? But after going through the emails, I went back. Out of all the folks who wanted Hamden to know how much they hated him, only one vehicle showed up in the area near the time of the murder."

"Patti Madden," Jenna concluded. Tyr nodded solemnly. Gone was the bouncing boy with his hip-hop music and boogie walk. Beside her sat an astute young man with cop eyes.

"You've got it. Now, the cam was at an intersection on the main street outside the subdivision and shows her turning in. Sure, there're at least sixty houses in that neighborhood, but the camera stamp showed her going in eight minutes before the 911 and leaving three minutes after. If someone was going to commit a drive-by shooting, that's about the right eleven minutes and is more than enough time."

Jenna scribbled "*#1*" beside Madden's name on her notepad. "Jamison."

"I know, get a warrant for her house too. Any others?"

"Might as well hit them up for Camila Diaz," Jenna answered. "Cite the emails with death threats."

"Monk, Madden, Diaz, got it." Even Jamison's chipper voice had faded to an exhausted wheeze.

Jenna glanced at Owens next. "Wake up. I can't have you falling asleep behind the wheel on your drive home. Let's reconvene at nine in the morning and start hauling in suspects. Good work, everyone."

The only people they passed on the way out were the night desk clerk and a lone uniformed guard at the front door. They all said good night, and Jenna plodded to her car, ready to fall into bed with Randi. *Would she wait up? Of course, she would.* Even though she had a headache and felt mentally drained, Jenna looked forward to a peaceful moment with her wife before going to sleep. She needed to decompress and unwind. She needed Randi.

8

Jenna slipped in quietly through the door from the garage, soon to be the new home of their Zen gym, to spy Randi asleep in the recliner chair with *Star Wars: A New Hope* playing on the TV. Randi probably had every line memorized. Byron, who lay on the floor beside her, lifted his head, gently wagging his tail. Bandit, who had made himself cozy beside Randi's head on top of the chair, stretched, lifting his tail into the air and extending his front paws. He yawned before hopping off and loping over to rub her legs.

"I know you ate," she whispered. Sitting on the little bench by the coat hooks, Jenna secured her gun in its drawer, slipped off her boots, and Randi's beautiful face turned to smile sleepily at her.

"Good. You're home. I waited up for you."

Jenna's lips curled as her eyes sparkled with her last ounce of energy. "I can see that. Did you have much nausea tonight?"

"A bit." Randi stretched and pushed down her footrest. "Not as bad as last night. I ate a sandwich and some grapes. I'm more sick about Judge Hamden. It's just ..."

"Awful? Disappointing? Dismal on so many levels?" Jenna supplied. Walking across the room, she leaned over to greet Randi with a kiss.

"Uh-huh."

"I'm grabbing a beer," Jenna said. "Do you want anything?"

"I've got a glass of water," Randi replied, "but it could use some ice."

Jenna returned from the refrigerator with three cubes and dropped them into Randi's glass. Randi pushed the off button on the remote. "I know how it ends. What can I do for my sweetheart before tucking you into bed?"

"Just be here." No sooner had Jenna sat down, Randi moved from the recliner and snuggled up to her, brushing kisses across her face and neck. They felt warm, comforting, and tingling with an abiding love. Jenna inhaled a deep breath and let out a sigh before gulping a sip of her beer. "What do you know about Judge Hamden?" she asked, sure that Randi had some insights into the man.

"Funny you should ask." Randi recounted her student, Noah's, story.

"One of our early suspects was accusing Hamden of being a racist, which sounded wrong to me. Noah's account contradicts that characterization. I think our suspect was just grabbing at excuses. But let's talk about something else. I don't care how high a profile case this is, I'll do everything in my power to be at your appointment on Monday. I'm excited to see the ultrasound. Will it even look like a baby?"

Randi chuckled, a smile brightening her face, and, with an arm around Jenna's shoulder, flexed her muscles to squeeze her. "It will look like a six-week-old fetus, so, babyish. It will confirm that I'm pregnant, but we won't be able to tell the baby's sex, and it probably won't look like a baby to you."

"But they can tell if it's all right?" Jenna asked anxiously.

"The doctor can probably detect a heartbeat and an approximate date of fertilization, which we already know. He'll use that to predict a due date, but some healthy babies come either early or late. We'll see tiny arm and leg buds, and maybe spots where the eyes and ears are starting. Later ultrasounds will show a lot more. We won't be certain about the sex until eighteen to twenty weeks, so you'll have to be patient."

Randi kissed Jenna's head and lowered her mouth to her ear. "When and how are we going to tell your parents?"

Jenna polished off her beer and set the can on the coffee table, her face going blank. She turned into Randi, circling her waist in her arms, and peered at her with trepidation. "They invited us to Thanksgiving dinner. I thought we—you, me, and Vince Jr.—could break the news to them then. In-person is better, right? And having Vince there too, I think."

Randi smiled at her questioning expression and pressed her lips to hers. "It will be fine, Jenna. They love little Eli, and he didn't arrive the way they would have approved of. Even if your mother passes out in a dead faint—bless her heart—it'll be all right. Your brother and sister will be thrilled, and I don't see your dad kicking up a fuss."

"Yeah," Jenna admitted with a sigh. "It's Mama I'm worried about." *She better not have a heart attack or stroke or something.*

"Are you still upset about her not attending our wedding?"

Jenna had to reflect for a minute. She'd put it behind her, hadn't she? After all, her mother had been in a cast for a broken ankle. *Mama said she would have come—after she didn't, of course, not before.* "I guess not. I mean, it is what it is. I can't expect her to turn a complete one-eighty after she's believed a certain way all her life. If only she could just be happy for us instead of agonizing over every decision I make, thinking, somehow, it's her fault I turned out 'wrong.'"

"You turned out beautiful, brilliant, and oh so right." Randi's lips captured Jenna's in a tantalizing kiss, loaded with appreciation. "I know you'll be heading to work in a few hours, so let me get you tucked into bed now."

Jenna relaxed. "That sounds like a plan."

***

Saturday, November 2

Jenna awoke to texts and emails that she scanned before rushing through a shower. The smell of bacon and coffee greeted her while she pulled on slacks, a long-sleeved button-up shirt, and her black leather jacket. Mornings had been a little frosty, and she liked the hard-hitting authority the coat projected. Plus, it matched her boots. She ran a comb through her hair, accepted the to-go breakfast Randi presented, and kissed her goodbye.

"It's going to be another late one," she warned in a disappointed tone.

"I know," Randi answered. "I'll catch up on essay grading and lesson planning. If it stops raining, I might take Byron for a run."

Jenna glanced out the window, her spirits sinking further. In her sleep-deprived state, she hadn't noticed. "Be careful with that running business," she ordered with a stern look. "There'll be no falling, you hear? On second thought, I forbid you to go for a run. There could be slick spots."

"Jenna," Randi responded, her eyes widening. "I'm supposed to stay in shape while I'm pregnant. It will make the birth easier and help prevent packing on pounds."

"Then stay inside and practice your forms, pump some weights, but no running on wet surfaces, understand?" Jenna flashed her most intimidating scowl at Randi. "And I almost forgot! Why didn't you tell me it was going to cost a million dollars to raise our child?"

Randi laughed—*laughed*—her eyes crinkling and cheeks beaming with warmth. "That's an exaggeration. We'll be fine. Now, go catch bad guys. I love you."

Jenna smirked and, hands full of a plastic food container and coffee thermos, struck off to face the day, calling over her shoulder, "I love you too!"

"Lieutenant Ferrari." Captain Myers caught her in the hallway before she made it to her office door.

"I sent an update last night," she answered, veering toward him.

"Yes, and I responded. I'd already assigned officers to the other judges, but that was a good thought. And I got a call from Judge Stroud this morning, complaining Detective Jamison woke her up at seven o'clock, standing outside her door with a bunch of warrants." He shot her a piercing gaze and twisted his lips before adding with a sigh, "And she was happy to oblige. You've got a firecracker with that one, Ferrari."

"I know. I'll send officers to serve the warrants right now," Jenna vowed, "as soon as I get them from Jamison."

"And I got a late note from Dr. Valentine," Myers added, rubbing the back of his neck. "He's finished the autopsy."

"Yes, he sent me one too, but I haven't had a chance to study it yet."

"He said you'd probably want to talk to him, see everything in person like you always do," he stated, as if irritated at Jenna's thoroughness. "He'll be in shortly but isn't staying all day."

"Yes, sir. I won't keep him waiting." Energy raced through Jenna from her toes to the top of her head. She was anxious to get into her office, get everything rolling, and drag suspects in to see whose story held up. "Anything else?"

He propped a hand on his belt, tilting his head at her, and grumbled, "I have meetings with the chief, the mayor, and they've scheduled a press conference. What am I going to tell them?"

"That the Roanoke PD is pursuing all leads in the assassination of Judge Hamden and expects to find the perpetrator, arrest and convict him or her in a reasonable amount of time, but refuses to rush the investigation, leading to errors. Tell them we extend our heartfelt sympathies to the victim's family and are employing every resource to bring the killer to justice. You know what to say—you were born for this."

He snorted, the tension easing from his taut features. "Go make it happen, Ferrari."

"Right away, sir." Pivoting, Jenna hurried into her office, where she found not four, but six team members awaiting her instructions. *I could get used to this*, she thought.

"I got the warrants!" Jamison announced. How could she look so good on less than six hours of sleep?

"We already busted in on Carter Mintz at his apartment," Officer Stone reported, a fist on her hip and holding a mug of coffee. A blonde tail dangled down the back of her uniform shirt. "The kid and I checked every nook and cranny," she said with a nod at Officer Murphy. "Mintz's abiding by the terms of his parole, it would seem. No gun, no contraband, but we can't rule out that he might have ditched it—thrown it in the river, or something. The car he's using is a clunker his cousin loaned him, and it's clean too. He claims he didn't go anywhere near Hamden's house yesterday or since being released, but he could be lying."

"OK, good work," Jenna confirmed. "He stays a suspect, and I'll want to bring him in, but there're a couple of folks higher up on the list. Right now, I need the two of you to head over to Luckas Monk's place, serve this warrant, comb his residence like you're searching for fleas, and bring him in for questioning. He's out on bail for a trial next week that Judge Hamden was supposed to preside over. He's a big brute, so watch your backs."

"We'll take care of it," Murphy answered with a smart nod.

"Owens," Jenna called, striding toward his desk. "I want you and Jamison to serve the warrant on Patti Madden, turn her residence and vehicle upside down, and bring her in for questioning. We'll get around to Diaz this afternoon if no one confesses by then."

"You've got it."

Jenna had to hand it to Owens. He sported a fresh shave and acted much perkier than she'd imagined, springing from his desk chair like a man half his age—and size. "What's the deal?" she asked as she studied him.

"I might have missed the game last night, but my wife videoed our boy scoring the winning touchdown." His grin spread as wide as his substantial girth. "Do I get to intimidate her?"

Jenna responded with a devilish look. "No. I want to be the one to intimidate her."

Jamison joined them. "What will you and Tyr be up to?"

"I've got an appointment with the morgue, then ballistics, and want to set up for the interviews, while Hendrix digs deeper into the judge's computer and cell phone for clues."

"Ferrari?" Owens asked with a withering look. "What do we do with the baby?"

"What baby?" Jenna peered at him in puzzlement.

"That's right," Jamison said, her green eyes widening. "Diaz has a baby, and I doubt she'll have a sitter on hand. When we get around to her, I guess she'll have to bring the tot along." A devilish grin brightened her creamy face. "Maybe you could hold it while Owens and I ask the questions. It would be wonderful practice, don't you think?"

Jenna narrowed her eyes to slits and jabbed a finger at Jamison. "You think that's funny?" She had to admit, Trish had a point. Jenna needed to learn to feel comfortable around babies if she was going to have one. But what did Jamison know about it? Had Randi blabbed to her during some female bonding in the restaurant restroom when they had dinner with Jamison and ADA Altman last week?

Jamison shrugged. "Just a thought. We'll sweep under every rock and bring Madden in."

"Yeah, you do that," Jenna glowered.

In the elevator down to the morgue, she texted Randi. *'I thought we weren't telling anyone yet.'*

'We aren't,' came the reply.

'Then how did Jamison find out?'

'She's an observant woman and a smart detective. Did you think she wouldn't put it together?'

The elevator opened. Randi was right, naturally, of course, always. How absolutely annoying—and yet reassuringly helpful. *'Sure you didn't tell her?'*

'I swear.'

Jenna shoved the phone back into her pocket. *I'd better hurry up and make captain,* she thought, *or Jamison will be coming after my job at this rate. Observant, smart detective. Damn if she ain't!*

9

Bright lights, soft jazz, and a chemical odor greeted Jenna when she pushed through the glass doors into the gleaming, sterile domain of Dr. Rudolph Valentine, chief medical examiner for Roanoke County and, Jenna supposed, a friend. The tall man with a sweep of black hair and matching glasses rolled a body, shrouded by a hospital-green sheet, from a drawer in the cooler and glanced at her entrance.

"Thank you for coming in this morning," Jenna said with genuine appreciation. "I got the email with the attached report, but hearing everything from you, being able to ask questions, is so much better." She stopped opposite Dr. Valentine with the body between them.

With an understanding smile, he responded, "I know. Besides, the judge was one of us—a purveyor of justice. We're part of the same team, and I don't take kindly to one of our own being gunned down."

"Right." Jenna steeled herself to see a familiar face looking up at her from the slab, and Dr. Valentine turned down the sheet. Hamden wasn't supposed to have that Y incision in his pallid chest; he was supposed to be heading to Washington to represent their district in Congress.

"The cause of death was a single gunshot to the back that struck his heart's left ventricle. The bullet lodged in a rib, therefore, no exit wound. I sent the slug to ballistics for analysis. No bruising or gunshot residue near the entry wound would suggest the shooter was at a distance. More curious was the angle of entry, with a slightly downward trajectory, indicating the killer was taller than the victim. Judge Hamden was five feet eleven inches."

Dr. Valentine turned the body so Jenna could examine the entry point. Taking a neon-colored straw, he gently inserted it into the wound tract. "See? I included pictures in my report for the lab."

"None of our current suspects are six-foot-four or taller," Jenna mentioned with a frown. "And this all but eliminates a drive-by shooting, which was our leading scenario."

With a shrug, Dr. Valentine suggested, "Perhaps the killer was standing on something or shot from a second-floor window or balcony across the street. I can't give you a precise distance. Initially, it appeared to be from fifteen or twenty feet but, considering the size of the slug and the propulsion force from a weapon, one would think at that distance a .45 would rip right through him, yet it caught in a rib. So maybe the killer was quite a distance away."

"He'd have to be a hell of a marksman to hit his heart with one shot from a distance," Jenna admitted. "We've been thinking handgun, but maybe the killer used a rifle, which might explain why none of the neighbors saw anyone. But the position of the body suggested he was shot from the road."

"It's possible he could have taken a step, twisted, or changed directions before falling."

He was right. "There are so many variables to account for. Owens and Jamison are bringing in a suspect we have on camera driving into the neighborhood around the right time. What if she stopped her vehicle and stood up, sat on the driver's door, and shot over the roof? Depending on the size of the vehicle ..."

"Like you said, many variables to consider," Dr. Valentine agreed. "Other than the hole in his heart, Judge Hamden was a healthy, fit man who could have easily lived another forty years. You know, we're all looking at the possibility of seeing a hundred now, if we exercise and eat right. The average lifespan keeps inching up, and who knows what cures lie just around the bend?"

Jenna instantly thought of Randi always trying to get her to give up sodas and lay off the donuts and fast food. Her wife often presented a lecture on the healthy qualities of each item she served, how this or that was organic, and the other loaded with antioxidants and vitamins or some crap. *She loves me! She wants me to live to be a hundred.* Then she thought of her mother, who, at only a few years older than Hamden, seemed to be on death's door and wracked with pain. She shook away the thought. *That doesn't have to be me. At least I never smoked, so I don't have those issues to deal with.*

"Nothing in his tox screen," he continued. "No alcohol in his system. Looks like he had lunch around twelve-thirty and nothing to eat since. No trace under his nails, no other insults to his body, and no signs of an altercation. I sent his clothes to the lab, but don't expect them to find anything probative. An assassin put a bullet in him, and that's it. I truly wish I could give you more."

"The bullet helps," Jenna said, "and the wound tract trajectory. I know we have to place someone shooting from a higher spot than where he was standing, and those facts narrow it down. For example, one suspect is shorter than me, so she didn't just run up in the yard and fire. Lying in wait in the front yard tree?" she pondered. "I'll have Murphy check it out. He was in that tree last night. Thanks, Doc."

"It's my job," he answered as he pulled the sheet back over the victim. "But helping you solve a case is also a pleasure. I'm headed home for the weekend if you don't need anything else."

"Thank you for coming in to show me, lay it out in words I can understand. Enjoy the fall weather before it gets too cold."

"You forget," he smiled and pushed up his glasses with a long, slender finger. "I grew up with winter weather and don't mind a little snow."

After her visit at the morgue, Jenna stopped by the lab, hoping to talk to CSI Wilcox. Upon scanning the space without catching sight of Destiny, she had to settle on the twiggy, younger Davenport, whose light brown hair fell in his eyes and whose white lab coat consumed him.

"Good morning, Davenport." Her greeting lacked enthusiasm. "What was collected from the crime scene yesterday, and what about the slug and clothes Dr. Valentine sent you? And where's Wilcox?"

"Well, it's Saturday," he said and blinked. "I'm sure CSI Wilcox would have come in if she were in the middle of something, but we don't have much to process. Over here." He threw a finger to the right, and Jenna followed him to a stainless-steel table under bright lights. "You see where the hole in the suit coat is. We used every process, checked under a microscope, and not a molecule of gunshot residue, nor any muzzle burning or scorching. Your killer must have been at least six feet away, maybe five, and, depending on whether the wind was blowing, possibly four."

"But he could have been a hundred feet away," Jenna speculated.

"Right you are." Davenport, who was built like Gumby, rocked on his heels. "Wilcox swabbed the front and back of it and sent the samples to the DNA lab. Dr. Gupta got them started before she left last night."

"What are those?" Jenna pointed to several clear plastic Ziplock bags.

"Oh." He spread them out with his long, spidery fingers. "This one is the grass clippings Officer Murphy brought in. I analyzed it, and the sample came back as a mixture of—"

"I don't need to know now," Jenna said, holding up a hand to stop him from reciting a litany of scientific grass names she wouldn't recognize anyway. "Hold on to it in case I can bring in a suspect's shoes. Where's the bullet?"

"Oh, Verbeck has it, but you might be interested in this." Davenport lifted another bag. "The CSIs and uniform officers combed the whole front yard between the body and the road. No shell casings, cigarette butts, seed shells—like sunflower seeds or peanuts. Hamden's must be one of the cleanest yards in the city. The only thing they scraped up were these tiny plastic shavings."

"Plastic shavings?" Jenna took the bag and held it up to the light. Four bits of gray polymers the size of fingernail clippings lay at the bottom of an otherwise empty bag. "How did they even find these with all the grass clippings? They're so small."

"People were on the ground, on their hands and knees," Davenport reported. "We know how important this case is, and everyone did their best to not overlook a speck. The metal detectors didn't pan out—only picked up one rusty nail buried about half an inch under the soil. Of course, we didn't bag the acorns and bring them in, and the plastic might not be anything, but ..."

Jenna laid down the bag and stared at him. "What?"

Davenport handed her a printout. "The analysis from the plastic flakes. They're polyamide-imide, or PAI, a high-performance polymer known for its heat resistance. It's used for hundreds of processes, such as automobile and aeronautics, industrial equipment, and injection molding applications, like for toy figures, decorative ornaments, and household products. It's a uniform, gunmetal gray pigment. Now, if I had the object they were shaved from, I could probably match the edges to see where these bits fit, but you'd have to find the thing they got scraped from."

Great, Jenna thought, *another thing I have to find before this evidence has context.* "Thanks. If we turn up anything from the suspect searches, I'll send it over. Verbeck, you said?" She slid her gaze through the glass separating ballistics from this part of the lab to spy Davenport's polar opposite. The man was short—not as short as Jenna, but that was nothing new—stocky, with a round face, rather than Davenport's long one. His bald head, ringed with a short, sandy-blond fringe, gleamed under the intense light, and prominent ears stood out from a face etched in age lines. With the addition of a jawline and chin sprouting a semicircle of fading beard growth, he rather resembled Randi's Christmas gnome.

"Is he new?"

"He transferred from Wytheville over the summer," Davenport answered. "You've been too busy honeymooning and solving murders to have noticed, I reckon. He's got your bullet."

"Thanks."

Jenna strode through the open doorway into the connecting room. "Good morning. I'm Lieutenant Detective Ferrari, and I don't think we've crossed paths since you arrived."

Glancing up from a sheet of paper, he removed his reading glasses and met her gaze. "Lieutenant Ferrari, I've heard of you. Jasper Verbeck, civilian ballistics specialist, at your service." He heartily shook her hand.

"The slug from Judge Hamden's murder," she stated, getting right to it. They could socialize later. "I need everything you've got. Is it a match to something in the system?"

With a severe grimace, Verbeck replied, "You aren't going to like this."

Jenna's shoulders slumped. "No match?"

"No striations."

"What? That's impossible!" Jenna's jaw dropped, then closed as her wide eyes narrowed on the new ballistics guy. *What happened to the old one? Does this troll have a clue what he's doing?*

"Improbable, but not impossible," Verbeck explained. He held up a bag with the bullet. "First, it went to fingerprints, but it was clean. Whoever loaded it must have been wearing gloves. Then CSI Wilcox swabbed it for DNA and sent the sample to Dr. Gupta."

Jenna knew the results wouldn't be back until tonight. *We need that new machine,* grumbled through her mind. "So, what? This was the first time a new gun was fired?"

"Even that should have left rifling marks on the bullet." Verbeck set the evidence back on the tray and passed Jenna the report he'd been reading. "Wilcox also tested a swab from the slug for trace and found this." He leaned close and pointed to a line in the report.

"PAI plastic polymer ... so what? It was fired through a homemade silencer? That doesn't make sense. Witnesses heard the shot."

"Lieutenant, I think this bullet came from a 3-D printer gun—unmatchable, untraceable, and probably melted down by now."

"Are you serious?" It was too early in the morning for this. Her only piece of evidence was a .45 caliber slug with no striation marks and plastic residue, suggesting it had been discharged from a fantastical weapon that should be so illegal. It made her head swim, and her stomach tightened into a knot.

10

Jenna took a moment to sit at her desk with a cup of coffee, breathing and preparing herself for the interviews with Lukas Monk and Patti Madden, unsure which would arrive first, while Hendrix hummed at his station, his fingers flying across his keypad. Although Monk's file was larger than Madden's, they both contained plenty.

I don't see either making a 3-D printer gun. Monk wouldn't have the knowledge and resources, and I'm sure Madden is anti-plastic. There must be another explanation. Maybe the shooter took a tool to the barrel and smoothed it out—a drill or tiny sander or something. Maybe he glazed the bullet in plastic before loading it so the artificial coating would absorb the grooves. That's why it flaked off as it shot through the barrel, and residue remained on the slug. He altered the bullet so it wouldn't pick up rifling marks.

"Lieutenant?" Officer Stone poked her head in the door. "We've got Monk, and his lawyer's on his way. Where do you want him?"

"Interview A," Jenna answered. "Find anything at his place?"

"Interestingly enough …" She lifted a clear plastic bag with a revolver, weighing it down as it dangled from her fingers. ".45 caliber hidden in a hole carved under the bottom of his mattress. I'll drop it off at the lab. What's next?"

Jenna's eyes lit. "Good work, Officer Stone. I guess Camila Diaz and Guerrero's family members are next. Employ some sensitivity, though. They just lost a loved one and will respond better to sympathy than gruffness."

"Me? Unsympathetic toward murderers who get murdered in prison?" she fake-scoffed.

Jenna winced. "Yeah, like that. Hey, just let Murphy take the lead when you talk to them while you watch his back and spy out their houses. The kid is so wholesome and drips with empathy, kind of like Jamison-light. Oh, and here's the warrant for Diaz's place. Maybe drop by there last and bring her in."

Stone let out a snorting laugh. "Yeah, I get it. Matt needs practice taking the lead anyway. Monk'll be in room A waiting for you."

"Thanks." It wasn't that Vicki Stone wasn't up to any task, but there was a reason she had reached forty without making rank, and it wasn't timidity. She was a great cop—just brusquer than necessary at times. Murphy, on the other hand, charmed everybody he met without even trying.

"Hendrix, you get to run the booth for your first interview," Jenna declared as she turned to him. "Let me show you the board."

"Wicked!" He spun, catapulting out of his seat like a grinning rocket. "Now I get to see how you operate. Dad interrogated this suspect one time and made the dude wet his pants."

Jenna stared at Tyr with a flat expression as she gathered papers into a folder. "I'd prefer to avoid the smell of urine or causing a mess the custodians would have to clean up. All you have to remember is to capture clean audio and video that can be used in court if necessary."

"Aw, piece of cake," he summarized and hopped to stand beside her. The kid wasn't Bauman tall, but Jenna still had to raise her chin to get her sarcastic expression aimed correctly.

She left Monk to stew while she showed the new tech specialist around the booth, only to discover he had repaired similar systems while still in elementary school. "Thanks, Lieutenant," he said politely. "I can take it from here."

Confident he could, Jenna stepped out into the hallway, where she almost bumped into a handsome, clean-cut Black man in a suit carrying a briefcase. "May I help you?" she asked.

He jutted out an angular chin, inspecting her with displeasure. "I'm Zachary James, Mr. Monk's attorney. Are you the overeager, ambitious detective who had him hauled in here for no reason?"

"I'm Lieutenant Detective Ferrari of the criminal investigations office, and your client was hiding a handgun under his bed after Judge Hamden, upon agreeing to his bail, explicitly ordered him to surrender all his weapons until after his trial. Were you aware he'd kept one back, Mr. James, in violation of the terms of his bail?"

The defense attorney, who appeared to be around Jenna's age, with a slighter build than ADA Bennet Altman, aka Trisha Jamison's new fiancé, sucked in a breath and brushed a hand down the front of his stylish suit coat. "I'm sure there is an explanation," he stated with less certainty than Jenna presumed he would have liked. "He must have forgotten about it."

Jenna pushed open the door, granting Mr. James a smug look. "We'll see. After you, sir."

With a guarded expression, the lawyer stepped into the room. "A moment alone with my client?" he asked.

"Just open the door when you're ready."

Jenna leaned against the wall and went over the pages in the file again. Soon, the door opened, and she joined the hulking Monk, a professional criminal facing his third strike, and his smaller, studious-looking representative. It struck her that Mr. James hadn't come from the public defender pool. Was Monk paying his tab, or did he still have ties to the gang he reportedly was no longer affiliated with? Maybe this professionally-performed assassination had been planned and carried out by a group rather than an individual.

Taking a seat across from the suspect, Jenna opened with, "Lieutenant Detective Ferrari in interview with Lukas Monk and his attorney, Zachary James, Saturday, November 2 at 10:15 a.m. Mr. Monk, did Officers Murphy or Stone read you your rights?"

She glanced up to meet his gaze for the first time. Fire blazed in his russet eyes, set in a scarred face that hid worlds of hardship and grief. A snake tattoo slinked its way up his thick neck, its fanged jaws opening toward a completely bald head.

He looked like a brown version of the old He-Man action figures—one giant muscle atop another.

"Yeah," he uttered in a gruff baritone. "Got my lawyer here, so I don't have to say nothin'."

"No, sir, Mr. Monk, you don't," Jenna affirmed politely. "However, since you were found in possession of a .45 caliber handgun—the same type that was used to murder Judge Hamden yesterday afternoon—in violation of the terms of your bail, I'll have to confine you to the city jail for the duration of your trial until a verdict has been reached. And I'm sorry to inform you that will probably be later rather than sooner, as your trial has been postponed due to the untimely death of your presiding judge."

"Hey, wait!" The hulk stirred, fear shooting into those rusty-brown eyes. He glanced from Jenna to Mr. James. "Can they do that? I paid the bail money."

"It's a technicality, but, legally, yes," he explained. "You should tell her about the gun, Luke."

The big man's gloomy face twisted back to Jenna, and his brows drooped. "I didn't kill Judge Hamden. I'm not crazy! I'm trying to get out of a third strike, not end up in prison until the day I die. Sure, Zach and me were upset after the jury selection and getting stuck with a White, political judge. We were hoping for better representation, more minorities on the jury, and maybe Judge Williams presiding, but it weren't worth throwin' away my chances by shootin' the guy."

Jenna studied his sincerity and wondered if he had done any acting when in high school. "The gun, Mr. Monk."

He sighed and hunched his shoulders. "I did turn in all my weapons, but then a friend showed up and needed somewhere to keep his revolver. He knew about the cutout in my mattress and begged me to let him keep it there, swearin' nobody would find out."

"And why couldn't this friend keep his own gun?" Jenna probed, unconvinced by his story thus far.

"Well, see, he found it, just lyin' in a dumpster a couple of weeks ago," Monk continued.

"Uh-huh," Jenna mused. "Just found it in a dumpster." She scribbled a note on her pad.

"That's what he said, and it happens," Monk gave her a credible look. "Anyway, he said his old lady would throw a fit and might even toss him out on his ear if she found a handgun in their house. They've got a couple of kids, and his woman's major rule is no guns in the house. She's scared one of the little ones might find it and get hurt." He rolled a shoulder and grimaced, folding his hands in front of him.

"She's right," Monk admitted. "It could happen. When I was a kid, a classmate of mine found his daddy's gun and accidentally shot and killed his baby sister. The boy was never the same again. He's gone now." He dropped a regretful look to the table between them.

"So, this 'found' handgun has been in your possession for two weeks now?"

"Around that, yeah." With a sigh, Monk leaned back in his chair, his hands retracting across the smooth, steel tabletop. He had tremendous hands, one displaying a faded gang tattoo.

"We aren't here to talk about the robbery you are accused of," Jenna stated. "We're here about Judge Hamden, who—by the way—would have granted you the fairest trial you could ask for."

"That's your opinion," Mr. James inserted, "not a verifiable fact."

Meeting his gaze with steel in her own, Jenna bit out a reply. "Well, now, we'll never know, will we?" The lawyer fell silent.

A knock sounded, and Jasper Verbeck, resident gnome, stuck in his head, followed by a hand holding a report. "Lieutenant? Sorry to interrupt, but I knew you'd want this."

Jenna left the table to retrieve the paper. "Thanks." The civilian specialist retreated, and Jenna returned, studying the findings.

"Your friend's name," she ordered.

Monk shifted uncomfortably in his chair. "I'm no rat, detective. I can't tell you and be the reason he gets in trouble."

"I thought you said he found the gun," Jenna coolly recalled. "If he wasn't involved in a crime using this gun, how could he get in trouble?"

The big man wiggled and scrunched his brows. "He *said* he found it, but how do I know? He trusted me. Do you understand what that means? My friend *trusted* me. I can't give you his name."

"Does that report clear my client?" Mr. James asked urgently. "Luke didn't kill Hamden."

"Ballistics tests reveal this was not the weapon used to fire the bullet that struck and killed the judge," Jenna confirmed. Both attorney and client breathed relieved sighs and exchanged a smile. "However," Jenna sternly stipulated, regaining their attention. "It has been used in several unsolved crimes, and the fingerprint lab is having a field day matching up everyone who handled it recently."

"I tucked it under the bed," Monk explained. "That's why my prints are on it."

"Along with Jabari Brown, Malik Kamara, Asad Habib—" Jenna paused when she spotted Monk's reaction to the third name on her list. A satisfied smile tugged at a corner of her lips. "Seems like this gun has gotten around. We'll be investigating everyone tied to the revolver regarding the unsolved crimes and any ongoing cases. I hope it doesn't come back to bite you, Mr. Monk. The district attorney's office has a slam-dunk case against you for the armed robbery you're being tried for. Honestly, all things considered, your attorney should be advising you to make a plea deal and save the taxpayers the time and money of a trial."

"My client deserves his day in court," Mr. James thundered, seeming slighted that Jenna even suggested he wasn't acting in his client's best interests. "We need the media to be present, to report on how Mr. Monk's rights have been trampled on—like this crazy accusation that he murdered Judge Hamden." He waved a hand in the air.

Jenna merely tilted her chin at him. "Mr. James, nobody has accused Mr. Monk of killing the judge."

"That's why you had his house searched in the first place, and I intend to file a suit against the RPD and whatever judge signed off on it. That search violated Mr. Monk's Fourth Amendment rights. He is to be considered innocent until proven guilty. You people regularly trample on the rights of persons of color and immigrants, assuming the worst of us, and imposing harsher penalties than on those who look like you. It's a disgrace to justice, and I've made it my mission to bring these inequalities into the light. This trial *will* go forward, and the public will see how the system piles misery after misery on members of the Black community."

She couldn't discount James's argument entirely. Jenna understood the justice system wasn't perfect and wasn't as colorblind as it should be. It was a complicated problem that Mr. James couldn't solve by arguing that everyone involved was out to railroad his client. Even if the lawyer's premise held merit, Lukas Monk would end up with a third strike, possibly proving James's point but at his client's expense. That wasn't fair either.

"Sit down, Zach," Monk grumbled miserably. His lawyer, who seemed not to realize he had bolted from his chair, sat and smoothed his tie with a dignified air.

"I robbed the check-cashing place but had nothing to do with what happened to Judge Hamden. Why didn't you say the DA would give me a deal? I don't want to be an actor on your stage—I want a deal." He shifted to Jenna. "Zach said he could get me off if I kept my mouth shut, but I didn't know I could have a deal. If it means less prison time, please, detective," he begged. "Can I still have the deal?"

II

After contacting the DA's office and instructing Monk and his lawyer to sit tight while someone came over to discuss terms, Owens and Jamison returned, escorting a wrathful Amazon, whose piercing cat eyes glared at Jenna when they met in the lobby. The woman about Jenna's age met Owen's height, sporting lean muscles and a butch haircut. The added details of her blue jeans, flannel shirt, faux leather lace-up boots, and lack of cosmetics on her stern, freckled face led Jenna to believe the woman just might be batting for her team—sexually, that is, not in her reckless lawbreaking to promote her cause.

"Interview B," Jenna clipped before her detectives could ask.

"Alright, Madden, you heard the boss," Owens rumbled and strong-armed her down the hallway.

Jamison hung back, giving Jenna a disbelieving look. "That's one scary woman, Ferrari," she whispered, her gaze following Madden. She lifted a large evidence bag. "We collected these firearms from her residence, along with two shotguns and a rifle. If she doesn't believe in hunting animals, you have to wonder why she keeps all this firepower around."

"Take them all to the lab, will you? Tell Davenport I want the barrels swabbed for plastic residue before Verbeck does the ballistics tests. It wasn't the shotgun, but we're looking at the possibility the shooter could have fired from a greater distance with a rifle."

"I'll take care of it. If she's still in there when they get results?" Jamison waited, nibbling her bottom lip.

"Then bring them on in. I bumped Lukas Monk from the list," she informed her partner. Jamison nodded.

"Thanks. Owens and I will take this one. Stay on top of the lab. There's some weird stuff I'll have to tell you about over lunch. Speaking of which—"

"Randi texted and said she'd bring by fruit, chips, and sandwiches for everybody." Jamison smiled, and Jenna frowned, drawing a tinkling laugh from Jamison. "She said you'd be too busy to answer her."

Jenna's brows lowered, and her lips twitched. "Yeah, yeah."

"I'll come see you when we get something." With a pert smile, Jamison spun on her high heel, her voluminous red tresses flipping around the shoulders of a stylish autumn sweater-coat, and strode toward the lab. The lack of watery spray suggested the rain had taken a break.

Deciding on an approach to use with Madden, Jenna swung by vending to grab a bottled water. She found Owens and Hendrix chatting in the hallway outside Interview B.

"There you are!" Hendrix enthused. "ADA Altman is in there with Monk and his lawyer. He said I didn't need to record it because, if they reached a decision, they'd be signing a contract. Mr. James looked peeved. And I don't know who's more dangerous looking—the Incredible Hulk in A or Lieutenant Ripley in B."

"Lieutenant Ripley?" Jenna asked, confusion masking her features. Why couldn't this kid speak English?

"Yeah, you know, the bad-ass who killed the aliens in *Aliens*," he explained. "Especially episode four, *Alien Resurrection*, when she had been cloned and infused with alien DNA."

Jenna had seen the *Alien* movies, and, upon Hendrix's comments, recognized a vague resemblance, only Patti Madden wasn't hot like Sigourney Weaver.

"I'll try to ensure she doesn't send crab creatures to shove eggs down our throats," she smirked. Hendrix shivered. "Come on, Owens. Let's find out what Ms. Madden was doing in Hamden's neighborhood while he was getting shot."

After introductions and reading Madden her rights, Jenna began with the threatening emails.

"They weren't threats," the woman replied smoothly. She leaned back in her chair, propping a booted foot over her knee. "They were food for thought."

The massive amount of dominant energy she projected engulfed the room, which was hard to do, given "Mr. Intimidation" Ron Owens and Alpha female Jenna Ferrari shared the same space. Jenna pondered how to use Madden's brazen confidence against her.

"Is that what you call promising to strap him to a table and perform excruciating chemical experiments on him?"

Madden shrugged. "I merely posed a 'what if' hypothesis, asking how he would like being treated like the mice at the chemical company's lab." She arched a brow at Jenna. "Don't sit there all smug, acting high and mighty like your law is the only one that matters. You have no right to judge me." Fire flickered in yellow-green eyes that hardened like granite.

"It's not my job to judge you, Ms. Madden," Jenna stated evenly, "and, frankly, I couldn't give a flip about you, your causes, your methods—"

"My lifestyle," Madden added bitterly.

"Are you referring to your choice to be a vegetarian or the fact you married a woman?" It was in the file. Patti Madden and Sophie Amato had been among the first couples hitched in Roanoke the month Virginia legalized same-sex marriage.

"Vegan," she clipped with derision and swung her foot. She rested one elbow over the back of her chair and one on the table, taking up as much space in the room as possible.

"My apologies, and, as for the other matter, I happen to have my own beloved wife at home."

A hint of surprise rushed across Madden's face before her features hardened again.

"It's true," Owens confirmed. "Her wife is a first-class woman who treats Lieutenant Ferrari right. We all love her." A smile lit his face, displaying LGBTQ+ advocacy. "But like she said, we don't care about any of that. These death threats, on the other hand ..." He tapped the folder.

"I don't kill any living thing, even despicable, disgusting humans," she seethed through gritted teeth. "I care about the planet and the other animals that occupy it with us. Sometimes I may come across as overzealous, but that's only to make up for the millions of people who turn a blind eye to how we're destroying the earth, or worse—those who are complicit, who know what they're doing and just love money more." Her eyes and tone darkened with the accusation. Her foot dropped to the floor as she leaned forward with both elbows on the table.

"It's not just carbon pollution and oil spills. They are poisoning our food and water every day. And have you seen the torture they put animals through in the name of progress?"

Jenna regarded her neutrally. She didn't approve of cruelty to animals any more than other sane, sensitive people, but radicals like Madden took their stands to unreasonable extremes. Should new cancer treatment drugs be tested on human subjects instead of mice? What about research and potential therapeutic applications for stem cells? Did she think theories should be tried on people first? How was that better? Or maybe she was one of those extremists who think humans are like a virus infesting the earth and should all be eliminated?

"And you believe Judge Hamden was complicit in the destruction of the environment? Did you even look at his stand on the issues?" Jenna caught herself. Aware her emotions were about to kick in, defending a man who supported weaning the country off fossil fuels in favor of clean sources of energy, she took a breath and waited.

Madden's scowl deepened. "He ruled in favor of that chemical company and against me. Actions speak louder than words, Lieutenant." She jammed her finger into the tabletop for emphasis, her features twisting with malice. "He's a hypocrite and a traitor to true liberals and doesn't deserve to win that election."

"You mean didn't," Owens corrected.

Jenna felt like tearing her hair out and yelling, "And you'd rather have Cochran, a born and bred conservative from Lynchburg who thinks women are too inept to tie their shoes, stands by the decision to put kids in cages on the border, and wants to revoke every legal protection for members of the LGBTQ+ community?" She bit her tongue before dropping her jaw in wonder at Madden's curious expression.

"What do you mean, *didn't?*" she asked slowly, the mask of bravado slipping away.

"Have you been hiding under a rock for the past eighteen hours?" Jenna blurted out in astonishment.

"Ms. Madden, Judge Hamden was murdered in front of his home yesterday afternoon," Owens stated. "It's been all over the news ever since."

"I," she stammered, "I don't watch television or subscribe to a paper. I didn't know."

Owens snorted and shook his head. "How convenient," he muttered sarcastically and rolled his eyes. Then, fixing her with a hard look, he charged, "You and your PETA buddies cut the lock on the gate of Chemical Secure Labs in the middle of the night, unlawfully entered the premises, and trashed the place. You weren't even smart enough to spray paint over the monitoring cameras until after they'd caught you in the act. When security guards approached you, y'all threw tear gas canisters at them and then set a fire in a dumpster. You caused thousands of dollars' worth of property damage and put employees' lives at risk, and you wonder why a judge ruled against you?"

"Nobody was hurt," she snapped back with a glare. "No lives were ever at risk—except maybe ours if a guard with an itchy finger had fired at us. But you don't know what they do there."

"Two wrongs don't make a right," Jenna replied. "Cliche, but true. Additionally, the RPD has evidence that you vandalized Judge Hamden's campaign billboards, posted an embarrassing AI-generated video of the judge and a chimpanzee, which, even if fabricated, suggests cruelty to animals, which seems to make *you* the hypocrite. Add in the death threats, and you're currently our number-one suspect."

Regaining her composure, Madden flipped her nose at them. "You have nothing. Besides, if I killed that sorry poser, I'd be bragging about it. I'd gladly stand up and tell the world I took him down, rid our town of one more two-faced lying politician who wouldn't know justice if it kicked him in the ass. You've got my guns," she clipped in irritation. "Your tests will show none of them killed anybody."

"That's another thing," Owens accused. "Why would a tree-hugging animal lover like you even have that arsenal in the first place? I'm an ex-military cop, and I only own my service pistol and a twelve-gauge."

Patti Madden crossed her arms and glared at Owens intently. "You never know when you'll need to protect yourself from vicious human varmints. I'm well within my Second Amendment rights."

"Where were you yesterday afternoon around four-thirty?" Jenna asked directly, studying her for any sign of deception. A tendon tightened in the woman's neck, and her jaw clenched.

"I don't recall," she replied curtly. "According to you, I must have been drawing mustaches on Hamden campaign posters."

"You don't recall," Jenna repeated in a dangerous tone. "Think harder."

Madden flexed her muscles as she balled her hands into fists before slapping them on her hips. Exhaling a sigh, she pronounced, "Lawyer."

"Fine." Jenna gathered her papers and rose. "Officer Girard will show you to the phone and then escort you to your cell to await his or her arrival, at which time we'll continue your interview."

"Wait, what?" Madden shot out of her chair. "You can't lock me up."

Owens, who now stood beside Jenna between Madden and the door, met her rage with cool confidence. "Of course we can. The police can hold a suspect for twenty-four hours before charging them with a crime or letting them go. Considering your record and the severity of the crime, twice that long. But don't worry, Ms. Madden, we'll have enough to arrest you for first-degree murder even if none of the guns we pulled out of your place match. Any smart killer would have ditched the murder weapon, and, while I might think you're off your rocker, I don't believe you're entirely stupid."

"Wait!" She raked long fingers through her short crop of honey-brown hair, her weight leaning on one foot. "We're living in 1984, Big Brother spy cameras everywhere. You probably know I drove by Hamden's house. I was calculating how to perpetrate a prank—you'd call it vandalism—so the whole neighborhood would see what a phony he was before election day. But then he pulled into his driveway, and I didn't want to get caught. He'd probably tell the police I was stalking him, so I sped on down the street."

Flipping through her folder, Jenna asked, "You own a 2023 four-wheel-drive Jeep Wrangler hybrid, correct?" She flicked her gaze to the lanky activist. The traffic cam showed her behind the wheel of a dark gray Jeep.

"That's right."

Jenna pictured how high off the ground the chassis stood—at least as high as Randi's pickup truck. Madden was a tall woman, and, if she raised her bum, sat in an open window, and shot over the top, it would put the trajectory at just about the right angle.

"And that's the vehicle you drove past his house?" Jenna followed up.

"You already know it was. I'm not lying to you, detectives." Madden dropped her attitude like a coat that was too hot to wear anymore. "Maybe I thought of and treated Judge Hamden like an adversary, but I didn't want him dead, and I certainly didn't kill him."

"No," Owens growled. "You wanted to strap him to a lab table and pump him full of deadly chemicals so you could watch him suffer."

"I was angry when I wrote that," she responded. "When my wife saw the email, she threw a fit and called me an idiot. Haven't you done something when you were furious only to regret it later?" Her jaw quivered as her eyes darted from Owens to Jenna. "They were only words. You can't just look at what people say—you have to consider their actions."

"Your actions say you go to extremes for your causes," Jenna noted. "Maybe eliminating Judge Hamden was an extreme you felt necessary."

Jamison stepped in with a blue folder. "Excuse me, but you wanted to see this." She passed it to Jenna and eased back out. Tension still hung in the air as Jenna read the results. None of the guns showed a match, and tests for plastic polymers came back negative. The report further stated that the amount of dust in the barrels suggested it had been months, if not years, since any of the weapons had been fired. However, just because it wasn't one of these guns didn't mean Madden hadn't built another one out of plastic parts, shot him with an untraceable bullet, and ditched or destroyed the evidence. However, not long ago, she'd jumped to a conclusion too soon and arrested the wrong person; Jenna didn't intend to make the same mistake again.

Raising a serious gaze at Madden, she said, "You might want to secure that lawyer. None of these guns fired the fatal shot, but you still had motive and opportunity. If you leave town or fail to appear when we call you in again, I'll put out an arrest warrant on you, and every police officer in the state of Virginia will be tracking you down. Do you understand?"

Looking like a scolded puppy instead of the rabid pit bull who'd strode in earlier, Madden cast her gaze to the floor and nodded. "I understand."

12

After three unremitting hours of marking essays with a red pen so her students would understand where their mistakes lay, Randi gladly vacated her office to whip up a batch of sandwiches. A news report played on the great room TV while she stacked sprouted whole-grain and wild-grain sourdough bread on a massive wooden cutting board beside deli meat, real cheese, lettuce, pickles, and tomato slices next to mayonnaise and mustard bottles. She knew to double the meat and skip the veggies for Ron, leave off pickles and mustard for Trisha, but she frowned when thinking about Tyr Hendrix. She didn't know what he liked. Confident Ron and Jenna would eat more than one sandwich each, and Jenna wasn't picky, she made extras with various combinations of bread and fixings. Grapes and apple slices were already in plastic bags, and a batch of fresh, gluten-free, walnut date chocolate chip cookies baked in the oven.

"And now for the latest in Judge Lester Hamden's murder. Tom?"

Randi glanced at the television to spot a reporter standing outside Jenna's building. "Police have been bringing in persons of interest to interview all morning, Kate," said the man in a raincoat holding a microphone. "So far, no arrests have been made, and Chief Clarkson has been tight-lipped regarding the investigation. Earlier this morning, he gave a brief statement."

The image transitioned to Chief Clarkson standing beside Captain Myers in the police station lobby, surrounded by journalists. "We are deeply shaken by the murder of Judge Lester Hamden, a respected member of the justice system, and wish to extend our deepest sympathy to his family and loved ones. I assure the public that the RPD is pursuing all leads and will not rest until we apprehend the killer. However, we will not rush to judgment or be hurried into overlooking a vital piece of evidence. Investigations of this nature take time. The press will be notified of any new developments or when an arrest has been made. Thank you, and God bless."

"Less than twenty-four hours," Randi muttered as the reporter came back to discuss how long the judge's killer might remain at large. "Do they understand nothing?"

She spread mayo on the bread and assembled another sandwich. When the timer beeped, she grabbed a mitt and pulled the aromatic cookies from the oven. At least Jenna's team would get healthy fuel to energize what was bound to be a long afternoon. Stacking the cookies between sheets of parchment paper in a Tupperware dish, Randi snapped on the lid, stowed everything in an extra-large picnic basket, and bade the pets goodbye.

"Be good while I'm gone, and we'll play ball in the backyard when I get home," she promised Byron, who regarded her mournfully. "Jenna says no going for runs on slick surfaces. Bandit, claws go on cat scratchers and your treehouse, not doorframes or furniture." She pinned him with a stern expression, which he ignored, choosing to lick his paws instead. He was usually good anyway.

When she sauntered into the criminal investigations office, Jenna and her team were so deep into it that they didn't notice her arrival.

"Hendrix, research every detail about 3-D printer guns," Jenna barked. "Fact or fiction. Do they work? Are they reliable? What is required to make one?"

"Are you serious?" Jamison spun her chair around, mouth agape. "Oh, hi, Randi. Hey, lunch is here, but I want to hear about this crazy 3-D printer gun theory." She whirled out of her desk chair and headed to the table where Randi set the basket.

"They've been around for over ten years," Randi replied easily as she laid out the goodies. Didn't everybody know that? "There have been all kinds of legal battles over them, and their creation is protected under the First Amendment."

"The First Amendment?" Owens gave her an incredulous look and selected two lettuce-free sandwiches for starters. "Thanks for remembering how I like them."

"That's right," Randi quipped, "and you're welcome. Tyr, I didn't know how you like yours, but there's a little bit of everything here, so take your pick."

"Thanks!" He beamed at her, putting Randi in mind of her student Noah. They were of a similar age, and she'd seen the same expression of appreciation on Noah's face.

"Go back to the First Amendment," Jenna said. Leaning in behind Randi, she whispered, "Thanks indeed. You didn't have to—"

"Nobody has to," Randi chided sweetly, batting her lashes at Jenna with a bashful smile. "I love you," she whispered, "and your team by extension."

Straightening, she opened the plastic bin of cookies and raised her voice to an instructional level. "A 3-D printer gun isn't a product—it's a recipe—and thereby covered under freedom of speech. People download the code, or recipe, online, feed it into their legally purchased printer machine, choose the plastic tubing they want to use, and the machine follows the blueprints in the code to create the parts, one layer at a time. Then the person has to assemble it and insert a tack or nail head as the firing pin. Now, it is illegal to make or create any gun that cannot be identified by a metal detector. So, to be a legal weapon, the Liberator—or whatever gun recipe the individual chooses—must include a metal plate to make it detectable. However, they are highly unreliable and tend to explode upon use. Some hobbyists experiment with their 3-D printer guns, using metal barrels they purchase as replacement parts, which are far less likely to overheat."

She paused for a moment, wondering. "Why are we talking about this?"

"How do you *know* all this?" Jenna asked in bafflement. "Byron, Shelly, and Keats, I'd understand, but how did you become a walking encyclopedia of untraditional firearms?"

"Well, it began when I started dating a cop," Randi offered honestly. "I had to bone up on all the dangers you might face on the job, and because there's no way to trace bullets fired from—"

It hit Randi in mid-sentence why Jenna asked for the research. Her heart leaped into her throat, and her pulse raced. "That's what the killer used?"

"No wonder none of the ballistics results were matches," Jamison voiced in astonishment. "Owens and I have been too busy this morning to read the lab findings on the slug."

"No striations," Jenna reported in sullen frustration, "and traces of plastic. I'm exploring a few possibilities of how that happened, and using a 3-D printer gun is one of them."

"Dr. McLeod is right," Tyr noted, "but I can find more in-depth information and all the most recent upgrades. Such a weapon would be unique, lightweight, and disposable. Even the best ones are only good for a few shots before they stop working." From his spot at the end of the table, he bit into his sourdough ham and cheese, his paper plate piled with sandwich halves, fruit, and cookies. His eyes lit, and the curve of his lips created dimples in his cheeks. "This is one wicked sammie!"

"Thanks!" Randi blushed.

The five of them sat around the table brainstorming ideas until Vicki and Matt walked in. "Hey, save some for us!" called Vicki. She rushed to the table, relieved to find food remained.

"We put Ms. Diaz in Interview B," reported Matt. "Hey, are those soft chocolate chip cookies?" His blue eyes danced.

"Gluten-free with dates and walnuts," Randi supplied. "And there's a turkey on sprouted grains and a ham on sourdough, if you like those."

"You bet!"

Officers Stone and Murphy squeezed in and helped their plates with what was left.

"Did you find anything suspicious at Diaz's place?" Jenna asked.

"No guns in her residence or car, but evidence she'd been drinking and threw a temper fit and smashed a bunch of stuff that she didn't bother to clean up."

"Are you sure an intruder didn't ransack her place?" asked Trisha.

Vicki shook her head. "She admitted to breaking things when she learned Guerrero had been stabbed to death."

"Where's the baby?" Jenna's tone sounded strangely anxious.

"She's holding him in the room," Matt answered. Wrinkling his brow with concern, he added, "Maybe we shouldn't keep them waiting too long."

"What did Guerrero's other family members have to say?" Jenna asked.

"His dad was on shift at the factory he works at and didn't get off until five," Vicki replied. "We verified that. His mother was at her employment with a hotel cleaning service, also verified. One of his brothers is serving day fifteen of a thirty-day lockup, and the other is in Atlantic City."

"We verified that, too," Matt added. "Security cameras show him playing blackjack at the time of the murder."

"Which only leaves Diaz," Owens concluded. "What'd she say?"

Vicki gave an irritated frown. "That she was home alone with the baby all afternoon and night—no visitors, no phone calls—hence, no alibi."

Randi knew what Jenna was thinking. First, she'd have to deal with a baby, and, second, she'd be wondering how an unwed mother of extremely modest means could have gotten hold of a 3-D printer, much less know how to use it. She glanced at her wife and spied her brain cogs turning.

"I don't suppose you found a 3-D printer at her house?" Randi ventured to ask.

Vicki Stone shot her a disbelieving expression. "Are you kidding? Her crappy apartment was doing good to have a working microwave. Where'd that question come from?"

Jenna shook her head. "Long story, but it's an avenue we're exploring. Murphy, did you establish a rapport with Ms. Diaz?"

"Yeah," Vicki answered for him. "You know the kid—everybody loves him." She rolled her eyes and stuffed the last bite of sandwich into her mouth.

"Come with me for the interview, then," Jenna invited. "Hendrix, I need you in the booth and then back to research mode. Did you turn up anything else on Hamden's phone or computers?"

"There are more concerning emails, but none rise to the threat level of those the PETA lady sent. One, about three months ago, claimed to be from a psychic who predicted if he didn't drop out of the race, he'd die before he could be elected to Congress, but I figured you wouldn't put any stock in it."

Jenna groaned.

Less than six months ago, Randi had brought Jenna into a case involving a genuine psychic amongst a cluster of charlatans. Jenna said it made invisible fingers crawl up her back just to think about anything supernatural. However, if Rhianon Hayes had foreseen danger clouding Judge Hamden's aura, she'd have contacted either Randi or the lieutenant.

"Randi, thanks for this wonderful lunch," Jamison said, a smile lighting her sweet eyes.

"Yeah, Randi," Owens agreed. "It really hit the spot, and my wife won't fuss at me for eating fast food."

"Even better than Mom's," Tyr added in chipper praise. "And that's saying something—believe me!"

"I'd better let y'all get back to work." Randi stood and gathered the containers into her basket.

Jenna's hand pressed to the small of her back and she murmured from behind her, "You're the best wife ever, and I appreciate you. No running in the rain, remember?"

Randi wanted to kiss her so badly. She longed to grab Jenna up in her arms, swing her around, squeeze her tight, and kiss her until her toes curled. Unfortunately, such wasn't an option. "I remember. You be safe too, and don't be afraid of the suspect's baby."

Glancing down, Randi caught the horrified expression on her wife's face. "I am no such thing afraid of babies," she rebuked in a hush, making Randi laugh.

"I'll see you when I see you." Lifting the basket, Randi's gaze passed around the room at Jenna's coworkers and their friends. "I won't wish you good luck, because a team this talented doesn't need luck. Instead, I'll say God's speed at catching the culprit and nailing him or her to the wall." With a wave and many goodbyes exchanged, Randi departed the office into the drizzle to go home, play ball with Byron, grade another pile of essays, and daydream about what she and Jenna could be doing if some nasty bastard hadn't murdered her favorite political candidate.

13

Jenna and Murphy sat down across the table from a petite Hispanic woman who looked younger than Matt. Clutching her baby, wearing cartoon-character footie pajamas, she bounced him gently, and scowled at Jenna. "You are a ripe bitch dragging me in here like this. I didn't do nothing!"

Responding with a nod of acknowledgment, Jenna asked Matt to Mirandize Camila Diaz.

"Yeah, I understand my stinking rights," she growled. The baby flailed an arm and made unhappy sounds.

Immediately, Jenna wished Randi hadn't left. Civilian or not, she would have been the perfect choice to hold the squirming baby while they interviewed Diaz. She forced a smile. "What an adorable baby," Jenna commented. "What's his name?" Mothers liked it when people bragged on their children, and he was kind of cute, with his round, chubby-cheeked face and little hands grabbing his mother's hair.

"Roberto Diego," she answered, a scowl still engraved on her face, "after my father and his."

"Robbie is sixteen months old," Murphy supplied with a friendly smile. "He can walk and climb on the couch, and even run, although his brakes don't work as well as his accelerator," he added with a charming grin.

"Ms. Diaz, I wish to begin by expressing my condolences on your loss. Nobody wanted Mr. Guerrero to end up dead in an altercation behind bars. I spoke with the warden of the Red Onion yesterday evening, and he has conducted a full investigation." She opened her folder and turned a report to face Camila. "The inmate who stabbed Guerrero with a shiv devised by sharpening the handle of a plastic spoon was identified. Manslaughter charges were added to his record, ten more years were tacked onto his life sentence, and he was sent to solitary confinement for the maximum time allowed. I know it isn't enough, but at least—"

"No, it isn't enough," she broke in, storm clouds brewing on her wrathful face. "Sly should never have been sent to that horrible place! He didn't mean to kill anybody; it was an accident."

"The homeowner died as the result of Mr. Guerrero's assault on him during the commission of a felony robbery," Jenna said in a tender tone. "Then he verbally attacked the judge, jury, prosecutor, and everyone else in the courtroom and had to be dragged out in handcuffs."

"No shit, he was angry about the verdict. Wouldn't you be? That rule isn't fair. My Sly should have gotten five years at Lawrenceville or Dillwyn, not been locked up with the worst of the worst. He wasn't a career criminal," the young woman argued. "He was just trying to get extra money for us after I told him I was pregnant."

"This wasn't his first offense." Jenna maintained some sympathy for the situation. Guerrero had priors for shoplifting and purse-snatching, but nothing violent. Still, he had struck the homeowner, causing him to fall and hit his head on a sharp hearthstone, resulting in his death. Rather than call 911, he had fled the residence. "He could have pursued legal means to earn more money."

Diaz set her fussy baby on her knee and bounced him, sneering at Jenna. "You don't understand how hard it is to break out of poverty. I'll bet you never went hungry a day in your life."

If she only knew, Jenna thought, then shook it away. This wasn't about her.

"Looking at everything from your point of view," Murphy proposed, moving the interview along, "you had a reason to be angry with Judge Hamden. Are you aware that he tried to place Diego in three different prisons before he was sent to Red Onion?"

The young woman's features drew together in confusion.

"Virginia, like most states," Murphy continued, "is suffering from prison overcrowding. The nature of Guerrero's crime prohibited him from being housed in a minimum-security facility, and the Red Onion had an opening."

Kid did his homework, Jenna thought appreciatively. She hadn't had a moment to dig deeper into Guerrero's story. *Unless he's making it up... naw, I don't see it. He couldn't lie to a grieving woman like that.*

Diaz's tension leveled down a notch, and sadness welled in her chestnut eyes. Little Roberto let out a squeal and waved fists in the air. "But, still, he sent Sly there, and some brute killed him. Now my baby doesn't have a father. What am I supposed to do?"

"What have you been doing, Ms. Diaz?" Jenna inquired. "Mr. Guerrero has been in prison for almost two years, so he couldn't have been providing for you."

"He provided love and encouragement, emotional support," she retorted as bitter tears stung her eyes. "I have a job, although it's only minimum wage. My mother watches Robbie when I'm at work."

"But you weren't at work yesterday afternoon," Jenna probed.

"My job is only thirty hours a week. The greedy boss doesn't want to have to provide benefits for employees, so almost everyone is part-time, so he doesn't have to. Cheap son-of-a-bitch lives in the same nice neighborhood as Judge Hamden."

Did she just let something slip? Jenna jotted a note, then asked, "You know where Judge Hamden lived?"

She shrugged. "He's a public figure. Lots of people know where he lives. I already told this officer I was at home taking care of Robbie when the judge was getting shot. Even if I'm not broken up that karma visited old Hamden, I didn't kill him. I don't even own a gun, and, if I did, I wouldn't be crazy enough to off some high-profile type and have the cops breathing down my neck. Yet here you are anyway." She waved her free hand at them.

While Diaz was clean and attractive—polished nails, hair brushed to a shine—she didn't sport expensive jewelry, and her clothes could have come from Walmart. As Jenna concentrated, she seemed to remember seeing that blouse on a sale rack.

"Look, officers," Diaz said impatiently. "My kid has already lost one parent. Do you think I'm eager for him to lose his other one too? I might look up a Latino curse to say over him, but I wouldn't risk getting locked up for killing him. I have to think about my baby first. You see?"

Jenna's gaze shifted to the tan little boy with a head of black hair, entertaining himself by blowing bubbles through slobbery lips. *The kid matters. Babies do come first.*

Murphy shot Jenna a questioning look, and she nodded. "Ms. Diaz, thank you for coming in to answer our questions. I might need to reach out to you again. Without an alibi, you still have motive and opportunity to have killed Judge Hamden, and, once we find the murder weapon, we'll need to match fingerprints and DNA. Would you be willing to submit your samples now, so we wouldn't have to disrupt your routine by calling you back in again?"

She narrowed her eyes at Jenna. "Sly said to never willingly give the police anything; they'll just devise a way to use it against you. You'll need a court order to get my prints and DNA. Can I go now? It's time for Robbie's nap."

"You may go." Jenna rose, Murphy right behind her, and opened the door. "He is a cute baby," slipped out of her mouth, with far more sentiment than she intended. Mother and child left without a reply.

Alone with Murphy in the interview room, Jenna asked, "Have you ever gone hungry before?"

His eyes widened, and his lips parted in mild surprise. Then his cheeks flushed an adorable pink as he flustered with his hands, finally stuffing them in his front pockets. "I could say I spent my entire teenage years hungry, but I know what you mean. There was this time our youth group went on a wilderness retreat—one of the most meaningful weekends of my life. We all struck out on a less-traveled part of the Appalachian Trail with nothing but water and our sleeping bags. The group leaders had supplies in case somebody got hurt or sick or fainted or something, but we didn't eat for three days. The point was to understand what it was like to go without, and also to commune with nature and God. We built campfires at night and sang songs, shared our thoughts and feelings. There were ten of us teens and three adults, and we all bonded over the experience. I guess you can't know how someone else feels until you've walked a mile—or twenty," he added with a laugh, "in their shoes. At the end of the three days, I felt hungry on the one hand and strangely satisfied on the other. Do you know what I mean?"

Pride in the young man swelled in Jenna's chest. "I do. What do you think of her story?"

"I think she's angry, grieving, and scared," he answered, moving one hand to scratch his head. "I realize anyone can commit murder, given the right circumstances, but I can't see it."

"She's too short," Jenna stated. "And I don't think she has the means to pull it off. Whoever shot Hamden was a marksman. I checked the registry, and Diaz has never owned a gun, legally registered, anyway. That's not to say she couldn't have had help, but I'm bumping her down the list."

"I'll buy that. But what do you mean about being too short?" He cocked his head at her.

"Come on." Jenna led the way out of the room, meeting Hendrix in the hallway. "We need a briefing to exchange all the information so far in the case and an action plan for moving forward."

"This is so much more exciting than cyber crimes," Hendrix said. He jutted a hand toward Murphy. "I'm Tyr."

Taking his hand, the uniformed officer chimed, "Matt Murphy. Pleased to meet you."

"You already met," Jenna grumbled. "Remember lunch?"

"But we weren't introduced," Tyr replied amiably.

Jenna pushed open the office door and asked over her shoulder, "Hey, Murphy, how easy was it to climb that tree in Hamden's front yard?"

"Not hard," he shrugged.

"Listen up, everyone," Jenna announced. "Gather around the table—no food this time," she stipulated with authority. "We need to share info and get on the same page. Then I have to update Captain Myers."

The team gathered around, notes in hand, and Jenna started. "Thus far, we've interviewed three suspects who could have killed him, but we've no hard evidence against any. I want to get Carter Mintz in here this afternoon, and, Jamison, you and I need to go to that horrible Purity Fellowship tomorrow morning and catch that Heckle fellow and all his followers on their way out. There's a host of potential suspects there. Now, here's what Dr. Valentine and the lab have given me so far."

She went through the one exacting, fatal shot, the wound tract trajectory, the plastic flakes from the yard, and the residue on the bullet. She then briefed the others with her notes from the interviews. Hendrix added an update on the other threatening emails and additional personal history about the victim and his family. Jamison presented photos and quotes by opposition groups she had found posted on social media, while Owens produced a list with more names of criminals Hamden had either prosecuted or sentenced over his career. Jenna breathed a sigh of relief when she received a call from Captain Myers saying there had been no suspicious activity or attempts to attack any of the county's other sitting judges.

"I think we're looking for somebody who's tall, or with a large vehicle to shoot from, or nimble enough to hide in the front yard tree," Jenna deduced. "They must be smart, an excellent shot, and most likely with access to a high-quality 3-D printer or work with polymer plastics. This unsub should also have a reason to target Judge Hamden specifically and the opportunity to do so. A couple of our suspects thus far have the motive and opportunity; it's the means we're having trouble with. Murphy, Stone, grab some more uniformed officers and return to the scene. I want a more exhaustive search of a broader area. Check every drainage ditch, trash can, neighboring woods, and vacant lots. We need to find that gun—one that doesn't leave striation marks—and then have the lab link it to one of our suspects. And the killer either blended in or disappeared in a flash because the neighbors saw nobody."

"Sure thing," Officer Stone replied. "Let's go round up the cavalry." She slapped Murphy on the shoulder, and he followed her out.

"I'll go pick up Mintz," Owens volunteered.

"Good. Hendrix, see if you can find more traffic camera footage with a suspicious vehicle and track Madden's jeep around town. Expand your search a mile—no, two miles—from Hamden's home."

"Yes, ma'am, Lieutenant Ferrari. I'm on it."

"Jamison." Jenna met her gaze. "Go by Mrs. Hamden's sister's house to check on the family. Ask them if they need anything and reassure them we're on this case twenty-four-seven until we've locked up the judge's killer."

Exchanging a look of compassion, Jamison nodded. "Thank you. That's important too."

"And while you're there," Jenna added sheepishly, "see if they remember anything else. We need a break."

With a sad smile, Jamison brushed Jenna's arm as she passed on her way to the door. "We'll get it."

With assignments given, Jenna strode down the hall to update Captain Myers in person.

14

Jenna and Owens sat across from Carter Mintz, convicted arsonist, and his parole officer, a woman who looked tough enough to bite nails—the construction kind. While Mintz was White, average-sized with stringy brown hair, a scruffy face, and a rather unremarkable appearance, in contrast, Ms. Lashay Jackson's warm, earthy skin, sharp angles, and a distinctive pattern of Fulani braids adorned with beads drew the eye to the sturdy woman around ten years Jenna's senior. The buttons of her red and white checkered shirt pulled snugly across her ample breast and muscular shoulders.

After introductions and reading Mintz his rights, Owens began. "We were glad to find no weapons or contraband at your residence, Mr. Mintz. That's a promising start."

"Carter better not be caught with a gun," Jackson bellowed, passing him a severe stare beneath narrowed brows.

"What exactly do you want with me?" Mintz barked in dissatisfaction. "Some suspicious fire you want to pin on me?"

"Not today," Jenna answered. "I understand that Lester Hamden was the district attorney who prosecuted your case, ending in a conviction and a fifteen-year sentence to a state penitentiary, that you served twelve years of that sentence, and were released from prison a week ago."

"Yeah, sounds right." Mintz crossed wiry arms over his flat chest and frowned, leaning back as if to distance himself from the rest.

"Are you aware of the pivotal role your conviction held in Judge Hamden's career?" Owens asked. "The acclaim he garnered for incarcerating 'The Match' helped him win his seat on the bench."

"Bully for Hamden," Mintz uttered in mock cheer and twirled a finger in the air.

"Straighten up, Carter," barked his parole officer, her menacing tone and scowl deepening. "The judge who put you away was just murdered a week after you got out of prison. Don't you see how this makes you a suspect? If you want to hang onto your freedom a little longer, you'd better cooperate."

Unremarkable Mintz glared at you-couldn't-miss-her-for-the-world Jackson before assuming a less combative posture. His lips twisted, and he clasped his hands together on the table. "What do you expect? I've been locked up for twelve years."

"We understand," Owens said, "and, while destructive and potentially deadly, your past fires never killed anyone."

"Did somebody catch the judge's house on fire?" Mintz inquired. "Did the arsonist use my signature? I doubt you ever released that detail to the public."

"No," Jenna responded, observing every tick and intonation originating from the suspect. "No fires were set. I'm sure you've heard the news and are aware of those facts."

Mintz rubbed his stubbly jaw and met Jenna's gaze for the first time. His dull amber eyes hardened like Carnelian stones—cold, lifeless, almost mechanical. "Then why hassle me? Guns aren't my style. Boring. Did I break out the tissues and sit down for a good cry when I heard about Hamden? No. Neither did I throw a party. Honestly, I didn't care about him one way or another. If Hamden hadn't prosecuted me, some other suit from the DA's office would have." He lifted a shoulder. "I never held a grudge against the man, and I certainly didn't spend my time locked up thinking about him."

"What did you think about, Mr. Mintz?" Jenna asked.

A diabolical smile slowly formed across his lips. "Do you know what it's like to get paid for doing what you love? I do. Arsonist for hire," he reminisced, "and I was the best—until that milk-toast client betrayed me. You cops never would have caught me. You caught the treacherous rat who hired me, and his testimony put me away. If I were going after anyone, it would be Patrick Malone, not a stinking lawyer." He stared at a spot on the wall past Jenna's shoulder, a faraway look in his eyes. "I might just do that. What a shame if Malone's boat was to just poof—go up in flames?"

"Shut your mouth, asshole!" Jackson rebuked. "Carter had psychiatric counseling on the inside. They worked with him on ways to suppress his cravings and satisfy his firebug in conventional ways, like lighting candles and keeping a safe fire pit in his backyard." She slapped a firm hand on Mintz's arm, bringing his attention back to the here and now. "Isn't that right, Carter? You don't need to set other people's property on fire anymore."

He lowered his gaze. "No. I can control myself like a normal person."

Jackson turned to Jenna and Owens. "It's just coincidental timing—Carter being released and then Judge Hamden's murder. I'd be right there with you if a fire had been involved, but Carter isn't motivated by violence or revenge. He just has an unnatural fascination with fires and took jobs where people paid him to burn down buildings."

Jenna granted her a nod. She was probably right. "Mr. Mintz, where were you yesterday afternoon around four-thirty?"

His gaze roamed as he scratched above his ear. "I haven't left my sister's house since she drove me home from prison. I'm not accustomed to being out in the world yet, with the traffic and the noise. Sometimes I sit in the back yard with a barrel and a lighter and burn leaves one at a time. It's soothing and doesn't hurt anything."

"Was your sister home to verify that you didn't leave the house?" Owens inquired.

Mintz shook his head. "She got home a little after five. Meagan's been good to me. She loves me and understands. But I don't have a car, and she had hers at work. How would I have gotten to Hamden's house? Is it on a city bus route?"

The upscale neighborhood was assuredly not on a city bus route.

"Detectives, Carter is required to check in with me weekly and to call if he experiences any urges to start a fire," Jackson explained. "While I know not all parolees strictly abide by their instructions, his sister, Meagan, is sincerely involved in his recovery and rehabilitation effort. She made a firm stipulation for him to live with her: he must abide by all the rules. I don't believe Carter will knowingly jeopardize his living arrangement or his relationship with his sister. But, if he does ..." Her tone sharpened as she twisted to glare at Mintz. "I'll haul his sorry ass back to jail so fast it'll make his head spin!"

Mintz winced and leaned away from her. "I don't want to mess things up with Meagan. She loves me. I can't lose her."

"Mr. Mintz, Ms. Jackson, thank you both for coming in this afternoon." They didn't need to ask for his fingerprints or DNA since they were already in the database, the same as Monk and Madden. *What is it with the suspects' names all starting with the letter "M"? Dial M for Murder—was that Agatha Christie or Alfred Hitchcock? Randi would know.* Jenna shook her head to refocus.

"I hope you find Judge Hamden's killer," Jackson said. "He was a reasonable man to work with—not too lax, not too rigid—and he always upheld the spirit of the law. I'll miss him."

"Me too," Jenna honestly concurred.

"I'm with the parole officer, and man, Ferrari!" Owens swore as he walked beside her on the short trek back to their office. "If I knew they made parole officers as stunning as her, I might have considered working for the opposing team."

Jenna snorted. "I'm telling your wife."

Owens shrugged. "We have a no-touching rule, not a no-looking rule. Besides, I've seen her drool over Captain Myers, so she has no room to chastise me." Both detectives laughed as they pushed through into the office.

"I don't think he did it," Hendrix commented as he followed them in. With Jamison still gone and Stone and Murphy heading up the continuing search for a murder weapon, it was only the three of them.

"Based on what criteria?" Jenna asked to test the young man.

"You said the killer needed to be tall, and Mintz is five-foot-ten, close to Hamden's height," he began, counting one finger. "Then he doesn't seem to have had transportation." Finger number two. "Maybe he could have climbed the tree, but the neighbors didn't spot anyone fleeing the scene on foot." A third finger shot out. "And the obvious—his psyche would demand he set a fire, and there was none." Pinky finger joined the rest. "Besides, that snatched parole officer was right—he wouldn't want to blow his sweet setup with his sis."

Owens gave Hendrix a slanted glance. "You know Ms. Jackson is old enough to be your mother, right?"

"So?" He shrugged and bopped back to his station. "I didn't say I wanted to hook up with her, just that she's like smokin', you know?"

Owens chuckled, shaking his head. "Let's see who else we can come up with, and hopefully Officer Stone and the others will bring back a murder weapon."

Research, reports, speculation, and more slugging through lists of individuals and organizations who published a negative word about the judge/congressional candidate, and the afternoon morphed into a late night. Exhausted, Jenna's senses awoke to the aroma of beef and vegetable stew when she entered the house. A pot simmered on the stove, and Randi occupied the recliner with an iced tea and a sapphic romantasy in her hand. Her glasses lay on the end table, as she always took them off to read. She had explained she was nearsighted and could see perfectly up close without them.

"Hey, sweetheart," Randi greeted with a sleepy smile. She set aside her book, pushed down the recliner foot, and moved to Jenna, arms open for a hug.

Jenna gratefully received the embrace and kissed Randi's cheek. "Dinner smells amazing."

"I left it warming for you, in case you hadn't eaten already." Randi's lips brushed Jenna's, and suddenly all was right with the world again.

"We worked right through dinner, though I had to get a snack from the vending machine," Jenna admitted. "I dread tomorrow." Sliding out of Randi's arms, she headed for the pot on the stove. Randi already had a bowl and spoon set out for her. As if by magic, a frosty can of beer appeared beside the bowl.

"Or would you rather have wine?"

Jenna couldn't help but smile, her insides warm already from the loving care radiating from Randi's nearness. "This is perfect."

"What's tomorrow?" Randi asked.

Jenna signed as she ladled out a healthy portion. "I'm taking the whole team to the Purity Fellowship excuse for a church to interview their protest-leading pastor and his ultraconservative congregation members. They had this vigorous campaign against Judge Hamden that was too blatant to be ignored."

"The same ones from the Royal Ivy murder case?" Randi followed Jenna to the table, a half-empty can of coconut water in hand.

"Yep," she answered as she slid into her seat across from Randi. "The resident 'we hate everyone who isn't us' crowd. It blows my mind that people like that supposedly worship the same God as the open-armed, open-minded folks at your church."

"Not to mention Jews, Muslims, Jehovah's Witnesses, and Mormons," Randi added. "A host of opposing groups all claiming the same God. In theory, it should draw the world together, not separate it into hostile camps. Ah, the good ole human flaw of always focusing on our differences instead of what binds us together."

"Yeah." Jenna picked at her food, sampling a bite. The tender meat, soft potatoes, firm vegetables, and burst of flavorful broth filled her mouth with such delight as to dissipate all apprehension about tomorrow's exercise. Randi smiled at the expression lighting Jenna's face.

"I'll shower in the morning," said Jenna. "I don't want to waste a minute of what's left of tonight by not spending it with you. Tell me about your day. Were you sick again, or is the nausea getting better? Did you get all your papers graded?" Stilling her spoon and narrowing her eyes, Jenna pressed, "You didn't go running, did you?"

Randi laughed and crossed her heart. "I think someone's been interrogating suspects all day!"

"We don't call it 'interrogating,'" Jenna specified. "And all right. I didn't mean to bombard you with questions. I'm just ready for some normal and to relax with my beautiful, talented wife."

Another laugh rang out from her partner across the table. "When do you ever get 'normal' with me? But if distraction from work is what you crave, I'm sure I can whip together something to meet your needs." Light danced in Randi's flirtatious gaze, her brows wiggling suggestively.

"And *your* needs," Jenna added. "I'm serious. How are you feeling?"

An inspired expression washed over Randi's features, and she beamed. "Like a new life is growing inside me, and it's wonderful!"

15

Sunday, November 3

Out of respect for herself, as much as anything else, Jenna wore her nicest pinstripe pantsuit with a conservatively cut powder-blue blouse to the Purity Fellowship Church that morning. She stood in the back foyer with Sergeant Detective Owens, typical gray, Detective Jamison, stylish yet frugal, Specialist Hendrix, a sports jacket and khakis, no tie, and Officers Stone and Murphy in their standard police uniforms, effectively blocking the exits.

"Well, folks, it would seem the long arm of the law awaits outside this sanctuary to once again harass us for exercising our First Amendment rights," said the man at the pulpit. Donning a navy suit, white shirt, and red tie, the tall fellow gripped the edges of the podium, leaning forward toward the microphone.

"Despite the fact we courageously act on God's behalf, according to his will, to combat the evil that so hideously surrounds us in the world during these troubled times, act in love, not malice, and never with violence, they always believe the worst of us. Do not be troubled, my brethren, brothers, and sisters in the cause of righteousness," he expounded with a preacher's flair. "The Lord told us we would face persecution, that we would be accused of all manner of wrongdoing, and that we should count it a joy and a boon to suffer injustice, even as Christ and the apostles suffered at the hands of the Romans and the Pharisees. Let us suffer patiently in holy reverence and answer their questions honestly and directly so that we will prove to the world our cause is just. Never, I say, will we convince the sinner by pointing a finger at his sins, but only by pointing the finger upward to God." He demonstrated by raising a finger in the air. A chorus of "amens" followed.

Jenna quelled her desire to roll her eyes at the thin, red-haired Heckle, whose prominent nose dominated a pasty, freckled face. She thought he looked more like a scarecrow than a pastor, but what did she know? Catholic priests had robes and collars to define them, but, as for the others? If a stranger passed Pastor Luna from Randi's church on the street, they'd never guess she was a minister.

Although Jenna had felt far less awkward the last time she visited Randi's church, she hadn't been back in the interim month. Still, it only took a moment for her to feel how different the atmosphere here was—chilly, select, unwelcoming—as if the chosen few gathered behind these walls and all others were sinners and deceivers out to get them. There was nothing Jenna could do to change that.

"Be on your best behavior," she instructed her team. "They're looking for a reason to fault us, so let's not give it to them—Owens, Stone," she stipulated.

"What?" Owens whispered innocently. "I'm polite."

As congregants filed through the inner doors into the foyer, Jenna announced, "Thank you all so much for cooperating with the RPD in our investigation into Judge Hamden's death. We apologize for any inconvenience, but anything you can tell us could help achieve justice. We promise to be brief. If you could form lines in front of these detectives and officers, they will take your statements, and you may go on about your day."

Jenna strode straight to Pastor Rod Heckle. "Thank you so much for agreeing to speak with us, Reverend," she opened with a serious yet amiable expression and extended her hand.

He glanced at it before agreeing to give it a limp shake. "Did we have any choice?"

"You had the choice as to where, when, and how the interviews were conducted, and I believe this is the easiest, less intrusive way to accomplish a necessary task. As you might assume, Mayor Tackett, Chief Clarkson, and the national media are pushing us to produce leads in the case. As one of many groups who support Congressman Cochran and have protested against his opponent, you and your congregation members might have seen or heard a member of those other entities issuing threats or behaving in a less holy manner than yourselves."

He gave her a disbelieving look. "You want to know if I killed him, and the answer is a resounding 'no.'" Heckle crossed his arms, peering down at her with disgust.

"Reverend Heckle, could we sit and talk for a moment?" Jenna motioned toward a pew near the back of the sanctuary. "Surely a good Christian man such as yourself—a follower of Jesus and leader of your flock—could spare a few moments to help uncover a clue to who violently shot and killed a fellow human being created in the image of God."

With an impatient sigh, Heckle relented, granting her a nod. "We are attacked so much that we tend to get a bit defensive. I suppose the police would know how that feels."

"Indeed," Jenna agreed.

Leaving plenty of space between them, Jenna took a seat on the same pew that Heckle landed on. "I assure you our intent is not to attack you or your congregation, rather only to uncover the truth of what happened to Judge Hamden. I know you had your differences. Could you explain why you found it necessary to mount so ardent a campaign against him?"

"At first, we weren't worried," Heckle answered in a less belligerent tone. "Representative Cochran has served several terms in Congress, and we suspected he'd win reelection. But over the summer, Judge Hamden rose in the polls to become a genuine contender, and we became concerned."

"Concerned he might win the election?" Jenna specified.

"Yes, which would be a terrible blow. Hamden is a left-wing extremist, a pro-abortion candidate with a stance for trans rights. What an abomination!"

Jenna stiffened but tamped down her temper. "As I recall, Judge Hamden was pro-choice, not pro-abortion. I dare say nobody is pro-abortion except people who want to slash the human population of the planet in half or more. Judge

Hamden was a faithful member of his Methodist congregation who believed a woman's reproductive choices were a matter between her and God, not for lawmakers and courts to decide."

He frowned at her, his eyes darkening with disapproval. "The sanctity of life takes precedence over a woman's right to choose, and the law should recognize the rights of the unborn. But I'll not have that conversation with you. I feel my words would fall on deaf ears, as your mind is already made up on the subject. Yes, Lieutenant, we march and protest—as is our First Amendment right, and our sacred duty—but we use the Word of God as our sword, faith as our shield, wearing the belt of truth, the breastplate of righteousness, the shoes of peace, and the helmet of salvation. We certainly don't kill people."

"Volumes have been recorded of good Christians killing people they believed were evil," Jenna mentioned. "The Crusades, the witch trials, the Holocaust, just to name a few."

"Ancient history," Heckle declared, slicing a palm through the air. "The conscientious dissenters in my congregation would never raise a hand in anger to a fellow human being, even if we are duty-bound to point out the errors of their ways and seek to bring them back into the fold. Hate the sin, love the sinner is our motto. It's even on the sign outside the building."

"And you believe Judge Hamden was a sinner who needed to be shown the error of his ways," she proposed.

"We are all sinners, saved by grace, lest any man should boast," Heckle recited in a manner suggesting anything but humility. "We fight for God's kingdom to come, for His will to be done on earth as it is in heaven. Jesus taught peace and love, not violence and murder. One day, God will judge all; He will dish out punishment to those who deserve it. It's our job to shine a light in a darkened world, to proclaim the Gospel, and to uphold God's infallible law. How can a man claim God made a mistake and go about trying to change himself into a woman? The same goes for a woman who tries to become a man. We are the sex we were at birth because God willed it to be so. Transgender is no better than blasphemy, accusing God of being wrong, and we can't support that kind of thing. It doesn't mean we go beat up trans people or kill those who promote their right to exist. We believe in the sanctity of life; what hypocrites we would be if we set out to kill people with whom we disagree. But ask your questions, take your notes, and find the person who actually killed Hamden, because you won't find him here."

Jenna couldn't be led into a religious or philosophical debate about how wrong Heckle was. Randi would come armed with scriptures, examples, and spiritual laws with which to oppose the conservative pastor; all Jenna had was a smoldering fury over why these people couldn't just live and let live without marches and signs and shouts of angry condemnation. She could still hear the insults ringing in her ears from their demonstration outside the theater where the drag competition had been held. She recalled the hurt on people's faces and understood the guilt caused by the accusations. It had taken her years to realize there wasn't anything wrong with her after the verbal and emotional abuse she'd endured in the past.

What will Mama think? popped into her consciousness. *Will she be like Heckle and be appalled at Randi and my decision to have a baby? And what about Vince Jr.? Will she find his role equally reprehensible?* She couldn't think about that now.

"Mr. Heckle, I understand your position," Jenna responded. "These are standard questions we ask everybody. Do you own a gun, particularly a .45 caliber?"

He stretched to his full seated height and glanced down his ski-slope nose at her. "I own a shotgun, a thirty-aught-six rifle, and a .22 handgun. Sometimes I go deer hunting—in season with a permit—and occasionally a rattlesnake or predator might come around my property. The police department is welcome to test my guns if you wish."

Jenna made a note on her pad, nodded, and continued. "Where were you Friday afternoon at four p.m.?"

"Engaged in a counseling session," he clipped sharply. "Even God-fearing Christian men and women can experience challenges in their marriages and seek a guiding hand to help ease them back on track."

"And two weeks ago, at the demonstration in front of Judge Hamden's campaign headquarters, do you recall other groups or individuals being present who were not part of your congregation?"

Heckle's defensive posture eased as a contemplative look crossed his sea of freckles, his jaw working back and forth. "It was a publicized protest and, yes, others took part. There were some PETA people," he mentioned, and rolled his eyes. "Some other conservative, pro-life advocates. I remember one fellow seemed unreasonably angry, ranting about potential voter fraud and fabricated poll numbers. That was right after the news reported Hamden had gained a two-point lead over Cochran."

Jenna sprang to attention. "Do you know his name? Can you describe the man?"

Shaking his head, Heckle answered in what seemed genuine disappointment, "I didn't know him, and I wasn't paying that close attention. He was White, average-looking, and he didn't have a sign or a group T-shirt to identify him."

"Any facial hair or tattoos?"

Heckle sighed. "I train myself not to judge people based on their appearance, so I don't pay close attention to hair, clothes, or tattoos. He only caught my attention because he sounded angrier than we, and he seemed to think there was a conspiracy to replace Cochran as our congressman. We don't believe that," he attested, raising a hand to his chest. "We know the prevailing attitudes of the folks around here, the liberal bias, and the propensity of residents to reach their hand out to the government wanting a free check. I know most of our elected officials are progressives and socialists, which is why we've worked so hard to get a conservative reelected. Maybe Cochran hasn't rid the country of gays and trans offenders or put a stop to abortions, but at least he's on our side on the issues. Do you really think somebody murdered Judge Hamden to keep him from winning the election?"

"It's a possibility, Reverend Heckle. Thank you for being patient and answering my questions. I'll let you return to wishing your members a good afternoon."

With thoughts of an angry, lone protester accusing Hamden of cheating playing through her mind, Jenna gravitated toward Hendrix, who looked completely out of place surrounded by the all-White congregation. To her surprise, she found him cheerful and coping well, even drawing smiles from the woman he interviewed. Confident he'd found his rhythm, she stepped up to an elderly woman waiting for her turn, greeted her, and proceeded to ask about the angry man at the demonstration, convinced the five-foot-two, white-haired grandma with a cane wasn't their prime suspect. Unfortunately, her failing eyesight offered no better description than she'd gotten from the pastor.

16

Randi spent most of the afternoon curled up in bed between a sympathetic dog and a cat she knew cared more than he let on. Church had been hard as shocked members grieved over Judge Hamden's murder. They prayed for his family and took up a special collection for flowers and food to go to Amanda and their children. Even though they belonged to a different church, Christ United Methodist participated in some of the same charities and projects, such as supporting the local food bank, a women's halfway house, and Habitat for Humanity. Many members of her church knew the Hamdens personally and recounted stories.

Coming home to a house without Jenna in it felt depressing. The cookies and coffee at after-service fellowship time hadn't settled right in Randi's queasy stomach, so she'd just taken some Dramamine and lay down. It might have been out of character for the active, driven teacher, but she didn't feel like doing anything. She just wanted to sleep until it was time to go to the delivery room.

Randi's eyelids fluttered open when she felt a warm kiss on her cheek and familiar hands on her arm and shoulder. It was still light outside.

"I'm home for the night," Jenna cooed into her ear.

A spark of life kindled in Randi's heart, and she rolled on her back to smile up at the woman she loved. Jenna looked as exhausted as Randi felt. "Hey, honey. Did things go all right today? I didn't expect you before dark."

"We made progress," she answered as she sat on the bed beside her, "but we're a long way from discovering the who and the how. You just lie here and rest while I take a shower and order us some dinner. What do you feel like eating?"

"Honestly?" A pained look crossed Randi's face. "Nothing. I've felt bad all day—no energy, nauseated, and not good for anything."

"That's to be expected, and you're good for plenty," Jenna said, making an exasperated face at Randi. "I'll get you chicken soup from the deli that you like and some Jell-O. Soup, crackers, and Jell-O—the staple foods for upset tummies." She brushed a kiss on Randi's forehead. "You'll have some energy after you eat a little something."

"I should be the one taking care of you," Randi moaned. "You're the one who's been thrown into the pressure cooker and had to work all weekend."

"No, sweetie, it's my turn to look after you. After all, you're the one who's growing a new person inside. Spending the day in bed was exactly what you needed. Aren't you the one who told me to listen to my body, to stop and take a break when I need it?"

"Yeah, yeah." Randi tried to produce a laugh, but it just wasn't there. "I love you, Jenna Ferrari. And I'll help you through this case in whatever way I can."

"Bringing lunch yesterday really helped," Jenna said, gliding her fingertips across Randi's cheek and around her chin. "Cuddling with me while I brainstorm later will also be a tremendous boon. And, if my neck and shoulders get too tense, I know I can count on you for a back rub."

"Oooh, a back rub." Life slowly returned to Randi's veins, pushing its way around her limbs. "So, I get to take off your shirt and break out the essential oils?"

Jenna's smile was tired, but warm and dreamy. "Whatever makes you happy, love. Shower, food, brainstorming, back rubs. Sounds like a perfect night." She touched her lips to Randi's and headed for the shower.

Randi liked watching her go, enjoying the playful way she disrobed, tossing clothing items in the general direction of the bed without ever hitting it. The luscious curves of her hips and breasts, the taut muscles in her legs, and soft pillow of her tummy sent arousal shooting through Randi, making her hungry for so much more than soup. And Jenna could complain about her butt being too big all she wanted; to Randi, it was perfection. She wanted to get up, run in there, and take a nibble of that delightful flesh. Thinking about how much she enjoyed showering with Jenna almost gave her the energy to throw off her clothes and do it—almost. When she moved to sit up, her stomach reminded her why she'd lain down to begin with. This had to end soon, didn't it?

Yes, Jesus, the spirit is willing, but the flesh is weak. I have a new understanding of that verse now, she thought and lay back down. *I won't ask why. People die every day—the good and the bad alike—because it's just part of living in this world. But sometimes I get a little angry, frustrated, maybe, or just confused when a human intervenes to bring that death about much sooner than it should have happened. I know not everyone makes it to their nineties, but, when a person who's just trying to do good is shot and killed by a person who's set on doing bad, it doesn't sit right with me. I don't know, maybe they think they're doing good because they have twenty screws loose in their head, but it still seems to buck against the natural order. Comfort Amanda and the children as only you can. Show Jenna the clues she needs to catch the person responsible. And help me accept the things in this world that I can't change.*

***

Monday, November 4

With coffee in mugs and bagels in a box, Jenna and her team gathered around the table in the Criminal Investigations office for a briefing on the case with Captain Myers.

"Where are we with the evidence and interviews?" Myers asked. He looked sharp in his starched beige shirt and bold striped tie, ready for cameras should reporters burst in. Hamden's murder had made national news over the weekend, and Randi had informed Jenna last night—while Jenna's muscles had relaxed so much under her wife's talented hands and fragrantly tingling oils—that the BBC and Canada's Global News had picked up the story. The blanket assumption was that tomorrow, with only the Green Party candidate and the Libertarian opposing him, Cochran would cruise his way to another term in the U.S. House of Representatives. It wasn't just Virginia's Sixth District at stake, but which party would control the most seats in the House, thereby tipping the scales of power.

"Officer Stone." The older woman in uniform straightened when Jenna called on her.

"Sir, we spent all yesterday in an exhaustive search for the murder weapon or any other viable clues," she reported, gloom weighing her words and darkening her visage. "We checked drainage ditches, trash cans, under porches, in bushes ..." Motioning toward Matt, she added, "Murphy and Washington climbed down into the sewer and walked the whole line with flashlights. The killer had to have taken the gun when they left. We brought in an old pair of gloves, a baseball cap, some old bottles, and assorted trash from the drains and bins and turned them into the lab, just in case."

"I've got the lab report that Deng, who took the overnight shift, turned in," Jenna said, holding up a folder. "He tested the items the search team recovered, but they were so old and degraded that he couldn't pull any fingerprints or DNA. Even though the lab is running various tests today, I doubt they'll turn up anything related to the murder. Hendrix?"

The young man looked nervous enough to puke, sitting at the opposite end of the table from the captain. "I checked out more traffic camera footage, and a neighbor down the street brought in his home security video, just trying to help. The most promising pieces feature a 2023 Jeep Wrangler driven by Patti Madden. While the neighbor's front door cam shows her Jeep driving down Judge Hamden's street, it doesn't give a view of when the vehicle was in front of his house. I asked if the Hamdens' house has video surveillance, but Mrs. Hamden said the security system only includes cameras pointed at the front and back doors, not the street. Then I made a list of all cars that turned off the main street into the neighborhood or pulled back out again between four and five p.m. and looked up their license plates. We haven't had time to contact every driver yet."

Jenna nodded at Jamison. "Yesterday, we, everyone present for this meeting, went to Purity Fellowship Church and interviewed the pastor and members. They were one of the most vocal protest groups against Judge Hamden's campaign. Most provided alibis for the time of the shooting, including Reverend Heckle."

"I contacted the couple he claimed to be counseling at the time," Jenna added, "and they verified his account. We also followed up on dozens of hate emails that had been sent to the victim and have divided the senders into lists of who did and did not have an alibi for the time of the shooting. Once we're done here, I've asked Hendrix to compare the names on the non-alibi list with the vehicle owners who drove into Hamden's neighborhood during the hour window."

"And you're certain he was shot from a vehicle?" Myers asked.

"Not one hundred percent," Jenna had to admit, "but witnesses reported not seeing anybody walking by. Our best eyewitness, the retired schoolteacher who called 911, stepped outside only minutes after hearing the gunshot and testified she looked and didn't see anyone walking or running. While it's possible that the killer escaped on foot unnoticed, according to Dr. Valentine's autopsy report, the bullet entered the victim's back at a slight downward trajectory, indicating the shot came from someone significantly taller than Hamden, or the unsub fired from a raised position, such as standing up in a car or from a four-wheel-drive Jeep with a high clearance."

"Several SUVs and full-sized pickup trucks were caught on the traffic cam turning into the neighborhood," Hendrix supplied, his knee bouncing like he was operating a foot pump with his heel.

Captain Myers nodded before pinning Jenna with a grave look. "Tell me about this 3-D printer gun theory again."

"The bullet has no striation marks, but it did have traces of polymer plastic, and a few small plastic flakes were recovered from the lawn near the sidewalk," Jenna recounted. "We've interviewed a couple of promising suspects who either had no firearms found in searches of their property, or the guns recovered didn't match. That's why I sent the crew out on the search yesterday. Our suspect might have thrown the murder weapon in the river or, if it was plastic, melted it down by now. This puts us in a tight spot."

"Making a murder charge stick will be formidable without tying the perp to a weapon," Myers stated and shook his head. "Who are these suspects?"

Jenna gave Owens the nod. "Captain, I'm still plowing through a list of criminals Hamden prosecuted or presided over their trials, so we might produce more persons of interest today. Thus far, there's Lukas Monk, whose trial was supposed to start today and has been postponed. He and his lawyer accused the judge of racial bias, but his motive started falling apart when Monk told his lawyer he wanted to plead guilty and make a deal with the DA. Then there's Camila Diaz, girlfriend of a guy Judge Hamden sent to the Red Onion. He was stabbed and killed in prison a week ago, and she's in a bad way emotionally. No alibi for the time of the murder, but she's a tiny young woman. No gun either, but we're figuring whoever did this isn't stupid enough to have kept it. Our most promising suspect is Patti Madden, the one who we know was driving through the neighborhood. None of her guns matched, but if she ditched it—"

"And this woman is the one you told me about," Myers clarified, glancing at Jenna, "the PETA and environmental protestor who regularly winds up in jail or being charged with fines for property damage and disturbing the peace?"

"Yes, sir. She's driven, intelligent, tall, and checks many boxes, but I can't tell you she screams 'murderer' at me. Except for petty payback, she didn't have a strong motive to kill Judge Hamden. I could see her slashing his tires or spray-painting graffiti on his house like she's been doing to his campaign posters, but fabricating a 3-D handgun and shooting him with it?" She sighed and shook her head. "We're going to keep digging in until we find a better fit, more evidence, a witness, something. We just won't have the case wrapped up for you today."

"Well, that would be asking a lot," Myers admitted. "What about Mintz, the arsonist who was recently released from prison?"

"We bumped him down on the list," Jenna informed him. "His parole officer is staying on top of him, he doesn't have a gun, and he's a classic firebug. Dr. Grayson would say, if he did it, he would have burned the judge's house down instead of shooting him."

Captain Myers nodded. "Keep bringing in folks off your lists and try to catch one in a lie. Then we can get a warrant to search for that printer machine or a weapon. There's one other dreadful, yet obvious, possibility." He let his words hang in the air a moment and then suggested, "The person with the motive isn't the one who shot him. We could be looking at a professional hit. Ferrari, I want you to ask our friends at the FBI if they have any information regarding assassins on their watch list who might be in a two-hundred-mile radius. And keep up the good work, everyone. We just need that one break," he emphasized, closing his basketball player-sized hand into a tight fist on the table.

"You got that right," Owens muttered under his breath.

The captain stood, and Jenna followed. "Lieutenant, walk with me a moment," he said, as more of a request than a command.

"Sure." Glancing around the table, she snapped, "Why are you all just sitting around? Get busy! Go—find some more suspects."

Hendrix and Murphy jumped, Stone moseyed, Jamison snickered, and Owens reached for another bagel. "On it, boss," he proclaimed.

Stepping out beside Captain Myers into the foyer, with Stewart faithfully manning the desk, Jenna dreaded the idea of seeing reporters. Instead, both she and Myers stopped short, taken aback by the surprise awaiting them. U.S. Representative Nash Cochran and his entourage had taken over the visitor area as if they were the conquering heroes of San Juan Hill.

17

Cochran lifted his smooth, angular chin and locked his Caribbean blue eyes onto Jenna's with an air of superiority. He appeared as she expected, his double-breasted charcoal suit crisp and sharp, the fog-gray shirt a perfect complement to the maroon tie and matching silk handkerchief peeking from his breast pocket, a picture of polished power. Every rustic brown hair of his fresh hundred-dollar cut shone like the fake smile he wore. Jenna hated to guess what he was doing here.

"Are you the police captain?" he asked, redirecting his focus to Myers.

After only moving one foot, Cochran's entire team shifted, the four men and two women surrounding the congressman protectively.

"Yes," Myers answered politely, stepping into the lobby. Jenna stuck with him like glue, curious about what performance Cochran was here to give.

Slipping past the blonde woman in the pink pencil skirt and heels and edging around burly bodyguard number one, Cochran extended a smooth, manicured hand to shake the captain's. "I'm Nash, Congressman Nash Cochran. My team and I are here to check on your progress in the investigation into my esteemed opponent's murder. Horrible, just horrible." He shook his head, assuming a saddened expression.

"Captain Jerome Myers and this is Lieutenant Detective Ferrari," he introduced. "She's heading up the investigation on the ground."

A flicker of surprise flashed across Cochran's polished face as if he couldn't fathom a woman being in charge of anything. His lips parted as his gaze shifted to her once more. "Well ..." Recovering quickly, Cochran retracted his hand and rested it on his belt. "I'm glad to see the city's finest are on the job. But tell me honestly, Captain—should I be concerned?"

Cochran returned his attention to the tall, muscular man in charge, his brows crinkling with unease. "Phil, my chief of staff," he said, shrugging a shoulder toward a bookish-looking fellow with round glasses and male-pattern baldness, "insisted on hiring extra security. I told him nobody was getting past Sam and Tony, but he brought on four more bodyguards in an overabundance of caution."

Jenna presumed the fair-skinned, younger man with an earbud and black suit snug around his shoulders could be Sam, while the older, stouter man with ebony hair, olive complexion, and the bulge of a shoulder-holstered weapon under his navy jacket might be Tony. For an instant, she wondered if he got his bodyguards from the mafia. There had been rumors.

"I suppose any public figure must be concerned with safety these days," Myers replied matter-of-factly. "There are a bunch of nutcases and radicals out there who fixate on celebrities and politicians. However, we have discovered nothing thus far to suggest Judge Hamden's killer has other targets on their list."

A fat fellow stood in the corner with a video camera, recording the exchange. *Of course, this is for publicity*, Jenna groaned inwardly to herself. *The nerve of that man!*

Relief brightened the congressman's face, and the blonde woman beside him smiled and relaxed. "See, Congressman Cochran? I told you everything would be fine."

"Yes, Nancy, you did, and I appreciate that." The insufferable show-off returned a serious expression to Captain Myers. "We are all so shaken up about what happened and have already reached out to Mrs. Hamden to extend our most sincere condolences. My wife, Alida, has been beside herself with worry ever since we heard about it on the news. I can't imagine the grief and suffering the judge's family must be feeling right now. I assured them I would come over here in person to encourage the RPD to find and arrest the murderer with haste so we can all put this terrible ordeal behind us."

A smart-looking woman with short, dark hair and a fall fashion pantsuit stepped forward, extending an electronic recording device. "Captain Myers, is there anything you can tell us about the case?"

He gave her a patient smile and held up a palm. "Only what Chief Clarkson has already told the press, ma'am."

"This is Jackie Thompkins, my press secretary," Cochran inserted apologetically. "She can be a little overeager." He shot her a quelling glance, and the woman slunk backward. "My staff is worried that, if someone is killing candidates, I might be next. Please excuse them."

"No problem," Myers said. Broadening his shoulders, he addressed the room. "While certain precautions are always in order, we don't believe at this time that Congressman Cochran is in immediate danger."

"How long have you been and will you be in town, Mr. Cochran?" Jenna asked. She was curious, and, honestly, he couldn't leave soon enough to suit her.

He angled a curious gaze her way, almost as if he'd forgotten she was present. Then a charming smile graced his lips. "We arrived Friday late morning, checked into our rooms, and prepared for the afternoon rally at the Roanoke Community College stadium. Afterward, we zipped over to Salem for a seven p.m. rally, and I didn't even hear about the shooting until returning to the hotel."

Cochran passed a perturbed scowl around at his staff. "They wanted to protect me," he grumbled. Returning a pleasant expression to Jenna, he continued. "Saturday, I had campaign functions in Staunton and Harrisonburg, but we returned here for a day of rest on Sunday. Tonight's big shindig before Election Day is happening in Lynchburg." He beamed with pride, probably because he knew he was going to win. There was nothing and nobody to stand in his way, and Lynchburg, home to one of the most conservative universities in the country, would be like the Promised Land for Cochran. Jenna had to deliberately stop her shoulders from slumping.

With a self-satisfied pat to his perfectly coiffed hair, Cochran drew his lips into a thin, thoughtful line and shook his head slowly. "To think, I was on stage giving a speech before thousands of cheering constituents—televised to boot—when my respected opponent was being shot to death in front of his home. Can you imagine anything more bizarre?"

When the cocky congressman's questioning gaze met Jenna's, it was as though everyone else filling the room faded away, and she and Cochran were the only two people sharing the same plane of existence. Mixed in with arrogance and entitlement, she detected a challenge in those exotic blue eyes. For the briefest instant, he smirked at her—*smirked*—like he dared her to breathe in his illustrious presence.

The realization hit her like a speeding freight train—*He did it! And he's taunting me because he's got an ironclad alibi. Smug bastard!*

The sounds of voices, footsteps, and the bustle of the foyer roared back into her ears as Jenna stood stunned in silence. Captain Myers showed the congressman and his team out, assuring them and promising to bring the killer to justice. Jenna wanted to scream.

When the wet-behind-the-ears, youthful page, the attractive personal assistant, the mousy chief of staff, the keen press secretary, the muscular bodyguards, the dumpy cameraman, and the slick-tongued, narcissist politician were all gone, Jenna pulled Captain Myers into his office and closed the door.

"He did it!" she declared in a hush, never more certain of anything in her life. "I don't know how, but that's the guy."

"Who, Cochran?" Myers's eyebrows shot up. "It's physically impossible. He was speaking on stage to a crowd of thousands during a televised rally. What's gotten into you?"

"He has more to gain than anyone by Hamden's death," she pointed out. "He had fallen behind in the polls and stood a good chance of losing his cushy seat in Congress. The guy has amassed power. He's on the Ways and Means Committee, has his finger in every political pie, and rumors have been flying around for years of the connections he's made, the under-the-table payouts and bribes. Sure, he hasn't gotten caught, but there was that photo taken of him on Jeffrey Epstein's island ten years ago. His people claim it was doctored to discredit him and he never associated with the creep, Epstein, but, Captain, did you see the look in his eyes? He smirked at me!"

"He smirked at you," Myers repeated, completely unconvinced.

"That man looked me in the eye and practically dared me to prove he killed Hamden." She stared up at him with conviction, slapping her hands on her hips.

Myers rubbed the back of his neck and sighed. "We can't accuse a sitting U.S. congressman of murder based on your perceived smirk, Ferrari. And I'm not sure we could convict him even if you had a pile of evidence, of which you have none. I know it's hard for a cop to ignore their gut, but I'm asking you to keep working the case with your head. Could your personal feelings for the man be getting in your way?"

Jenna had to pause and consider his point. She didn't like Cochran's politics but had never met the man until today. Nevertheless, his slimy, arrogant energy had filled the lobby like synthetic fibers in an overstuffed pillow. He had regarded her as nothing, nobody, and he had brushed his female press secretary aside. *Not only a narcissist but a misogynist too*, she pondered. *And interesting how every aide on his team is as white as bleached flour, not counting the Italian, but he was still white. Maybe I just don't like him.* Her gut still screamed that he was the guy.

"We'll keep working the case, pursuing every lead," Jenna agreed. "But *every* lead includes investigating people with motives, and Cochran has a shiny, bright motive."

"Ferrari," Myers declared sternly. "Tread carefully. If you produce a pile of evidence and want to bring Congressman Cochran in for questioning, or—heaven forbid—ask a judge for a search warrant, you pass it by me first, and I'll have to get clearance from Chief Clarkson. Do you understand me, Lieutenant?" He jabbed a pointed finger her way and scowled, making Jenna feel small in his presence.

Without backing down one inch, she nodded. "Yes, sir. We will keep hunting until we can prove who killed Judge Hamden and how he did it, and I know that won't be easy. You've given me a smart team, so we'll find a way."

"Don't ignore normal suspects to go on a wild goose chase, Ferrari," he added.

"You know I won't ignore a single clue, Captain."

Being dismissed, Jenna left his office and strode back to hers.

"Jamison, whatever you're working on, table it," she ordered. "I want everything there is to know about Congressman Nash Cochran, from the time he entered kindergarten to what he ate for breakfast this morning."

Glancing over her shoulder with a bewildered expression, Jamison replied, "Sure, boss, whatever you say."

Every eye in the room flicked to Jenna in surprise. "Ferrari, he was on stage—" Owens began.

"I know," Jenna barked, cutting him off. "Do you have lists of suspects for Stone and Murphy to go interview?"

"I've got two license plate matches," Hendrix cautiously supplied. "One for an SUV and the other for a pickup. One is for a protester and the other is for a felon Hamden prosecuted his first year with the DA's office."

"Give them to Officer Stone." She shifted her gaze to the veteran and the no-longer-rookie. "Please," Jenna offered in a gentler tone. "We must keep working the case as if I don't believe Cochran killed off his competition to ensure he'd win reelection. At the same time, we have to find proof he did."

"Right," Stone answered uneasily. "You know, I voted for him last time around."

"A lot of people did," Jenna stated. "Otherwise, he wouldn't have won. This has nothing to do with politics, Vicki. I looked into his eyes and saw it. You know what it's like when your gut screams at you to pay attention."

"Yeah." She bit her lip and swallowed. "I hope your gut's wrong because, if it's right, I don't see how we prove he killed the judge while he was on live TV."

"Maybe it's like Captain Myers said, a professional hit," Jenna speculated. "Anyway, you two keep looking into less high-profile suspects, and we'll see if we can turn up a connection or a payoff or something to tie anybody to the murder."

"I can't recall ever having less to go on," Jamison lamented. "It'll be a miracle if we can produce a viable suspect at all."

Murphy's brows furrowed as he stood to join his partner. "There was nothing in the tree, nothing in the sewers, grass clippings that probably no killer walked through, a bullet without rifling marks," he enumerated sullenly. "We'll check out every name you give us, Lieutenant, but whoever did this was smart and resourceful. I hate to say that, even if your gut is right, we'll never prove it."

"Just keep collecting clues, Murphy," Jenna charged him, "and let me worry about proving it."

18

While her team worked on their assignments, Jenna pulled up a recording of Congressman Cochran's campaign rally and watched the entire hour and a half of shouting, flag-waving, music, and speeches. It got underway at four o'clock in a packed stadium. Parents brought their kids, local bands and church choirs showed up to perform, and it appeared like everyone behaved themselves and had a good time. Pans of the audience showed hands holding soft drinks, corn dogs, and popcorn bags, as well as "Smash the Libs with Nash" signs, American flags, and a sea of red hats. After a prayer, the national anthem, a country band, and two introductory speakers, Cochran took to the podium at exactly four-thirty-two, grinning, waving, and holding his fingers up in the victory sign. Then he speechified as enthusiastically and eloquently as a Baptist preacher at a tent revival for the next half hour, only pausing for the occasional sip of water.

Frustrated, Jenna combed the internet for any hint Cochran might have an identical twin or a doppelgänger out there somewhere. The crowd in the bleachers was plenty far away, and the TV camera only showed the occasional close-up, so maybe his chief of staff was in on a switch. Nothing. No TikTok videos of Cochran impersonators, and his mother's birth records listed Nash as an only child. Besides, she couldn't imagine a foil performing so well in front of the audience.

Jenna had focused on Cochran himself, not what he said. All politicians were full of hot air, and who could know if they actually believed what they spouted from a podium? But she had worked with Judge Hamden for years and thought he'd be different—at least until Washington corrupted him.

Her frustration grew palpable. The man walked out, waving to the crowd, at four o'clock and never left the platform erected in the middle of the football field. Rolling her chair away from her desk, Jenna pushed up to pace. Then she glanced at the clock—less than an hour before Randi's appointment. She sent a quick text: *'I'm coming.'*

"Jamison, what can you tell me so far?" Jenna crossed to the coffee station near Jamison's desk and listened while she poured a fresh cup.

"Many interesting tidbits," she replied, "none of which point to Cochran growing up to become a murderer."

"Tell me." Jenna rested her bum on the edge of the table under the action-hero mural, nursing her coffee, and focused on Jamison.

"Nash Jefferson Cochran grew up in a middle-class home as an only child. He was born in Enterprise, Alabama, and his family moved to Williamsburg, Virginia, when he was ten. He was a talented student, especially in science. In his senior year of high school, Nash won the state science fair with a robotics project. Here's an old newspaper clipping."

Jamison brought up the image on her screen for her to study. "Nineteen-eighty-five," Jenna read while peering at a seventeen-year-old boy with floppy hair and bright eyes standing beside the black and white robotic arm he had created. The article explained the practical uses of the arm, which could aid people with disabilities in reaching and manipulating objects. It was operated with a remote gadget that resembled an old game controller. The young Cochran's joyful grin stretched from ear to ear.

"Why didn't he become a scientist?" Jenna asked, baffled by the juxtaposition between the geeky kid in the photo and the dubious politician he was today.

"I don't know," Jamison replied, "but his father was a successful businessman, who today is worth millions, so maybe he influenced his son's life choices. Nash earned his undergrad business degree from Liberty University and his master's from Columbia. He moved straight into company management with Dominion Energy in Richmond, then took a CEO position in Harrisonburg.

With corporate and church backing, he dipped his toe into politics in 2000, winning the race for mayor of Harrisonburg. With four years as mayor under his belt, he ran for and won a seat in the Virginia Senate. From there, he made his bid for the U.S. House of Representatives, where he's served for twelve years. According to the readily available biography, he's never lost an election."

"Then he was about to lose his first," Jenna mused. "From science to business to politics—not the usual route, but who's to say what's normal?" She frowned at the picture of the boy with his robot, wondering what had happened to steer him in the directions he had taken. An overbearing father? A desire for popularity or power? Greed?

"I haven't delved into his family life or political fires where his name popped up yet," Jamison said, "but he has an ex-wife hardly anyone knows about. I'll see what I can discover about her too."

"Good. Ex-wives can harbor a world of information about their former husbands. Owens, Hendrix, y'all keep doing what you're doing. I have a doctor's appointment I can't miss."

"Oh?" Owens shot her a surprised look from across the room. "You don't look sick to me. Oh," his eyes widened more. "One of those female doctor appointment things?"

Jenna returned a sarcastic look. "It's personal. No cause for alarm. And Hendrix, see if you can finagle that network footage of Cochran's rally to zoom in on him the whole way through. I want a cut version of only Cochran video, got it?" She wanted to make sure it was indeed him and not a double on the stage.

"Yes, ma'am, and I've got another vehicle owner for Officers Stone and Murphy to check out when they get back."

"Good." Jenna's brain continued to hum while she pulled on her jacket. "Hendrix, can you legally poke around Cochran's finances, you know, without a warrant?"

"His campaign money has to be open to scrutiny," he answered, "so that, for sure. Personal bank accounts require permission or a court order." He lowered his voice conspiratorially. "That's not to say I couldn't hack into all his records in ten minutes or less; you just wouldn't be able to use the intel in court, and if people found out—"

"Hush!" Jenna scolded, pushing a finger to her lips. "We'll pretend for now you didn't say that. Comb through the campaign account with special attention to the biggest contributors and any funds paid to an individual or an unlikely vendor. I'll be back."

***

Randi sat in her OBGYN doctor's waiting area with butterflies crashing into each other in her stomach. It was too early for her "afternoon sickness" to kick in; these were purely nerves. While the faith side of her psyche instructed her that everything would be all right, the doubt side—that, try as she might to dispel, refused to be vanquished—posed the worrisome question, *What if it wasn't?* Wanting to remain positive, Randi focused on how normal her first weeks of pregnancy had been while ignoring the list of potential complications.

She wasn't alone. A highly pregnant woman, who looked ten years younger than her age, appeared ready to pop. She had an attentive man with her, presumably the baby's father, who kept asking what he could do for her. It made Randi smile. A riot of pastel paints, fluffy cushions in sunshine hues, and charming artwork gave the waiting room the feel of a giant nursery, a welcome change from the typical hospital atmosphere.

She said she's coming, Randi reminded herself as the wall clock ticked another notch. She bolstered her emotions to prepare herself if Jenna ran late or didn't make it. After all, she had known what she was signing up for when she married a police detective. Hadn't she assured Jenna hundreds of times that she understood her being called away and having to change plans at the last minute? And Randi had lived many years on her own with nobody there at all, taking care of everything for and by herself, so why should this be different?

Because I need her, she thought, holding disappointment at bay. *And she needs to be part of this. She needs to understand it's her baby too. I don't want her to feel left out of a single moment.*

A nurse appeared in the doorway with a clipboard. "Miranda McLeod?" she called, scanning the waiting area. Randi's emotions jerked up and down like a yo-yo on a string.

Standing, she opened her mouth to answer when a harried voice behind her belted out, "We're here!"

Relief washed over Randi, a wave of contentment that eased her worries and lifted her spirit, making her feel as light as a feather. "You made it." She beamed with delight at Jenna as she trotted up beside her, winded from rushing.

"Well, yeah," she replied, her blue eyes brimming with anticipation. She grasped Randi's hand as they approached the nurse, whose blush accompanied her smile.

"This way."

Randi's heart flew somewhere over the rainbow, and she felt she could face anything with Jenna beside her, holding her hand, loving her. It was the greatest feeling in the world! Just the assurance of her hand in hers and the sight of her eager expression made Randi stronger inside. Everything *would* be all right.

Together, they entered the examination room, Jenna taking the chair beside the padded table with a white paper cover and two stupid stirrups sticking out of the foot end. Randi realized they were necessary; she just never liked them. At least now doctors had warm, lubed speculums instead of the horrid, cold metal ones she'd started out with as a teenager. But this wasn't an annual checkup, so maybe that part wouldn't even happen.

"You alright, sweetie?"

Jenna's concerned voice arrested Randi's thoughts, and she smiled, if only half-heartedly. "Better with you here."

"I said I'd be here." Jenna's bravado teased a chuckle from Randi, helping her relax.

When the door opened, a matronly sixty-year-old marched in, a file in her hand and glasses on her nose. Randi had been seeing Dr. Bette Swansen for her female health checkups since she'd moved to Roanoke years ago. She had bright eyes and a professional touch, not to mention loads of experience—just the kind of doctor any woman would fight to have.

"Miranda." Her warm greeting accompanied a winning smile. "How are you feeling today?"

"Pregnant," she answered with a nervous laugh. "Dr. Swansen, please meet my wife, Lieutenant Jenna Ferrari. Her brother is the biological father of our baby."

"So pleased to meet you," she said.

When Jenna stood to shake her hand, Randi noticed they were the same height, though Dr. Swansen had at least twenty or thirty pounds on Jenna. "Randi tells me you're the best."

Dr. Swansen blushed. "Well, I don't know about that, but she tells me the same about you, and I hope it's true. So terrible about Judge Hamden's murder." She furrowed her brows and shook her head. "Now, Dr. McLeod, we will see if you actually are pregnant. You told the nurse when you called to make the appointment that your home test read positive. While they are generally reliable, they can give false readings, so let's check you out."

The older woman pulled a raised stool around and sat in front of Randi. "When was your last menstrual cycle?"

"About eight weeks ago."

The doctor checked a box on her sheet. "And have you ever had a pregnancy or miscarriage in the past?"

"No."

"Smoke, drink, or any marijuana use?"

"No," Randi answered. "Well, the occasional wine or alcoholic beverage, but not since we did the insemination." She bit her lip.

"Are you on any medications?" Dr. Swansen asked, glancing up at her. Randi shook her head. "What dates did you do this and what was your process?" She looked genuinely interested.

Randi was ready for this question and straightened on the table, taking a deep breath. "I checked my calendar and used a basal thermometer and the prediction test that came with the kit to calculate when I'd be ovulating. We called Vince, Jenna's brother, and had him stay with us from September 26th through the 29th, four days for maximum chances of success. We used a sterile,

FDA-approved ICI kit, collected a fresh sample each day, and performed the procedure in an intimate setting. It's not just more fun that way, but arousal hormones couldn't hurt, right?" She grinned nervously, hoping her doctor didn't think she was a nut.

"I know you can't just refrigerate sperm and the more the merrier, so we had plenty of movies and magazines for Vince. He's already fathered one child, who turned out to be the most wonderful and amazing little boy, so we knew his swimmers were up to the task. A few weeks later, my period didn't come. Then I started feeling hungry—you know, *really* hungry—only I was also getting sick to my stomach. Naturally, I have to be different and enjoy morning sickness in the evening. It's not just that the home test said positive, Dr. Swansen—I *feel* pregnant."

The doctor's lips parted, and she regarded Randi with skepticism. "If you got pregnant so easily, I might have to write a paper on you." Standing, she took her stethoscope and listened to Randi's chest, then her back, and finally her abdomen. Her lips pursed, brows scrunched, and mouth twisted. "You could be right," she suggested. "I'm going to do an ultrasound to be sure, so change out of your blouse and trousers and put on this gown open down the front. You won't need to remove your undergarments. I'll be right back."

Randi effervesced like two Alka-Seltzer tablets in a glass of water. "Jenna!" she squealed. In an instant, Jenna was hugging her.

"I know! Here, let's get you changed. You're going to be the subject of a medical paper—the ovulating wonder, the most fertile woman in America."

"I don't know about all that," Randi dismissed and pulled off her shirt. "All I did was follow the directions." She slipped off her pants and gazed teasingly at Jenna. "You're the one who operated the insemination syringe, or fancy turkey baster, and set the mood." With a laugh, she slipped her arms into the thin paper gown.

Dr. Swansen returned with an ultrasound technician wheeling in a silver cart loaded with equipment. "Now, Tina and I will spread the nice, warm gel all over your tummy, roll the transducer around, and you can both watch on the monitor. We'll also take some pictures if there's anything to see. Ready?"

"Yes, ma'am!" Randi could hardly wait.

Jenna circled to Randi's other side and held her hand while they watched something resembling sonar waves disperse across the monitor.

"Well, I'll be," Dr. Swansen uttered in wonder. "There he is, or she—too early to tell. See?" She pointed to the screen. There was indeed something there—*their baby*!

"Jenna!" Randi squealed.

"I know!" Jenna voiced in awe.

"What you're looking at is a miracle if I ever saw one," Dr. Swansen proclaimed. "We have a strong heartbeat, two arms, and two legs, nothing abnormal at this juncture. I'd say you're about six weeks along. That would put your due date sometime around June 20 or 21st. I'll order you some vitamins and see our receptionist about scheduling your appointments. We want to keep a close watch on you, and you must call if you have any concerns, no matter how minor. You aren't old like me, but still old to have a first child, so we want to take every precaution. Congratulations, Miranda and Jenna—you're going to be parents!"

19

"That must have gone well," Jamison observed. She did a poor job of hiding a knowing grin, sticking her tongue into the side of her cheek. Jenna realized she must have been glowing because the guys gave her curious looks.

"Like I said, I'm as healthy as a horse," Jenna declared, trying to rein in her ultimate delight at the news from Randi's appointment. She left her hard copy of the ultrasound picture in her car, away from prying eyes. *We've got to finish the first trimester before making announcements.*

"What all have you lackies discovered while I was gone?" Jenna plopped into her chair, the crash to the reality of an impossible-to-prove case feeling like a plunge from the Empire State Building to a concrete sidewalk after her moment of elation with Randi.

"Stone and Murphy called in to report the first two POIs they visited didn't pan out," Owens said. "The ex-con with the pickup truck was in the neighborhood to do lawn work. The homeowner verified he was operating a noisy leaf blower at the time of the murder. The protester in the SUV was there to drop off her kids at her parents' house so she could go hug a tree somewhere. Her mom says they argued from four-fifteen to a quarter of five over her life choices. Neither one could be our shooter. We gave them Hendrix's other match to visit."

"Good," Jenna replied. "We're dotting all the i's and crossing all the t's."

"Nothing unusual turned up in Cochran's campaign finances," Hendrix said, "unless you consider the exorbitant prices he pays for hotels, travel, and food on the campaign trail. His entourage isn't staying at the Motel 6—I can testify to that. But nothing that would appear to be a hitman's payoff, if that's what you're looking for."

Jenna frowned, her unfocused eyes peering at her blank computer monitor. "I didn't expect he'd use a public account. He's smarter than some politicians who shuffle campaign money to pay for prostitutes and get caught doing it. Jamison?"

"I have a phone number and address for Sarah Barnhill, the ex-Mrs. Cochran, in Charleston, West Virginia, a 3-hour drive from here. Do you want to call or go see her?"

Inspired once more, Jenna answered, "Both. I'll call, make sure she's there and willing to talk to us. Are you up for a trip?"

"Today?" Jamison gaped and glanced at the clock.

"It's only twelve-thirty," Jenna chided, "and I don't see the remains of lunch sitting around here. We can pick something up on the way, and you'll be home in time to tuck Altman into bed tonight—that is, unless we get a hot lead to pursue."

Jamison offered her a pained expression. "OK. I just need to send Bennet a note and run to the ladies' room before we head out."

Jenna gave Jamison a nod and dug her phone out to text Randi. *'So psyched about our little jellybean. I won't be home until late. Hugs and kisses.'*

'JELLYBEAN?' lit up on her screen, causing Jenna to snicker.

'Well, we don't have a name yet, so I have to call him or her something. Besides, that's what the ultrasound looks like to me.'

'I've got to run to class. Will discuss names soon. Love you the most!' Randi sent with a heart emoji. Jenna ached to spend tonight celebrating with her wife, who was having *her* baby—or the closest she could manage.

Next, she called the number Jamison had sent her for Sarah Barnhill and found the woman eager to talk about her ex-husband. She spouted off the address of a deli near her workplace where they could meet during her factory "lunch" break at four o'clock. If they hurried, they'd make it with a few minutes to spare.

Glancing up, Jenna asked, "Hendrix, where does one buy a 3-D printer fancy enough to create a gun with?"

"Lots of places," he replied as he munched on an apple at his desk, his eyes bright with enthusiasm. "You can order one online from an array of outlets or buy one at a printing or office store. They're pretty mainstream these days. The prices range from a few hundred to around twenty-five thousand on the super high end."

"I'm sure Cochran could afford the best," Jenna speculated. "Hold down the fort, Sergeant, and keep checking the boxes. We'll be back in about seven or eight hours."

"And you expect us to be here?" Owens's face shriveled like a disgruntled prune.

"I have more reason to want to be home tonight than you, so cut the whiny act." Jenna spun out of her chair and met Jamison returning from the restroom.

"Yeah, about that ..." Owens lifted a finger and aimed an inquisitive glance at her.

Jenna half-grinned, ignoring his question. "Get your coat, Detective; it'll be cooler up in the mountains. See y'all later."

***

Jenna and Jamison grabbed chicken tenders and fries from a drive-through because they'd be easy to eat behind the wheel. Jenna refused to confirm or deny that she and Randi were expecting a baby; she didn't fool Trisha, who beamed at her like the Cheshire Cat. Thinking of the Cheshire Cat reminded Jenna of Randi's skimpy—delectably naughty—Alice in Wonderland-themed lingerie with "eat me" and "drink me" floating over the coordinating top and bottom. And all that sexy playfulness and Randi's endeavour to excel at pleasing Jenna—well, the woman strove for perfection in everything, but especially that—is how Jenna ended up soon to be a mom. Would she be Second Mom? Maybe one of them would be Mama and one Mom. Mother?

Mama is Italian but also Southern. Mom is casual while Mother is more formal. I don't want to be formal, distanced, or authoritative. Well, I am those things, but not with Jellybean. I want him or her to know I love them from day one—before day one. Randi was telling me all about things to do before the baby's born, like playing classical music, stroking her belly, and telling Baby I love him or her.

"I know where your mind is, Lieutenant," Trisha cooed with a mischievous grin. She leisurely munched on her last fry. "And it isn't on the case!"

"Hush," Jenna scowled, pulling out of her vortex of baby musings. "Nobody is supposed to know, and Randi will have my hide if she discovers you found out." She shot Jamison a look as sharp and cold as a lethal icicle. "She wants to wait another six weeks to be sure everything goes OK. The doctor said she's at higher risk because of being over thirty-five."

Trisha made a zipping motion across her mouth. "My lips are sealed. It's got me wondering about what Bennet and I will do when the time comes. It's one thing for a teacher to work while pregnant; what will *I* do?" Her brows furrowed, and her lips twisted. "We talked about it, and we both want to have at least one child, maybe two. And we're working on a plan. You know how families who are from Spanish and English backgrounds will raise their kids bilingual?"

Jenna nodded. The Guptas raised their children to be fluent in English and Hindi.

"Well, we're going to try to do that with Christianity and Judaism. We plan to observe all the holy days for both traditions, attend synagogue and church services when we can, and teach them that God loves them. It seems both his and my parents have finally agreed to it."

"You've got a good plan," Jenna said. Randi would want to bring Jellybean to church and probably get Protestant baptized. *Mama wouldn't approve. She'd want the baby raised Catholic, except for the fact that her church would reject the entire idea of little Jellybean's conception, birth, and having two moms. I can't worry about that now. Jellybean is our baby, not hers.*

"Thanks!" Jamison smiled and sucked soda up her straw until it made that empty, slurpy sound.

"And being pregnant won't affect your ability to excel at detective work," Jenna added. "We just won't let you chase suspects down the street or be anywhere close to where shootouts are happening."

"I can deal with that. It's hard to chase suspects in the heels I normally wear anyway. I'll let you do all the dangerous stuff." Jamison flashed Jenna a satisfied grin.

"Thanks," she replied sarcastically, rolling her eyes.

***

Jenna bought Sarah Barnhill lunch, and the three of them huddled in the back booth of the eatery. The air was crisp on a cloudy day in the capital of West Virginia. Although it was the largest city in the state, Charleston was about half the size of Roanoke. Still, the golden dome of the capital building stood vigil over the Kanawha River before a majestic backdrop of ancient, weathered peaks, giving it charm and a sense of status.

"So," Sarah smirked. "You want to know about Nash, do you? What'd he do besides the usual crooked politician trash?"

The woman in her fifties, with gray-streaked ash-brown hair and crow's feet to prove it, bit into a club sandwich. Decked out in a factory uniform, she looked like someone who'd worked hard her whole life.

"We aren't at liberty to discuss an ongoing investigation," Jenna answered, "but anything you can tell us about him while the two of you were married could be extremely helpful."

"OK," she clipped in a satisfied tone. "Let me tell you about Daddy's little golden boy." She took a swig of her iced tea to wash down the sandwich bite while Jenna and Jamison waited, attention riveted on Sarah.

"We went to high school together," she began, "then, being good Baptist youth, headed off to Liberty University. The difference was, Nash's family could afford a college like that, and I had to work, barely able to keep up. After one semester, I knew it was too hard, and I wasn't getting any sleep. I'd have to drop out because, even with help from my folks, I couldn't pay the bills. The thing is, Nash was a big nerd in high school—smart as a whip, don't get me wrong—but not popular with the girls. I had been popular, and he'd developed a crush on me. I'm not saying I married him for his money—clearly, I didn't get any of it." She motioned toward herself, smelling like chemicals.

"Anyway, he was thrilled to have any female attention, but they watched the students real close to make sure we weren't, you know ..." Sarah rolled her eyes. "Having sex. He wanted it, so he asked me to marry him. Nash was cute, bashful, and impressively smart, so I said yes. I thought I'd have a promising future with a husband like him."

Sarah might be haggard, but she wasn't homely. Jenna could see why young Nash would be attracted to her.

"Then he changed." The light of fond reminiscence faded from her eyes, replaced by bitter shadows.

Jamison sighed and reached a hand across the table, covering hers. "I've heard this story before. Tell us how it happened for you."

"Our first six months were great," she admitted. "Then, from somewhere, Nash grew confidence, even arrogance. He began walking, talking, and acting differently. It was subtle at first, guiding and directing me on what I should wear, what groups I should and shouldn't join on campus. By the end of our sophomore year, he told me I had to quit school and devote all my energy to being his wife, that he was the authority figure, and good Christian wives obeyed their husbands. Naturally, I wanted to be a good Christian wife, so I did everything to please him. Looking back, I think he brainwashed me to believe everything he did was right and good and in my best interests."

Producing a disgusted expression, Sarah shook her head, sighed, and took another bite of her sandwich. "He decided I should go to work to support us while he got his MBA, since New York was such an expensive place to live. He was on scholarship to Columbia, and his dad sent us money, but by then Nash had become concerned with his appearance and needed the best clothes, a fancy car, so I got a job in an office building. Dominion Energy hired him right after graduation, and he filed for divorce."

"On what grounds?" Jamison looked both aghast and furious at the same time. "After you dropped out of school to please him and worked to pay for his upscale lifestyle?"

"Yeah, that's what I thought too." Sarah downed the last of her tea. "I was shell-shocked, lost, and terrified. He claimed I didn't meet his expectations as a wife, that, for his status, he needed someone more polished than an ex high school cheerleader. Of course, he pointed out small failings, mainly that I hadn't devoted enough time and energy to him, nor was I smart enough or good enough to keep up with him."

"But if he pressured you into taking a full-time job, how could he expect you to devote the same amount of time to him as when you weren't working?" By Jamison's tone, Jenna recognized her ire was up.

"I guess he wanted Wonder Woman, and I suppose that's who he got several years later," she grumbled. "He married a younger, more splendid model who came with her daddy's trust fund."

"Tell me you were treated fairly in the divorce," Jenna demanded, although from the looks of things, such hadn't been the case."

Sarah laughed. "You're kidding, right? I got nothing. We were renting an apartment, so there was no house, and the car was in his name. He filed the papers before his big salary kicked in, so alimony was based on what we had in New York—me working and him a student. I'm surprised he didn't finagle it, so I'd have to pay him!"

Jenna shook her head. She understood things like that happened, especially when one party blindsides the other with divorce papers. Lawyers excelled at lunging for the jugular and hiding important details in unintelligible lawyer language. She probably didn't even have someone to represent her, and was indeed lucky she didn't end up paying him alimony.

"What a scumbag!" Jamison proclaimed. Jenna tacitly agreed.

"Ms. Barnhill, was Cochran ever scary or violent? Was he ever rough or physically abusive to you?" Jenna asked.

"No. I think I could have dealt with that better. I stayed in good physical shape and would have felt justified fighting back," she explained. "It was his undermining of my self-worth that reaped the most damage. I went into another marriage believing I was worthless and only after it failed, too, did I start to get my act together. I finally met a nice, simple man who didn't need to put on airs or put me down. We only have a little trailer in a mobile home park, but we're happy. He treats me like a princess." A genuine smile filled her face.

"I'm so glad to hear that, Sarah," Jamison gushed, looking relieved. "You deserve some happiness after all that Nash Cochran put you through. When he got into politics, did you ever think about coming forward and telling your story to a reporter?"

A sour expression returned to Sarah's face, and she crumpled her napkin. "He didn't want me talking to runway-worthy heiress Alida. So, before they got married, he came to me with his lawyer, a nondisclosure document, and a big, fat check. I needed the money and didn't care to talk to or about Nash again, so I signed it, not knowing he would ever consider running for office. Now I'd be up a creek without a paddle if I took anything public. It said I can't even tell people I was ever married to him." She rolled her eyes. "Like it's not in public records at the Lynchburg Courthouse! But I've still got a copy in a fireproof lockbox under the bed, and it never mentions talking to the police if they show up asking questions." She sat back in her chair, eyes sparkling, with a look of immense satisfaction.

"That's good to know," Jenna said. *I'm so glad I never have to worry about any of that crap. Concerns over what Mama thinks of me pale in comparison to what she's had to put up with.*

A waitress took the empty plate and glass and laid a ticket on the table. Jenna picked it up. "Thank you, Ms. Barnhill. Covering your lunch is the least we can do."

"Thank you, Virginia detectives." The gleam in Sarah's eyes magnified as she sat forward, crossing her arms on the table. "Please tell me Nash is in trouble for something. I wish I could be there to see you wipe that smug look of self-importance off his face."

Jenna liked Sarah. She admired her for pulling herself up by her bootstraps and retaking control of her life. Not all women could do that. Sure, she'd gotten sucked in by the misogynistic phony in the first place, but you don't always know ahead of time. Some people excel at disguising their true intentions, and some who start out OK do change.

"If that day comes—and I sure hope it will—I promise to take a picture and send it to you," Jenna vowed in solidarity with Cochran's discarded wife.

20

"I'm on board with you now," Jamison declared as they drove down a winding road toward the highway, away from the little diner. "Even if he didn't kill Judge Hamden, I want to nail that sleazy jerk for something!"

"Good." Jenna pondered everything Sarah had told them, wondering what had happened during his second year of college to change a shy, nerdy young man into a domineering controller with visions of grandeur. The influence of his peers? Nonsense about men being over women some teacher pounded into his head at that conservative school? A desire on Nash's part to please his father and make him proud?

Jenna understood the power of influence others could hold over an individual, which is why it was so important who a person chooses to listen to and spend time with. If you keep hearing the same message over and over, you can become indoctrinated; Sarah had. Nash had conditioned her to believe she was nobody without him—then he dumped her. *Randi has sure had a big influence on me; Captain Myers and Dr. Grayson too. Only their influences had the opposite effect,* she considered. *They make me feel more worthy, not less. Ultimately, a person chooses for himself, though. Maybe Nash had some of that in him all along, just waiting to get out.*

"But how do we get around his alibi?" Jamison's question snapped Jenna's mind back to the dilemma at hand. "And the election is tomorrow," she moaned.

"I'm not sure," Jenna answered. "If we can come up with a sound theory and some circumstantial evidence, what judge could you get to sign off on a warrant?"

A blank look crossed Jamison's face. "Not Judge Vance. He's conservative and ready to retire. He wouldn't want to be in the middle of something controversial. Judge Stroud or Judge Williams might go out on a limb—if we can bring them strong enough grounds. Nobody wants to cross a member of Congress," she lamented. "I mean, if we don't get enough for an arrest or he wins at trial, Cochran could turn around and ruin everyone who stood against him. That's what power gets you."

"Yeah," Jenna groaned, "bigger ways to be a bully."

"If he hired a hitman and we can find *him*, then we could pressure him into naming Cochran," Jamison suggested.

Jenna pulled out her phone and pushed a button. "I've been meaning to do this," she mentioned. Setting her phone on the console, the call routed through her car.

"Special Agent Pane," answered a voice Jenna recalled from an investigation a few months ago.

"Hi, this is Lieutenant Detective Ferrari from Roanoke PD," she said. "We worked a case—"

"Yeah," her tone brightened. "How was the honeymoon?"

"Quite spectacular," Jenna answered, performing her obligation to engage in small talk before getting down to business. "Hey, we're investigating Judge Hamden's murder—"

"Oh, that was awful," returned a demoralized voice. "Is there something we can do to help?"

"Actually, it's looking like this might have been carried out by a professional. Can you check your intel to see if someone on your assassin watch list might have been in the area on Friday? See if there's been any buzz about a big hit."

"Yeah, yeah, let me get on that." Agent Edan Pane sounded sincerely invested over the phone. Jenna recalled her impressive look in her mind's eye—tall, lean, dark skin, sharp eyes, angular face, tousled pixie cut, a hundred and fifty pounds of muscle all rearing to go—just the kind of law enforcement agent they needed on their side.

"Thanks. I appreciate it."

"Say hello to that tall drink of water of yours," Pane requested. "I'll give you a call back soon—might take an hour to be thorough."

"I will and no problem," Jenna replied. "I owe you one."

"Nail the no-good bastard who killed my choice for Congress, and we'll call it even."

"That's the plan." The call dropped, either because Pane was off to search for assassins' whereabouts or because of the mountains flanking the highway.

"Good thinking," Jamison praised.

"Now, what about another idea?" Jenna posed. "We always need another idea."

"OK," Jamison answered, assuming her thinking pose. "If we believe a 3-D printer was used, not only could Cochran afford one, but, with his science background, he'd know how to use it."

"Good! That's good, Jamison. He would. So, maybe he prints up the gun, gives it to the assassin, and says, 'Here's an untraceable gun. It only has one shot, so don't miss.' But then what? If the shooter threw away the gun ..."

"Matt would have been extra thorough on that search," Jamison assured her.

"Yeah, but the unsub could have ditched it in another state or thrown it on a burn pile. We need to get inside Cochran's house, check if he owns a 3-D printer machine. Wouldn't it have, you know, chips, memory, some record of what actions it performed?"

Jamison shrugged. "That's a question for Hendrix. But before we can get inside his house, we need enough for a judge to grant a warrant."

"I guess saying he's an asshole isn't good enough," Jenna grumbled.

"If it was, the police could walk into half the people's houses in the country with impunity."

"*That's* the truth! OK, we'll keep thinking while Special Agent Pane tries to find us a suspect assassin."

It was a beautiful drive; Jenna couldn't deny it. They stopped at a rest area for a washroom and vending machines. One Diet Coke wouldn't poison Jenna, even if Randi feared it would. She'd been drinking them for years, after all. Randi said that, with prolonged use, the aspartame, phosphoric acid, and potassium benzoate had been proven to cause health issues. She'd cut way back, hadn't she? Yes. Jenna was mindful of her health now, and one Diet Coke didn't mean she was diving back into bad habits.

When Pane called, she couldn't confirm any suspected assassins on the FBI watch list had been in or near Roanoke on Friday. There was one, Dante Booth, who they couldn't account for as he'd been off the grid and off their radar for three months. Would he risk exposure to pull a job for Cochran?

Jenna had then asked Pane to check on any Mafia connections to Cochran.

"We've looked into that off and on for six years," she answered. "Don Nicolò Gucci is a regular contributor to Cochran's campaigns, but the amount of his donations doesn't raise a red flag. We know when he's in Baltimore, Cochran will have lunch with Luka Gambino. Some photos paparazzi took of them laughing together over hoagies at an outdoor café made it to the tabloids, but there's no solid evidence linking the congressman to organized crime. Still, I can see if anyone notable was spotted in Virginia on Friday. What makes you think a pro was your shooter?"

Jenna hesitated. She wanted Pane's help without violating Captain Myers's directive. "Let's just say between witness accounts, physical evidence, and the lack thereof, Bubba didn't do it."

"Uh-huh. Gotcha. And since you're looking into Cochran, I assume he's a person of interest?"

She couldn't let it slip that Cochran was their prime suspect. Had she actually mentioned his name? Horror shot through her when she realized she had. "We're looking at a multitude of people with motives to kill the judge. Cochran is just one of many on that list."

"Well, he had the most to gain by eliminating his competition," Pane concluded, "especially given he'd dropped out of the lead in the polls and faced losing his seat. But he was giving a speech at a rally Friday afternoon." Both the timbre and intensity of her voice rose. "That's why you're asking about hitmen and goons—because maybe he hired someone while giving himself an alibi!"

"That's one possibility among many," Jenna answered in a steady tone. "Hey, can you please keep this inquiry between you and me? We don't want word to get out we're looking into a congressman, even if it's along with a host of other suspects. OK?"

"Hey, I'm no Chatty Cathy," Pane retorted as if offended. "Nobody needs to know what you and I talk about on the phone. And if any wise guys pop, I'll let you know."

"Thank you," Jenna said with relief, "for everything."

When they arrived back at the office, Owens, minus a coat and tie, and Hendrix, with a slurpee and earbuds, still worked at their stations.

"This lab report came in," Owens said as he made a big show of stretching and yawning. Jenna shot him a perturbed look and picked up the folder. "Was the trip worth it?"

"It was," Jamison announced. "We learned about what an asshole Nash Cochran was to his first wife. I'd bet he's treated other people just as poorly, but, even so, it gets us no closer to proving he killed Hamden."

"What's in that report might." Owens glanced at the folder Jenna was reading.

"Dr. Gupta got two DNA profiles off the bullet," Jenna uttered in amazement. "One belonged to Judge Hamden, as you'd think. The other came back unknown."

"Which means," Jamison deduced, "if we can match a suspect's DNA, we'll have some hard evidence."

"She ran it against everyone we had in our suspect pool except Camila Diaz, who refused to contribute a sample," Jenna continued. Then dismissively added, "I don't think it's her anyway, for all the reasons. But Cochran wasn't ever in the military, never arrested, nor worked in a job that required DNA testing, so his wouldn't be in any database."

"Unless he did one of those ancestry things," Owens suggested. "Maybe Dr. Gupta would reach out to them, like she did on that other case?"

"I'll ask tomorrow," Jenna said. "Hendrix, how are you coming along?" Then she frowned at him. "Doesn't that slurpee have too much sugar in it for you? Randi would have my hide if she caught me with a cup full of frozen sugar like that."

Tyr bounced around to face her, plastic drink cup in hand. "Nope." He beamed like a little kid. "My mom found this recipe, and I made this myself with the new blender I put over there by the coffeepot; I hope you don't mind. It's a fruit slushy made with real frozen fruit, sparkling and coconut water, and ice—no artificial sweeteners, added sugar, or other assorted unhealthy ingredients. Want one? I could whip it up in a wink."

"Hey, Tyr, this is terrific!" Jamison veered over to check out the blender. "We could make superfood smoothies with this too."

The drink sounded tasty to Jenna—the strawberry slushie, not whatever Trisha was babbling about. "Maybe later. Case first."

"I made this shortened, zoomed-in version of Cochran's campaign rally for you and time-stamped each cut, so you'd know when it went down. Dude sure flexes all his mid ideas," Hendrix commented, rolling his eyes, and handed her a flash drive.

"Thanks. We'll wrap up soon," Jenna promised as she returned to her desk and plugged in the USB drive. "I don't suppose Murphy and Stone turned up any leads?"

"They checked out the other driver turning into the neighborhood and requestioned everyone on the street. Nobody recalls a suspicious vehicle or a person walking or running down the block."

And that was the real kicker. Whoever shot Hamden did it without anybody noticing. "Hendrix, I don't suppose it's possible to fabricate a long gun with a 3-D printer, is it?"

"Pretty much anything is possible," he answered with a shrug. "Nobody's done it successfully, but it wouldn't stop a creative mind from trying. Size is an issue. You'd have to print out all the parts individually and assemble them, but the long barrel is the real problem. The heat and force from firing a slug through a long barrel? I just don't see it holding up—unless the barrel was steel and only other parts plastic. But if that was the case—"

"There would be rifling marks on the bullet." Jenna sighed and tried to focus on the arrogant SOB in her video. It was him—she had no doubt. *So much for the double theory. If I could just find a shooter to tie to him ...*

Jenna paused and rewound the footage, examining what she saw. In the enlarged version, it was clear that, moments before stepping up to the microphone, Cochran had his phone out, looking at the screen, then moving his fingers over it. She played it again. Excitedly, she yanked out the thumb drive, raced to Hendrix, and ordered, "Here. Play this on the big screen. Look at this, everyone, and tell me what you see."

Hendrix brought up and played back the fifteen seconds she indicated. "There it is!" Jenna pointed excitedly.

"He's texting somebody," Owens declared.

"Or doing something on his screen." Jamison sidled up beside Jenna for a better view of the wall monitor. "We can't see exactly what."

"We need that phone!" Jenna demanded.

"If he doesn't hand it over willingly, we'd need a warrant," Owens reminded her.

"And I don't have enough to get a judge to sign off on it," Jamison lamented.

"Phone records!" Hendrix shouted in inspiration. "What about contacting his cell phone provider and getting the number he communicated with? He had to have been giving the assassin the go-ahead. Look at the time! He makes that communication at exactly four-thirty, slips his phone back into his pocket, and takes to the podium amid thundering applause. See the smug look on his face? The spring in his step, the gleam in his eyes? Bastard! He knows he's going to win because he just ordered his guy to fire."

"It's tricky," Jenna supplied. "Cell phones are covered under the Fourth Amendment, and, even with the third-party doctrine, a warrant is usually required to tap CSLI data and definitely for retrieving the contents of text messages exchanged. Exceptions are made for immediate life-and-death situations or a hot pursuit of an armed suspect, and this doesn't qualify."

"Plus," Jamison added, "he might not have been using telephone text. Most likely, he used an app like Snapchat, WhatsApp, or Telegram that erases messages after you send them."

"Nothing is ever truly erased," Hendrix inserted, "if you know where to look."

"Good to know, Hendrix," said Jenna. "If we ever get a warrant for his phone, you'll need to put your best skills to work."

Jenna rubbed the back of her neck as frustration mounted. She knew he did it and was close to discovering how—if they could only get a warrant for his phone, his house, find out who he texted, and prove the 3-D printer she was confident he owned had produced a gun.

With a weary sigh, she pronounced the words, "Go home. We made progress today. We'll make more tomorrow. Dream of bright ideas to help solve this puzzle, and I'll see everyone back at eight o'clock—eight, not nine, got it?"

"How's criminal investigations working out for you, kid?" Owens asked Hendrix. "Everything you dreamed of?"

"It's wicked!" His enthusiastic response was coupled with a toothy grin. "Dad will be so proud of me if we catch the guy who murdered Judge Hamden. See y'all in the morning."

Jenna followed the others out and flicked off the lights, her mind continuing to churn. *How did he do it, and how can we prove it? And will I have to bend the rules to get the evidence we need?*

21

It was almost ten p.m. when Randi heard Jenna's car pull up. Reminding herself she should be happy her wife made it home at all, she stepped over a stretched-out dog and a balled-up cat to position herself languidly leaning against the interior doorframe Jenna would need to pass through from the laundry room into the rest of the house.

Her day had been a mixed bag of joyful teaching moments and dull reminders that Judge Lester Hamden was dead, would not be her next representative, and, more importantly, would never see his daughter get her medical degree or his sons graduate from high school.

At karate, Noah had told her that Anna was back from Duke, and he'd talked to her. The family had returned to their house, still with a police detail watching over them, and were overwhelmed by the compassionate response the community extended toward them.

Randi had finished her beginners' class before a wave of nausea sent her home. After two hours in bed, she felt fine and made a baked ziti for dinner; it would reheat easily for Jenna when she was ready to eat.

She heard the garage door close, and Jenna shambled through the doorway without flicking on the light, leaving Randi, draped in a forest green kimono embroidered with a yellow, orange, and red fire-breathing dragon, blocking her path in shadow.

"Jellybean?" Randi raised an amused brow.

Jenna glanced up at her, and Randi watched tension and dismay sweep away like twigs in a raging current. Jenna's blue eyes softened, and a beautiful smile graced her lips. They parted as Jenna flicked a glance up and down Randi's length. When her gaze at last locked onto hers, it brimmed with playful appreciation.

"Damn straight," she quipped. "I have to call our baby something until we settle on a name. And, based on the delicious aroma and the delectable you, am I being treated to dinner and a show tonight?"

Randi laughed, abandoned her attempt at a sexy pose, eased her palms onto Jenna's cheeks, and kissed her soundly. Then she wrapped her arms around her, drawing her into a loving embrace. "Dinner, at least. We'll have to see about the show."

"You teasing minx!"

With a grin, Randi released her hold on Jenna and walked with her into the entry hall. "Progress?"

"Yes and no," came Jenna's cryptic reply. She stowed her sidearm in its drawer and followed Randi into the kitchen. "I'll have to find somewhere else to keep my gun once a kid is running around in here."

"Indubitably," Randi answered and popped Jenna's filled plate into the microwave.

Jenna leaned her perfectly rounded bum against the opposite cabinets and crossed her arms. "I know who did it but am at a loss to prove it."

"Tell me."

All through Jenna's dinner, she expounded on how she knew it was Cochran and how impossible it would be to prove. "It's like going to the bank to ask for a loan," she explained. "You can't get one until you prove you don't need the money. Stupid, right? But that's how it feels. I need a warrant to gain the proof, but, to get a warrant, I need enough evidence to convince a judge he's guilty. Catch 22—whatever that means."

"It's a famous book title by Joseph Heller, and it means exactly what you've described—a paradoxical situation from which an individual cannot escape because of contradictory rules or limitations."

"Can't your brain figure a way out of the paradox box?" Jenna shot a pleading glance across the table, and Randi nibbled her bottom lip.

"I'll think about it," she promised, not having a clue. "But back to this Jellybean situation." She held Jenna's gaze skeptically for several seconds before caving into a smile. "It's adorable, now that I've thought about it. And you're right; baby needs a name. And since we don't know if it's a boy or girl yet ... have you thought about a name *you* want for our baby?"

"What do you like?" Jenna asked thoughtfully. "I know you probably have already made a list."

Randi winced with guilt. "Actually ... I wanted you to add some names to the list so we can go through them together." She flashed Jenna what she hoped was a winning grin.

Jenna emitted a half-hearted laugh, shook her head, and forked up the last bite of her ziti. "I'm too tired and distracted tonight. And I want to get started on the nursery once this case is closed. I'm sorry it's consuming all my time. I really missed you today."

"I missed you too," Randi concurred, "but you're here now, and I get to hold you all night."

"Not if I hold *you* all night." Jenna's lips quirked, and her dancing eyes sparkled. "I have to be up early, and I'd hate to waste you in a sexy kimono."

"Go, get out of those clothes," Randi ordered, pointing down the hallway, "while I let Byron out one more time. I'll bring water in case you get thirsty," she added with a playful wink.

"Now, see," Jenna mock-complained as she rose to put her plate in the sink. "This is how you got me to agree to having a baby. You seduced me, you vixen, wore me down with your delightful games, pushed all my buttons."

"And I'll push them again," Randi promised, wiggling her brows.

"Million-dollar babies," Jenna muttered behind Randi as she took the dog to the back door. "Ironclad alibis, irresistibly sexy wife ... it's a wonder I have any lucid moments."

Satisfaction surged through Randi from her toes up to the crown of her head. *I do that*, she told herself with loving pride. *I make Jenna happy.*

***

Sweating, her breathing jagged and way too fast, Jenna jerked awake, sitting up without realizing she had. Something was wrong; everything was wrong. "It's OK, sweetie," cooed Randi's voice in her ear. Her firm embrace encompassed Jenna's nude body, reassuring her she was safe.

Jenna swallowed and glanced at the clock—three-twenty-four. She tried to catch her breath as the disturbing images faded.

"It was just a dream." Randi's voice was tender, the kisses on her neck and cheek comforting. "It's been a while since one woke you up like that."

"I know," Jenna responded, leaning into Randi's strong body pressed to hers. "It was me shooting the guy at the junkyard, then everything was jumbled up. I was running through the weeds, the wrecked cars, and all the tires and parts. I'm not sure why I was running. Then there was Cochran, his smug mouth smirking at me while he told me how worthless I was, that I couldn't beat him even if I were a man. He had this plastic gun—it looked like a toy. It's all fading now," she admitted. "Mostly, I remember being scared, then you holding me, and everything was all right. I'm all right."

"Shh, of course you are," Randi soothed.

"Is it progress that the nightmare wasn't about Riley?" Jenna raked her fingers through her hair and allowed her breath to calm.

"You've made tons of progress." Randi's words were like a light in the darkness, and they resonated with Jenna. She believed she'd made progress too.

"I had to make the shot," Jenna stated. "I know I did. Dr. Grayson said no guilt, I followed the rules. I need to talk to her in the morning about Cochran. Maybe she can publish a profile that will help me get a warrant to search his house and phone, to get his DNA. He's laughing at me, Randi—*laughing*—because I'm not smart enough to catch him."

Randi's palm circled Jenna's back, rubbing her skin with reassurance. "You are, and you will. I believe in you, sweetheart; I always have."

Jenna shifted in Randi's arms and claimed her lips in fierce solidarity. "Thank you. I want a holiday when this is over. I want to take you somewhere special, just the two of us, to celebrate and escape crime and murder for a few days, maybe on a beach somewhere."

Randi's gaze sparkled in the pale moonlight streaming through the window. "I would love that!"

"Then it's happening." Jenna kissed Randi again to seal the deal before settling back onto the pillows, entwined together, limbs and torsos. She nestled her head into Randi's shoulder, nosing beneath her sweep of hair to nuzzle her neck. "Why do bad things happen?" she asked. "If there's a God, then why—"

"Shh, my love," Randi whispered, pulling her closer. "There is no why. There's only what we do with what is. Some things happen for a reason, and sometimes we can find a reason in what's occurred. Nature operates under principles and patterns, but when it comes to people ..." Randi's word faltered. She shook her head and dropped her lips to Jenna's.

"God is. Either you accept it, or you don't, but God still is. God isn't at fault for the evil a man nurtures in his heart and acts on. Should an impartial Creator step in to strike him down, taking sides with one of their children over the other? I can't explain it because I don't understand either. Do we attract good or bad manifestations to ourselves, or do they drop at random? I believe in the power of believing, but nobody can say for sure why certain things happen. Those who try invariably get it wrong. I love you. God loves you. Jellybean loves you. Whether you solve this crime or if the perpetrator gets away with it, those three facts will remain true."

"How can you know Jellybean loves me?" Jenna asked. "They're just a tiny mass of cells."

"Intelligent cells with a heartbeat," Randi corrected. "And I know because my DNA and their DNA are linked. My blood flows in and out of Jellybean's tiny form, so my body is in communication with theirs. Even if they can't talk, they can let me know how they're feeling. Everything will be all right."

Snuggled in a bed filled with fond memories, held in Randi's arms, hearing impossible utterings issue from her sweet lips—lips fired with tantalizing kisses, that had tasted every part of her and still begged for more, that laughed and smiled with such ease, that spoke often of inscrutable truths—Jenna believed that even the impossible could be possible.

"I know *this*," she answered. "I love you and Jellybean, and they can carve it into stone and put it in a magic arc." Relaxed again, Jenna drifted back to sleep, hoping for better dreams this time.

22

Tuesday, November 5, Election Day

"I'm not saying your theory doesn't hold merit," Captain Myers admitted. "I'm saying it lacks concrete evidence."

Jenna had worn her best professional blouse and blazer with her newest black slacks and even polished her dressy boots after an early shower that morning to look impressive. Appearing impressive was a daunting task next to Captain Myers, who wore authority like an expensive aftershave. His pinky finger possessed a more imposing air than Jenna's entire body.

"But look at this again." Jenna prodded an electronic tablet into his hands and pushed the play button. "See? He's on his phone at the exact time of the murder, before he takes the stage to secure his alibi."

"I see, Lieutenant," he answered impatiently. "Unfortunately, being on one's phone isn't a crime or suspicious. People are always on their phones. He could be checking the notes for his speech instead of giving the green light to a hit man."

Jenna's shoulders slumped, and her lips pressed together in a thin line. She knew he was right; so was she. He returned the tablet and rested a large hand on her shoulder.

"If Cochran had anything to do with this murder, you'll find proof of it. But we can't call him in for an interview on Election Day or convince a judge to sign a warrant for a sitting congressman without solid evidence."

"Yes, sir. I'll see what we can do."

Jenna stopped by the DNA lab and discussed the report with Dr. Gupta. Since the slug tested negative for fingerprints, she supposed the DNA came from a drop of sweat rather than a sloughed-off skin cell. Because it matched no one in the database, the report cleared activist Patti Madden and all the ex-convicts, leaving them only one current suspect—Cochran.

"Thanks, Dr. Gupta," she expressed, despite her frustration. In her peripheral vision, Jenna spotted Dr. Grayson gliding down the hallway in shoes Jamison would probably envy. "Can you ask the ancestor search registry people or whoever, like we did in that other case?"

Dr. Gupta smiled, her dark eyes tender and understanding. "I can check the public records, but we can't access clients who tagged their results to be kept private. I'll do that this morning. Who knows? You could get lucky."

Jenna returned a flat expression. "We could use some luck. Thanks."

Rushing, Jenna caught up to Dr. Grayson unlocking her office. "Do you have a minute?"

The distinguished psychiatrist lifted a brow and angled her head at Jenna. "I have five minutes, to be precise. But I can schedule you—"

"I'll take the five now," Jenna answered before she could finish. "It's about the Hamden case. Are you working on a profile for our unknown suspect?"

Jenna followed Dr. Grayson—Jane, if she was going to insist—into her invitingly professional office. This time, her gaze didn't wander to see if a new plant, photo, or book had made it to a shelf; all her focus was on the department shrink herself.

"I've received little to work with, Jenna," she admitted. "We don't know gender, race, age, motive, or much else."

"May I make a suggestion?" Jenna asked urgently.

Dr. Grayson held up a hand. "However, before you try to poison the well with your theory—which I've heard about, by the way—let me tell you what I've concluded."

Jenna should have known. Nothing got past Dr. Jane Grayson. "OK," Jenna grumbled, shifting a hand to her hip.

"Despite what we don't know, I can confirm the individual we're looking for is smart and organized. This was no spur-of-the-moment murder. It was meticulously planned, as apparent by the lack of witnesses and physical evidence. The killer is also patient, as he waited for a time to strike when Lester would be alone. Maybe the unsub didn't want the wife and kids around because he possesses a partial conscience and wished to spare them from seeing their loved one killed, or because he didn't want to risk striking one of them, or simply to avoid potential witnesses. But he or she did plan the attack for when Judge Hamden would be alone. This lets us know he researched Hamden's schedule, including his sons' after-school cross-country practice. Then there's the technology and expertise to create a 3-D printer weapon. Since they are notoriously unreliable, our killer likely practiced his shot, tweaked his printer recipe, or took other measures to ensure success. This tells us he's patient and detail-oriented. That brings us to the matter of being invisible."

Dr. Grayson set the armload of folders she held onto her desk and peered at Jenna speculatively. "Either the unsub blends exceptionally well, or he secured Harry Potter's cloak of invisibility. He got into and out of the neighborhood without anyone noticing, even though he fired a handgun in broad daylight. That, Jenna, is the riddle left for you to figure out. Discover how he did that, and you'll have him."

Jenna took a moment to ponder Dr. Grayson's observations. "Did you know Nash Cochran has a background in science and won a robotics contest in his younger days? He has to be organized to excel at his position. He's a patient planner. Jamison and I talked to his ex-wife, the one he screwed over and backed into a corner to sign an NDA. He waited until the exact moment to blindside her with divorce papers to get out of paying alimony. I'd say your profile fits him like a glove."

Dr. Grayson scrunched her brows and adjusted her glasses. Her silver-brushed brunette hair swept back from speculative green eyes. "It would fit a multitude of other suspects as well."

Under the scrutiny of her enigmatic gaze, Jenna second-guessed her gut ... for about five seconds. "Look, Dr. Grayson—"

"Jane."

"Look, Jane," she corrected, "I don't care about politics. My only goal is to put a killer behind bars. There are plenty of honest, well-intentioned politicians on both sides of the aisle, as well as corrupt, greedy ones. It wouldn't matter to me if Cochran were a bleeding-heart liberal or a staunch conservative. I looked into his eyes, saw the snarky smirk he gave me, and sensed the entitlement roll right off him. He practically challenged me to prove how he did it while standing on a stage in front of America."

"To keep you from straining something under that defensive posture, I'll let you know I'm an independent voter, not tied to a party or dogma. Most of it is BS anyway. I vote based on what I perceive about the individuals, not the labels they hide behind. In the past, I've voted for and against Nash. Today ..." She leaned back, almost sitting on her desktop. "I'm not sure how I'll vote today. I met Lester and Amanda. They're good people ... were, are ... you know."

With her sharp eyes shining with the fire of polished stones, Jane charged, "You find who killed him, but, if it was Cochran, you'll need a literal smoking gun, and, even then, he could end up getting off scot-free."

A police officer, whom Jenna didn't know by name, eased in through the open door. "Am I interrupting? I think it's time for my appointment."

"No, you're good, Officer ... Talbert," Jenna read from his uniform. "I'm just leaving."

Jenna marched into her office as if charging enemy lines. "Hendrix, get me Cochran's schedule for today. Owens, Jamison, how do you feel about going fishing?"

They looked at Jenna like she'd grown a second head. "Fishing?" Owens gaped.

"That's right. Murphy, Stone, I want you to go to every office supply and print shop in the county and use your best intimidation to make the clerks give you the names of everyone who's bought a professional-grade 3-D printer in the past year. I know our guy might have purchased it online, but, if he wanted to examine it in person, maybe watch a demonstration, he'd have to go into a local store." Jenna paused. "On second thought, start in Lynchburg."

"Lynchburg?" Stone questioned. "Because that's home base for Congressman Cochran when he isn't in Washington?"

"That and because I don't have jurisdiction in D.C. I know he has a home in Lynchburg, and it's only an hour's drive. You can come back and hassle everyone here when you're done," Jenna allowed.

"You heard the boss, kid." Vicki Stone didn't look thrilled, but she obeyed without complaint. "We're going on a field trip." She flung her uniform jacket over her shoulder, dangling it from two fingers, and declared, "Matt and I want ice cream when we get back. And five bucks says Cochran didn't buy a 3-D printer at any of the stores."

"Last of the big spenders, I see," Jenna countered. "I'll see your five and raise you five, and, yes, you deserve ice cream." Vicki and Matt both laughed as they exited. A pang in Jenna's gut reminded her of why she hated politics. All it did was split people apart, herding them into camps, no better than applying straight, gay, and trans labels, no different than warring over religion or any other stupid reason.

"I've got it, Lieutenant," Hendrix proclaimed, like he'd won a free, all-expenses-paid trip to Geekville. "Cochran's schedule has him visiting all the polling places in Lynchburg, making a quick stop by the college, and then heading to his campaign headquarters to watch the results come in."

"All right, then," Jenna proclaimed. "We're going fishing in Lynchburg."

***

It was hard to find parking at the middle school where Cochran's schedule showed he'd be at 10:30 a.m. Jenna and Jamison's police-issue SUV squeezed in where a hatchback pulled out, leaving Owens and Hendrix in a matching squad car to circle the lot again. Captain Myers had given her strict orders not to harass, confront, embarrass, or in any way antagonize Congressman Cochran; she'd taken the official vehicles to ensure nobody accused them of sneaking around.

The two-story brick building appeared inviting, with happy, child-oriented banners and blooming colors. The American and Virginia state flags flew from poles planted in a flowerbed on the front lawn. Also sprouting from the grass were red, white, and blue signs advertising every candidate for each position on the ballot. Jenna purposely ignored the ones for the presidential race. She couldn't allow herself to become distracted.

I did the early voting, she reminded herself. *Nothing to do today but catch Cochran saying or doing something dubious.*

"Turn on your body cam," Jenna instructed in a hush. Men and women of all descriptions made their way back and forth along the wide sidewalk while children romped in the grass, some not caring if they disrupted a sign. A man in a security uniform scolded one group of rowdy youngsters, and they scampered away.

Jenna peered at the faces of the voters. Some looked like her, some like Hendrix. Some were brawny older men with crew cuts, like Owens, while others wore attire announcing their religion. They were all there to vote, whether they championed a candidate or simply wanted to exercise their right and put a mark by whatever name grabbed their attention. One smiled, another frowned. Some seemed happy and carefree, while others glared at their watches, pushing past amblers in their haste to cast their ballot and get back to work.

Some countries make Election Day a holiday, so people don't have to worry about getting in trouble with their bosses, she considered. She should be glad it looked like a big turnout, yet she worried things might not go the way she'd like. *Politics are irrelevant,* she tried to convince herself.

Slowing to a crawl behind an old woman with a walker, Jenna practiced being patient. "Look." Jamison poked her and flung her chin to their right. "Outside the door."

There he was, the smug bastard, with his polished grin and winning handshakes. His cadre of caretakers encircled him, letting through fans who wished to congratulate the congressman and keeping out scoffers.

"We finally found a place to park," Owens huffed as he and Hendrix wormed their way to Jenna's other side.

"He's over there," Jenna said, shooting a glance at Cochran, his aides, and bodyguards. "We're going over casually to wish him luck. Keep your eyes and ears peeled."

"Just what are you up to?" Owens asked with concern. "He isn't going to simply confess."

"No, but maybe I can get him to slip up somehow," she answered. "I hope he'll let us see his phone."

"Like that's going to happen!" Jamison rolled her eyes.

"Let's just walk over casually to say hello, shall we?" Uncertain what might happen next, Jenna primed her intuitive senses and led the way.

23

Jenna and her team waited several yards away while Cochran basked in the praise of husband-and-wife supporters. Both were middle-aged and conservatively dressed. He shook their hands and grinned like the head chef at a barbecue. This time Jenna noted a runway-worthy, younger woman at Cochran's side and a teenage boy loitering nearby, looking out of place in a sports suit and dress shoes.

"Alida, his wife, and son, Liam," Jamison whispered, as if reading her mind.

The brunette press secretary and balding chief of staff stepped away to speak with reporter types, but the bodyguards remained firmly in place. As the couple shuffled off, Jenna spotted Cochran handing a takeout coffee cup to his blonde personal assistant. "Be a dear and throw that away for me, will you?" He must have thought no one was watching as his lustful gaze followed her swishing hips.

Jenna nudged Jamison. "Trash at ten o'clock."

She nodded and casually slipped away to follow Nancy somebody to the nearest public trash can. A swell of anticipation rose in Jenna's core. *If we can match his DNA to the bullet, we're home free! But surely he's smarter than that ... unless he's arrogant enough to believe he's above suspicion. Maybe he thinks he's so important that he could shoot somebody on Fifth Avenue at five o'clock and not be convicted of the crime.*

Flanked by linebacker Sergeant Owens and scarecrow Hendrix, Jenna stepped forward with a congratulatory smile. "Good morning, Congressman Cochran. So, today's the big day, huh?"

"Detective from Roanoke," he uttered, surprise evident in his expression. "I'm sorry, but I forgot your name."

"No worries," Jenna dismissed. *After today, you'll be remembering it for a very long time.* "Lieutenant Detective Ferrari. I'm joined by Sergeant Detective Owens and Tech Specialist Hendrix. We just wanted to check on you, make sure you haven't experienced any trouble, received threats, or had any close calls since we saw you on Saturday."

"Oh." His anxiety relaxed, and the surprise melted from his face, replaced by a practiced smile. "This is my beautiful wife, Alida, and my handsome son, Liam. Liam, come say hello," he instructed.

The lanky teen, with his mother's dark hair and a deeper shade of blue eyes than his father's, trudged forward with the enthusiasm of a bored sloth. "Hello. Thank you for voting Cochran," he recited. The kid must have been doing that most of his life.

"Liam is my pride and joy!" Cochran reached an arm around the lad's shoulders and squeezed. Liam dipped his chin, shuffled his feet, and looked like he wanted to hide under a rock.

"Thanks, Dad," he muttered.

"I have a boy his age," Owens said, pride scrawled across his blocky face. "Don't worry, Liam; it's better than if he ignored you."

"I suppose." The slightest gleam of relief blossomed in Liam's gaze as he looked up at Owens.

"No, Lieutenant," Cochran said, releasing his son, who retreated into his father's crowd. "We've had no trouble—thank the Lord—no death threats, no attacks. At first, Alida was so worried, you know, after what happened to poor Judge Hamden. But all my rallies have gone off without a hitch. So kind of you to come all the way out here to check on me."

"It's our job, Congressman," Owens replied in a friendly, we're-both-fifty-year-old-White-guys-with-sons manner. "It looks like a good turnout."

"We're hoping for one," Cochran answered. "It's great to see our citizens exercising their right to vote. Makes me proud to be an American. Have you voted yet, Sergeant?"

"I'll be swinging by my polling place as soon as we get back to Roanoke. The RPD is flexible enough to accommodate our force members getting to the polls. I'm glad to hear you've encountered no problems."

"Are you any closer to finding the murderer?" asked Alida, whose perfectly made face bore lines of concern.

"We've made some progress, Mrs. Cochran," Jenna confided, "though we've yet to obtain the evidence we need. Unfortunately, our unknown suspect has proven extremely smart and cunning. But I apologize. We're not allowed to discuss an ongoing investigation, even with other potential targets."

Alida's long, painted nails flew to the gold cross necklace at her throat as her dark eyes darted nervously to her husband. "You don't still believe the killer could be after Nash, do you?"

"Probably not," Owens assured her, "since he hasn't made a move for him yet. I think the Lieutenant is just being overly cautious, isn't that right?" He gave Jenna a quelling look, as if, being the man, he was actually in charge.

Jenna rolled her shoulders, as if she was brushing off his inappropriate comment. Based on Cochran's misogynistic tendencies, they had planned this approach in advance.

"Congressman, do you think our tech guy here could take a look at your phone?" Jenna asked. "I watched the recording of your rally in Roanoke. It was quite the shindig, and you are such an accomplished speaker. You had the crowd eating out of your hand, hanging on your every word."

"Well, thank you," he beamed as he retrieved the phone from his coat pocket. "But why do you want to see my phone?" He handed it over to Hendrix, and Jenna drew on all her self-control to keep her mouth from dropping. She hadn't expected it to be so easy.

"I noticed on the film you were looking at it just before you took to the podium," she replied. "I wondered if you were texting somebody or taking a last look at your speech notes—maybe even soaking in an inspirational family photo or some lucky charm. Public speaking isn't my forte, but Captain Myers tells me that, upon my next promotion, I'll have to give press conferences for the department and things like that. Do you ever get stage fright?"

Now that Hendrix had his phone, Jenna wanted to distract Cochran for as long as possible.

"Well, actually, Alida texted me a sweet good luck message, and I had to respond." He beamed and reached for his wife's hand. She entwined her fingers with his and leaned into his shoulder with a nervous smile. Jenna suspected this was the first she'd heard about the text message exchange.

"Would you believe, after all these years, I still get stage fright?" Cochran pretended to admit. "Getting an encouraging word from Alida always calms me right down. With her at my side, I can do anything."

"This is a brand-new phone," Hendrix blurted in a confused tone.

"Of course it is, young man," Cochran replied in a cocky, I'm-in-charge tone. "Clumsy me, dropped my other one in the pool Friday night. Silly, really, but these things happen. I just picked that one up Saturday. Of course, my old phone was a total loss—had to throw it away. And before you ask, Lieutenant," he said, pinning her with a steely gaze. "The trash truck picks up at the hotel we stayed at on Mondays. I'm afraid that old, waterlogged phone is gone for good."

He held out a hand, palm up, and Hendrix placed the clean new phone into it. Then Cochran did it again—he smirked at Jenna.

"I don't understand why you care about my husband's phone," Alida said in confusion.

"Could I see your phone, Mrs. Cochran, to view your inspirational good luck wishes?"

She sniffed, stiffened, and raised her head. "I didn't bring my phone with me today because I didn't want to be bothered by interruptions. This is a special day for us."

Cochran crossed his arms over a puffed-up chest, jutted out his chin, and sneered at Jenna with the exaggerated self-importance of a medieval high king. "The lieutenant is fishing in a bathtub, darling. Nothing to worry about." He turned to Jenna, rife with smug satisfaction. "Now, if you'll excuse me, I have constituents who wish to congratulate me on my imminent victory." He made a shooing motion toward Jenna, Owens, and Hendrix before deliberately stepping away to greet the group of folks who'd walked up.

Hendrix's mouth dropped while Jenna's jaw stiffened. "Let's go," she muttered, spun on her heel, and strode away. Owens caught up to her in no time.

"OK," he conceded. "After that, I'm on board with you. Dropped his phone in the pool? What a load of BS! Too convenient, too damn convenient."

"Thanks for buying me a minute to check out his phone," Hendrix said as he bounced beside Jenna. "I learned a few things that might be important."

Jenna glanced around until she spotted Jamison chatting with an old man sitting on a bench in front of the school. She clutched her oversized purse in her lap, her attention brightening his day. *She got it!* Jenna predicted as excitement bubbled up inside her.

"What things?" she asked Hendrix.

"It could have indeed come out of its box on Saturday," he confirmed. "Mint condition, only a few text messages, all from staff about his schedule."

"Wait," Jenna commanded. "*All* from his staff? No good luck notes from his wife? He had rallies on Saturday and Monday."

"Nope, nada," the bounding twig confirmed. "But there were a few photos of him and his son at the Roanoke Valley Model Flyers' Club, time-stamped for Sunday afternoon. They were holding these cool remote-control airplanes, historical replicas of famous aircraft, totally fab. I've got a basic flyer, not as cool as theirs—"

"Yes, Hendrix, that's fascinating. But you're sure no texts with his wife?"

"Positive," Tyr confirmed. "I didn't have time to check if he'd deleted them, but why would he if they were just good luck notes?"

"Exactly." They stopped in front of Jamison and Rip Van Winkle, chatting away. "Trish, are you ready to go now? We're all done."

"Oh, yes, of course." She rose and shot the old man one last dazzling smile. "It was so nice to meet you, Sam, and I wish you the best with your new hip."

It didn't matter how old, how young, how male, how female—Jamison made everyone fall in love with her. Maybe she secretly practiced white magic and had potions and spells she pulled out when nobody was looking. No. She just had a kind heart, a beautiful face, and, thank goodness, a shrewd intellect.

Together, the team marched into the parking lot. "You got it?" Jenna asked.

"I do," Jamison quipped, flashing Jenna a wicked grin. "And my body camera filmed continuously from the time Cochran handed the cup to his assistant to when I plucked it from the trash can. It's in a sealed evidence bag in my purse. Did he let you see his phone?"

"Yeah, but it wasn't the same one." Jenna deflated.

"He conveniently dropped his other one in the pool, if you believe in the Tooth Fairy," Owens declared and rolled his eyes.

"His new one is extra bussin'," Hendrix enthused, "all the bells and whistles."

"It's a piece of junk if it doesn't have what we need on it," Jenna complained. "When we get back to town, y'all go get your lunches and vote, and we'll meet back in the office when you're done. I'll be taking that cup to Dr. Gupta and standing over her shoulder until our not *extra bussin'* DNA machine spits out its results."

"Sounds good to me," Owens said. He stopped beside Jenna and Jamison's vehicle and handed his keys to Hendrix. "Tyr, you're young and loaded with energy. Run, get our ride, and pull around to pick me up."

Flashing Owens a toothy grin, the "Boy Wonder" snatched the keys. "You got it, boss!" He scampered away, cavorting like a gazelle in a minefield.

24

The afternoon dragged on. Jenna phoned Randi during lunchtime to check on her while she paced around the DNA lab, driving Dr. Gupta crazy. Then she headed back to her computer to read more background on Nash Cochran.

Around three-thirty, Officers Stone and Murphy returned from their store search. "Well, I have to hand it to you, Lieutenant," addressed Vicki Stone in a voice saturated with defeat. "I was sure that would be a wild goose chase." She plopped into a chair at the general table near the middle of the office space and shook her head. "I used the five I owed you to buy our ice cream."

"It was ten," Jenna corrected with a gleam in her eyes, "but forget it. Tell me what you've got."

Stone signaled Murphy, who stepped forward to pass a photocopy sheet to Jenna. "We thought it would be more efficient to start with the stores in Roanoke. That way, we'd only have to drive out to Lynchburg if nothing turned up here. But we ended up making the trip. The assistant manager at Liberty Copy and Printing Supply was eager to help."

"The young woman was smitten—smitten, I tell you," Stone said. "Couldn't take her eyes off Matt, kept blushing and batting her lashes. She thought he was the bomb."

Murphy's cheeks reddened like ripe cherries, and the curve of his lips broadened his dimples. "Anyway," he said, "she looked through their records going back two years and came upon a credit card purchase for a twelve-thousand-dollar, upscale 3-D printer. She had remembered the item because all the others they sold were under a thousand, the more run-of-the-mill variety. This one had to be special ordered. She hadn't remembered the customer—just the machine. But there's a copy of the receipt, and Nash Cochran's credit card paid for it."

"Hot damn!" Jenna cheered.

"Now he can claim he bought it as a gift," Stone argued, "but he did buy it. The thing is, the purchase was made two years ago. Surely, he didn't buy it with making a gun to kill Hamden in mind back then. The judge hadn't even announced he was running for the seat yet."

"That's true," Jenna agreed. "He probably bought it as an expensive toy. He likes science things. Maybe he only got the idea for the gun recently."

"*If* he made a gun with it," Stone pointed out. "At this point, Congressman Cochran is only a person of interest."

"You wouldn't be saying that if you were with us talking to him today," Owens countered. "Guy's as guilty as sin. I was skeptical too, until he smirked at us, claiming he dropped his phone in the pool and then went so far as to tell us the time the trash truck arrived at the hotel to haul the evidence away. He might as well have called us witless flatfoots. Jamison collected his DNA from a discarded coffee cup, and it's running right now."

"What should we do next, Lieutenant?" Murphy asked. "Oh, and thanks for the ice cream."

Jenna met Matt's eager gaze, the wheels of her brain turning. No. Asking him to go to the landfill and rummage through a ton of Monday's garbage would be too much. Besides, Cochran could have lied about throwing the incriminating cellphone away. She shook the request from her mind.

"We must continue to pursue other suspects," Jenna voiced thoughtfully. "We already searched Patti Madden's house, but, Owens, did you scour the yard, any outbuildings, vacant land near her house, survey her neighbors? She's our next best suspect."

"Her cabin is in the middle of nowhere," he answered, "surrounded by twenty acres of woods. Jamison and I ran a standard search of the house, jeep, garage, shrubs near the house, and a tool shed."

"We brought in all those guns," Jamison said, "the ammo, and a few other suspicious items. We didn't spend all day exploring the woods or digging up the yard."

"She didn't have a 3-D printer," Owens said.

"But she could have access to one. OK, Murphy, Stone, I'm putting the two of you on Madden for the rest of the day. Find out if she had access to a 3-D printer through one of her activism headquarters, and then go back out to her place. Jamison, did the warrant specify the house and vehicle only?"

"It says 'property,' which would include the land," Trisha replied. She produced a copy of the warrant and walked it over to Officer Stone. "You shouldn't need a new one. In fact, make her happy by returning all her firearms. The lab is through with them, and she might be more inclined to say something informative."

"Thanks, Detective," said Stone. She flicked a glance at Jenna. "No bets this time. I swear, if Cochran did this after I voted for his ass, I wanna be the one to throttle him," she growled.

"You'll have to get in line," Jamison quipped.

After Stone and Murphy left, Jenna sat staring at Tyr Hendrix's back while he conducted various legal searches. A part of her wanted to take him up on his hacking suggestion. If she only had Cochran's phone records, bank records, credit card purchases, internet searches, downloaded programs, or recipes, he called them. But it would do her no good if it were all inadmissible in court for being illegally obtained.

Jenna, Jamison, and Owens read article after article on Nash Cochran, chasing every rumor, researching each impropriety, all ending in "he said, she said" scenarios. Without his bank records, reporters had been unable to prove any payoffs were made or bribes accepted. The FBI had monitored but not gotten involved. Speaking of the FBI, Special Agent Pane hadn't turned up any known mafia affiliates in the area on Friday. Hendrix was doing something with videos at his station.

Owens groaned, Jenna's neck hurt, and Jamison's perfect, pert hair drooped wearily around her shoulders. Jenna glanced at the clock when her stomach growled. It was 7:00 p.m. The polls were closed, and results would start coming in. Any minute, every news outlet in the country would light up with early voting numbers, predictions, and a host of commentators pretending they knew what they were talking about. A sick ache kicked aside hunger as Jenna thought about Nash Cochran keeping his seat because of a lack of competition. *Hamden deserved to win, not to be murdered.*

Yet the largest hurdle to overcome wasn't who or why; it was how. How did someone get to Hamden without being seen? If Cochran had given the go-ahead to a paid assassin, the guy must have been a ghost.

"Hey, Lieutenant?" Hendrix—who had to stop earlier and get juice and vending food when his monitor beeped his blood sugar had gone too low—called to her in a timid voice.

Jenna leaped up and ran over to him, worried he might pass out or something. "Are you all right?" she asked. "We'll go home soon; I promise."

"No, I'm fine," he protested. "It isn't me, it's what I found. I've been re-watching it for half an hour just to be sure before I pointed it out to you."

Jamison and Owens walked over to huddle around the tech guy, probably glad to stretch their legs. "What'd you find, kid?" Owens asked.

"I was re-reviewing the neighbor's security footage hoping to spot a shadow or a rustling shrub or anything to indicate a person moving by, maybe just out of the camera's range," he explained. "I enlarged every square and scrolled through them frame by frame. That's when I saw it, but it was still fuzzy. So, I employed every trick I know to clean up the pixels and make the super-enlarged image clear enough for a jury. This is what I have."

He clicked his mouse to transfer the image onto the big monitor. "In the original, it looks like a bird. Here, you can tell it's a—"

"Drone!" Owens completed, his eyes round and jaw slack. "It's a frickin' drone!"

"Something is hanging underneath." Jamison pointed at an attachment a little smaller than the drone's body.

"The plastic gun," Jenna said.

"It doesn't look like a gun to me." Jamison frowned.

"Because it doesn't need a grip," Jenna explained. "You can see the barrel, frame, trigger, and cylinder. And that," she pointed. "A tiny camera?"

"Probably," Hendrix agreed. "He would need one to see what he's shooting at, even though the drone was most likely sent on autopilot to the desired coordinates."

"But mounting a gun on a little drone like that?" Jamison was either amazed or appalled as she gaped at the enlarged image on the screen.

"They're the next big thing in the military," Owens answered. "UAV—Unmanned Aerial Vehicle, aka drones, are in full use in conflicts around the world. They provide an inexpensive, easy-to-operate way to take out multi-million-dollar tanks and, equipped with thermal cameras, fly through spaces as small as an air vent to accurately target enemies without danger to the operator miles away. Equipped with a camera, gun, and remote-control device to pull the trigger, it can easily become a murder weapon."

"So, he'd need a remote control to operate the UAV, the camera, and to activate the trigger," Jenna mused. "Hendrix, could he do that all on his phone?"

"Heck, yeah!" he replied. "People are always accessing their nanny cams and home security cameras from apps on their phones, and some high-tech drones come with downloadable apps rather than separate radio controllers. I suppose a guy who built an award-winning robot in high school could figure a way to fire his gun remotely too."

"I must bring Captain Myers in to see this!" Jenna rushed for the door in her excitement. Then she turned back to her team. "Remember all that. Tell him what you just told me."

Racing down the hall, Jenna called through his office door, "Captain Myers! Come see what we found!"

He came, listened, and studied the newly discovered evidence. "We've got the receipt from when he bought an upscale 3-D printer, the DNA sample from his discarded cup is running right now, and see the gun mounted on the drone flying on a course to Hamden's front yard? The video of Cochran's rally shows him on his phone moments before he took the stage, at the same time as the shooting. Here," she added excitedly. "Let me play you this bodycam footage of our conversation earlier today."

Captain Myers watched patiently, an unreadable expression on his dark face. Then he glanced around at her team, listening to each share their expert take on the various pieces of evidence. His chest heaved, and he rubbed the back of his neck. "I really wanted you to find another perpetrator," he confessed, "but I feared this is how it would play out from the moment you mentioned your gut, Ferrari. While you might have convinced me, everything you have so far is still circumstantial. Even though we now know how the killing shot was made, you can't prove Cochran was on his phone, lining up the drone strike. Just because he bought a 3-D printer two years ago doesn't mean he used it to create a ghost gun. Without a witness or physical evidence, we don't know whether he purposely destroyed the phone he had on Friday afternoon or accidentally dropped it in the pool like he claimed."

"But, Captain—"

Myers held up a hand. "I said I believe your version of events; we just don't have enough to go after a sitting congressman—not yet. But, if you're right, the DNA sample Jamison collected will match what Dr. Gupta pulled from the bullet that killed Judge Hamden. That will at least give me enough to take to Chief Clarkson and get the go-ahead to apply for a warrant to search Cochran's house and bring him in for questioning. In the meantime, Ferrari, do not tip him off. If he suspects we've got anything, he'll destroy whatever evidence he hasn't already."

"His narcissism and misogyny will be his downfall," Jenna predicted. "He was so careful to create the perfect alibi, use an untraceable weapon, and avoid detection with that ingenious drone idea. He even got rid of the phone with the controller apps. But if he still has the drone, we can trace its movements through GPS. Hendrix said even deleted information isn't gone."

"The same with the drone camera," Hendrix added. "Even if he deleted the part where he lined up his shot on Hamden from the device, even if he threw the camera away, it's still in the cloud. Nobody remembers to wipe their cloud account."

Jenna nodded at Hendrix, beaming even brighter. "Then a couple of women cops show up, and he gets careless. He should have known that leaving a cup in a public trash bin made it eligible to be collected and tested by law enforcement, but he did it anyway. Maybe his mind was completely on his pending victory, or he thinks he's above touching, but we'll get him."

"Go home, everyone," Captain Myers suggested. "You've done a hell of a job on this—all of you. There's nothing more to do until the DNA results come in." He shifted his gaze to Jenna and pointed a finger. "Not a word about slow analysis times, Ferrari. I'm aware if we had the best of the best, we'd already have the match."

Jenna clamped her jaw closed and took the win. Feeling lighter than air, energized by the satisfaction of inevitable victory, she led her team out of the office, and Captain Myers turned out the lights.

25

It only took thirty minutes of election returns before Randi had to turn off the TV and take a shower, hoping the steam and hot water would ease her anxiety. While it helped her smell better, even her stress-relieving body soap didn't help her feel better. Exhausted after doing nothing but teaching her regular classes and going to vote, her hormones running amok, Randi slipped into a terrycloth bathrobe and curled up on the bed. Byron, who rarely ventured onto the mattress, as he was big and relegated to sleeping on his dog cushion, gingerly climbed up to lie beside Randi in solidarity. Not to be outdone, Bandit proved he could one-up the competition by cozying close to her head, purring to soothe her.

Although Randi's nausea was usually better by this late hour, it refused to ease, leaving her stomach as upset as her heart. At least in Virginia, the liberal party was leading in the national election, but District Six had already been called for Cochran. Even though she knew this would happen, it still left her feeling numb. Randi couldn't bear to think about what the presidential outcome would be. She just wanted to remain curled in a ball in the bed between her pets for the next four years.

It's not like you to let elections get to you, she reminded herself. *You know that, whatever happens, you, Jenna, and the baby will be fine. Your faith is stronger than this. It's the hormones—it has to be.*

Randi was trying slow, calming breaths and envisioning butterflies and hummingbirds when Jenna came in. "Randi, sweetie? Where are you?"

After a moment, her footsteps padded down the hall. Byron stepped off the bed, trotting to meet her, and Bandit stretched up with a solid, "Meow."

"In here," Randi moaned into her pillow.

In an instant, Jenna's reassuring hand was stroking her hair. She sat behind her on the edge of the covers, bringing her other hand to rest on Randi's thigh. "I'm sorry you don't feel well. Baby sickness again? I'd take some of it for you if I could." Randi tried to smile. She believed Jenna meant it.

"Partly."

"Yeah, I know." Jenna's tone fell in sympathy. "I listened to the election news on the way home." A warm kiss fell on Randi's cheek. "But I have good news that might help you feel better."

Inspired by the cheerful lilt in Jenna's voice, Randi rolled onto her back to peer hopefully into her wife's beautiful face and stunning blue eyes. "You found proof?"

"We did." Jenna grinned, leaned down, and kissed Randi's mouth. Folding her arms around Jenna, she found the strength to pull her all the way over, so she lay in her spot on the bed, boots and all.

"Tell me," Randi instructed. When her robe gaped from the movement, Jenna's gaze traveled down to the exposed cleavage that dipped to Randi's terrycloth belt, and half of one modest breast that lay bare.

"You're beautiful," Jenna proclaimed, her cheeks flushing with emotion. She wiggled a hand under the cloth to press lightly on Randi's belly. "Is this the right spot? Can I transfer my feelings of love for Jellybean like this?"

Randi beamed with joy at the unexpected gesture. Placing a hand atop Jenna's, she inched it down just a tad. "Here, I think. Yes, my love, my joy, and my delight, just let love for our baby swell in your heart, and the vibrations will flow down your arm and hand, through my flesh, and Jellybean will feel it."

Jenna focused on Randi's abdomen, scooted down her side, raised her hand, and kissed the spot, spreading kisses in a circle so she didn't miss Baby's resting place. "I love you, little one," she uttered in a timbre so angelic and reverent it could have been a prayer. Sliding back up to the pillow, she caressed Randi's cheek, riveted her gaze onto hers, adding, "And I love your mother."

Randi moved into a sultry kiss, savoring the feel and taste of Jenna's lips, the bond that grew ever deeper between them, until thoughts of anything else fled like a frightened fawn when faced with the power of their love. Her nerves and nausea waned, awakening her to what truly mattered. Relaxing every muscle, Randi's fingertips swirled on Jenna's lips, chin, and jawbone. "Tell me this wonderful news."

Jenna's grin widened in triumph. "We don't have Nash Cochran tonight, but we'll have him tomorrow."

With unchecked enthusiasm, Jenna relayed the mounds of circumstantial evidence they had gathered, the encounter they had with him in Lynchburg, and topped it off with the enhanced video image of a drone fitted with a small camera and a home-crafted, 3-D printer styled plastic gun flying across the street toward Hamden's front yard two minutes before the fatal shot was fired.

"The only thing more amazing than Cochran's plan was you and your team figuring out how he did it," Randi said in wonder, beaming her congratulations to Jenna. "I'm sorry I wasn't up to making dinner. I just burrowed into bed to feel sorry for myself—well, for the entire country. But knowing Cochran is going away for murder makes me feel better."

"Well," Jenna said guardedly. "The DNA still has to match, and I wouldn't put it past a politician with connections and a team of lawyers to win at trial. It's happened before."

"I'm sure the DNA will match," Randi responded. "As to the lawyers and connections, Jenna, that's out of your control. You did your job, and you did it splendidly."

"A confession would be better," she asserted, then shook her head. "And don't worry about dinner, darling. I'm a big girl and can fend for myself. Hey, now that you're feeling better, can I bring you something to eat? Crackers and cheese, soup from a can?" She lifted an amused brow, getting a laugh out of Randi.

"I think a banana and some cheese and crackers would go down good now." An adoring smile formed across Randi's lips. "Jenna, I appreciate you, all you're doing to take care of me and Jellybean—"

"It's hardly enough," Jenna protested as she rolled out of bed. "I should be doing more and will be as soon as this case is over. Hey, while I'm getting dinner together, why don't you look up what beach you want to lie on? See if the rooms come with little pails you can carry around to throw up in whenever you need to," she teased from the doorway.

"Brat!" Randi called as Jenna slipped out of the bedroom.

"I love you!" echoed her sing-song reply.

Lighter in spirit, Randi picked up her phone from the nightstand and started researching Florida beach resorts.

***

Wednesday, November 6

Jenna arrived at work early, wearing what she considered her next best outfit—a navy blue blazer and slacks with a pinstripe, button-up shirt, and polished boots. She reviewed the affidavit Jamison had written to present to Judge Stroud as soon as they had approval. Changing a few words, she passed the paper back to Jamison. "What do you think?"

"Oh, yeah," she agreed. "This gives it a stronger voice. I'll make those changes."

While Jenna watched the wall clock tick, Hendrix weaved around the office to hand her an envelope full of printed photos. "To go with your warrant request," he said. "They say a picture's worth a thousand words."

"Thanks." Jenna browsed through clear enlargements of Cochran on stage, fiddling with his phone, the drone fitted with a homemade gun, and others.

Officers Stone and Murphy walked in, drawing her attention. "The PETA warrior was happy to get her guns back," Stone announced, "but searching her woods and gardens was a waste of time."

"I can see why she's a suspect, though," Murphy added, cringing. "Remind me not to cross paths with Ms. Madden."

"Do you have any more busy work for us?" Stone asked, appearing bored.

"Soon I'll have vital—not busy—work for you," Jenna predicted. "I'll be back."

Leaving her team to their last-minute details, Jenna marched down the hall to the DNA lab. Dr. Gupta worked at her desk while the machine hummed. "When will it be ready?" Jenna felt like a kid impatiently waiting for Christmas morning. She hadn't gotten much growing up, but one year she awoke to find a shiny new bicycle standing in the living room by the fireplace. She never forgot how it made her feel, touching it for the first time, eyes wide and mouth open as she slid her fingers along the smooth metal of the handlebars, or the feeling of freedom riding it had given her.

Dr. Gupta glanced up with a sage chuckle. "When it's ready. It shouldn't be long now."

"I've spent a year dropping hints with the captain about getting us a new, rapid-response machine. If we'd had one, I could have arrested Cochran before he gave his acceptance speech last night."

The specialist with her PhD and years of experience raised a questioning brow. "Are you that certain he's guilty?"

"At first it was my gut," Jenna explained, "intuition, a vibe, you know? But the evidence has been growing. Still, it won't be enough without a DNA match to what you pulled from the bullet."

"You understand that my findings will be impartial," she reminded Jenna.

"I expect them to be pure science." Jenna leaned her elbows on the counter and stared at the DNA analysis machine as if she could force it to work faster by the power of her will. She jumped when it beeped, and the hum faded. The printer sprang to life, and Dr. Gupta walked over to await the pages it spat out.

In her enthusiasm, Jenna rounded the counter and hovered over her shoulder, thankful Dr. Gupta was shorter than her. "What does it say?" she inquired urgently.

"Be patient, Jenna," chided the older woman. She took the printout and returned to her desk with Jenna tight on her heels.

A range of emotions zigzagged through Jenna like two lightning bolts playing hopscotch. She rolled her fingers together anxiously, trying to catch glimpses of the page.

Dr. Gupta held up two sheets, making a visual comparison. "We have a 99% match between the bullet and the coffee cup samples. I can confirm they both originated with the same donor."

"Hot damn!" Jenna cried, looking at graphs and words she didn't completely understand. "But why do you always say 99%? What didn't match?"

"Oh, everything matches," Dr. Gupta assured her. "We can't say 100% because there's always a margin of error, a possibility of another explanation for a positive match. Identical twins, for example, are born with identical genes. However, over time, environmental factors can cause mutations, leaving slight differences in their DNA profiles. Also, if subject A had donated bone marrow for a transplant for subject B, their blood might produce the same profile. However, since these samples were from sweat and saliva, that wouldn't be the case. And if your coffee cup was Cochran—"

"We have a video that shows Cochran take the last swallow, handing the cup to his aide to throw away, the aide placing it in the trash bin, and Jamison taking it out," Jenna interrupted. "And his birth records show no siblings, a twin or otherwise."

Dr. Gupta nodded. "Like I said, it's a match."

"Copies! Your report stating they match," Jenna rattled off. "I need them now!"

"OK, OK." Dr. Gupta laughed at Jenna. "You Italians are always so emotional. I'll have them in five minutes—that is, if you stop pestering me long enough."

Jenna raised her palms and stepped back. "I'll go tell Captain Myers," she declared with an electric grin. "Thank you! I'll be right back."

Assuming her butt-wiggling, bouncy dance down the hall must resemble Tech Specialist Tyr Hendrix, Jenna didn't care. They were about to take down a Goliath as another twiggy young man had done thousands of years ago. She pictured Tyr standing up to the giant with a little sling and some stones. *I couldn't have done it without him,* she conceded. *Maybe he'll do after all.*

26

An hour later, as Jenna read through the warrant proposal for the fifth time, Captain Myers stepped into the criminal investigations office with professional ease. All eyes in the room shot to him in anticipatory silence so still you could hear a hair fall to the floor.

After scanning six pairs of eyes, his commanding gaze met Jenna's. "Chief Clarkson gave his approval for you to ask a judge for a search warrant of Congressman Nash Cochran's home, vehicle, electronic devices, phone service, credit card and bank records, and to ask politely if he would come in for an interview. This is to be carried out with the utmost respect and privacy. Ferrari, if a single reporter shows up—"

"We won't take cop cars," she began. "No lights and sirens. Nobody in this room is to breathe a word of this," she commanded, catching each eye. "But I would like to loop in Dr. Grayson and ADA Altman after we have him here, sir."

Inclining his head, Myers agreed. "And I will be present for the interview as well. Chief Clarkson wants to watch from the booth. But first things first. You'll have to convince a judge to issue the warrant."

"Yes, sir," Jenna replied, her posture straight and energy busting at the seams to be released. "Jamison and I are on that. The rest of you get ready to go. We'll need evidence boxes and bags for what we find, and I need you, Officers Stone and Murphy, as our muscle."

Rather than flush, Vicki Stone's face shone with pride as she adopted a Superman pose, while Matt Murphy's cheeks reddened. "Yes, ma'am, Lieutenant!" Stone affirmed. "But you don't want us to drive over in a squad car?"

"I'll authorize you to take an unmarked, comfortable SUV," Myers said. "We can't risk a media field day if a neighbor reports police cars pulling up to Cochran's home. Ferrari, I'll let you make the call, but, if Cochran wants to drive himself or have his lawyer accompany him, I'm fine with that. I'd like to ruffle his feathers as gently as possible, and we don't believe him to be a flight risk."

"I agree," Jenna stated. "He's too sure of himself to run." Turning to Trisha, she asked, "Jamison, are you ready?"

"I was ready yesterday!" Slinging her purse strap over her shoulder, Jamison glided to Jenna's side in an eye-catching onyx and snow geometrically patterned blouse, black skirt, and elegant, asymmetrical dolphin-gray blazer. Yeah, this woman was born ready.

***

Jenna wrapped a firm knock on Judge Stroud's carpenter-crafted front door, rang the bell, and stepped back to let Jamison take the lead. Admiring the planks and grooves, she recognized this was no cookie-cutter door the builder snatched up on the cheap. The entire mansion, if you wanted to call it that, glowed with refined sophistication, from its white columns to the two-hundred-year-old live oak spreading across the front yard.

The door opened to a petite, middle-aged woman with short, curly hair, still stark in its chestnut brown. "Detective Jamison," she greeted with surprise. "I wasn't expecting to see you back so soon. I see you've brought Lieutenant Ferrari with you this time—must be important."

"Yes, your honor," she replied, "and thank you for signing those other warrants for us. It was an important step in the investigation that helped eliminate several prime suspects. I fear the truth we now face is rather bleak. But, first, how are you holding up?"

"Oh, come in, you two," she invited with a charming Southern drawl. "Can't have you standing out on the front porch all morning."

The inside of her home spoke of style, achievement, and world travels—meticulous in cleanliness and décor. "Let's go in here to the front sitting room. Would you like some tea?"

"Oh, no, thank you, Judge Stroud," Jenna responded, knowing the woman had to ask per protocol. "Your home is exquisite, and we'd love to come for a visit sometime, but this is an urgent matter."

"Isn't it always with you, Lieutenant?" She winked and showed them into a room with gleaming white walls, a lush red and gold Persian rug, and new, recreated antique-style furnishings. "And thank you. My late husband and I spent a lifetime collecting meaningful pieces. Now, what do you want me to sign, and do I want to?"

She raised a brow, and Jamison passed her the affidavit. Judge Stroud put on her reading glasses and studied the paper. "Nash Cochran," she stated flatly. "Why am I not surprised?"

"Look at the photos and the DNA report," Jenna added, trying to hold back any semblance of desperation.

"I know it's tricky," Jamison said, empathizing with how the judge must feel. "But we believe we'll uncover vital evidence at the congressman's home and in his phone and bank records."

"People have tried to catch him in a shady deal for years," Judge Stroud admitted. "They're afraid of him and for good reasons. A few words from a man like that, and a law enforcement officer, an elected official, or even a judge could lose all credibility, their job, and possibly even their life."

"I'm aware." Jenna's tone was robust, and she was indeed aware of the backlash and consequences—risks she was willing to take.

Judge Stroud sighed and looked up at the detectives. "I watched his acceptance speech last night. Did you?"

Both women shook their heads.

With hard eyes bright as fire and an aspect of insult, the woman, shorter than Jenna and thinner than Jamison, spoke with the strength of a golden glove boxer. "He was so arrogant—not a word of sympathy for Judge Hamden, no mention of his untimely death. He acted like he had held the lead all along, and nothing could stop him."

Jenna thought she spotted steam when Judge Stroud's nostrils flared. "Among his campaign promises was to support a voting rights bill that would require a birth certificate or passport in addition to a driver's license or other photo ID, bearing the exact same name, for a citizen to vote. My birth certificate lists me as Susan Hogan, while my driver's license shows my married name—Susan Stroud. Without a passport, I wouldn't be allowed to vote. This bill, if passed into law, could end up restricting millions of married women from casting a vote. It is purely a sexist effort to disenfranchise women across America."

She clamped her hands on the warrant request, her face pained with decision. "I was thinking about retirement anyway. Maybe the only thing that can stop him is a few determined women." The judge signed her name and passed the paper to Jamison. "Find something good," she directed with the full authority of her office.

Jenna nodded, pushing rapidly to her feet. "Thank you, your honor; we will."

***

At ten 'til one, Jenna, Owens, Jamison, Hendrix, Stone, and Murphy all stood outside Nash Cochran's estate home in Lynchburg. While the officers drove there in unmarked cars, Stone and Murphy still wore their uniforms. All had their badges out and body cameras on. Captain Myers had called and informed the Lynchburg Police Department about the visit out of courtesy. The police chief had laughed, saying they were wasting their time and would end up with egg on their faces, but he didn't try to stop the execution of the warrant.

Jenna rang the bell and Liam answered. His eyes rounded at the sight of the official crowd. "Dad?" he called tentatively over his shoulder.

Cheerful voices rang from within the towering halls of the mansion, some male and others female. It seemed Cochran had company.

Liam stepped back when his father, chief of staff, and another fellow Jenna hadn't seen before approached the door as proud comrades. Instantly, Cochran's expression hardened. "Roanoke police, what do you want now?" Jenna held up the official paper. "Congressman Cochran, we have a warrant to search the premises and take your electronics and 3-D printer back to our lab."

"What? How? Why?" he stammered without budging from blocking the doorway. "You will do no such thing!"

"Now, Nash, settle down and let me handle this," said Phil Kensington, the chief of staff. He gave Jenna a hard eye and puffed up his chest with an air of importance.

"I'm calling Richard," Cochran grumbled and yanked a phone from his pocket. Glaring at Jenna, he barked, "That's Richard Wurth, of Albrecht Attorneys at Law in D.C." He stomped away and put the phone to his ear.

"Of course, Mr. Cochran is happy to cooperate with law enforcement," Kensington said unconvincingly. "But you caught him unawares. If you had called ahead and let us know you were coming—"

"That isn't how this works," Jenna clipped. She brushed the insubstantial chief of staff aside and strode over the threshold, followed by her entire crew. "Congressman Cochran, we are exercising this duly authorized search warrant, and your objections have been noted," she called, following him as he made his way deeper into the house. "Stone, Murphy. Stay on him and escort him outside. I don't need him 'accidentally' destroying more evidence before we can box it up."

"Yes, Ma'am," came Murphy's smart reply, and the two trotted after Nash.

"Owens, you take the garage and vehicles, and Jamison, Hendrix, and I will cover the house. Remember, plastic guns, drones, 3-D printers, and electronics, plus anything else suspicious that looks related."

"Got it." Owens stepped out, heading for the garage, which couldn't be seen from the front of the estate. Jenna had viewed a satellite image and knew the expansive building was around the back.

"But, really, officers, is this necessary?" Kensington inquired anxiously. He pushed up his glasses and followed Jenna.

The other man put an arm around Liam's shoulders, leading him away. "Let's go tell your mother."

"Yes, it is very necessary," Jenna stated. "And if you don't stop trying to interfere, I'll have to have you taken into custody, restrained, and placed in one of our vehicles until we're finished. Do you understand, Mr. Kensington? This is official police business."

A frightened look overtook him, his weak chin seeming to weaken more. He held up his palms and stepped back. "I'm not interfering; I'm just trying to—"

"Mr. Kensington." Jamison moved between Jenna and the annoying little man. "Why don't I show you out. There's a lovely seat on the veranda where you can wait until we're finished. That will keep you out of trouble. But I'm going to have to ask you to let me hold on to your phone. We can't have you calling people and telling them about the search. It's our duty to protect Congressman Cochran's privacy so that the press doesn't know we're here. We wouldn't want unwarranted, nasty rumors to get started, and we sure don't want Congressman Cochran to learn you were to blame."

His eyes widened, and he gulped. Handing Jamison his phone, the administrator uttered, "No, ma'am. I don't want anyone to know about this."

Jamison returned from showing Kensington out around the same time Stone and Murphy escorted Cochran past Jenna. "Here," Officer Stone said, handing Hendrix the suspect's cell phone. "His lawyer is arranging a private flight to Roanoke and should be there waiting when we arrive."

"Thanks," Jenna said.

Cochran blasted her with a fiery glare, hot enough to melt iron. In barely contained rage, he snarled, "You're going to pay for this! You and your whole damn department. Your chief will be lucky if he can get a job scrubbing toilets when I'm done, and you—" He wiggled an arm between Stone and Murphy to jab a finger in Jenna's direction. "You're done for!"

"You hear that, Jamison?" Jenna answered pleasantly. "I believe the congressman just threatened me, my boss, and the entire Roanoke Police Department.

That will provide such a great character witness video to play for the jury at his trial."

"Trial?" he fumed, launching an open fist toward Jenna. Matt and Vicki grabbed his arms and practically dragged him the rest of the way as he shouted. "There isn't going to be a trial! You can't prove anything!

"I didn't *do* anything," he corrected himself before Jenna stopped listening.

27

It was four that afternoon by the time all had been accomplished and Jenna was ready to start the interview with Congressman Nash Cochran, aka the perpetrator of the crime. She had allowed him the dignity of riding in his car, with Kensington driving between hers and Owen's vehicles. Stone brought up the rear, ready to give chase if Cochran tried to dart out of line.

The team had hit the Jackpot at the Cochran estate, causing confident rays of elation to pulse through Jenna on the ride back to Roanoke. Owens recovered two drones from the garage, both with cameras mounted, and one with a bracket and a couple of screws underneath. Jenna and Jamison found the 3-D printer in a hobby room in the basement and boxed it up to bring with them. Hendrix spent hours prying every byte of information from all three devices.

To Jenna's disappointment, and despite a comprehensive hunt, no gun, plastic or otherwise, turned up on the premises. However, Jamison found a small box of .45 caliber bullets tucked away in the back of a drawer in the hobby room, half of which were missing. Print Specialist Marcus pulled Cochran's fingerprints from all the items, but the most compelling piece of evidence remained the DNA match. For the record, CSI Wilcox had officially collected Cochran's DNA before he sequestered himself in a room with his lawyer.

"I found it!" exclaimed Tyr as he rocketed out of his swivel chair, a fist pumping in the air and a grin as wide as the Grand Canyon beaming across his face. "This is lit! You are so goin' slay that poser."

"What?" While Jenna thought she was up on teen slang, she wasn't exactly sure what Hendrix said. It must be good, though. She wove around Owens's desk, heading for her computer guy.

"You know how I told you things mostly don't get deleted and there're ways to get them back?"

"Yeah."

"Well, Cochran erased video from his camera; we never found the phone," he added in disappointment. "But we don't need it. I pulled the whole thing off the cloud. People always delete photos and stuff from their devices, but they forget about cloud storage. All newer technology automatically backs up pictures, videos, and documents to the cloud to protect them in case your device is lost or stolen and to free up memory and disk space. Anyway, look at this."

Clicking his mouse, Hendrix played a ten-second clip of Judge Hamden walking from his driveway past the tree toward his front door. Then, a small jolt in the video, probably caused by the gun firing, and a tear ripped through Hamden's suit coat, throwing him forward to the ground. That was it—the murder on streaming video shot from Cochran's camera and uploaded to his cloud account.

"How is he going to dispute this?" she asked, as another nail drove into the murderer's coffin. "Though I'm sure he'll try. Good work, Hendrix!"

"Oh, that's not all." He plunged a skinny finger into the air while his other hand danced across his keyboard. "He wiped the memory of the 3-D printer, but I was able to reconfigure what was on there and found the plans for a Liberty model plastic gun and the changes he made to it. I have to hand it to the guy," Hendrix admitted as he brought up a bunch of code Jenna would never in a million years decipher. "He's really quite brilliant. He improved on this classic design and used superior quality plastic tubing. The lab tested samples taken from the machine, and this polyamide-imide can withstand temperatures surpassing five hundred degrees Fahrenheit. Firing a single shot from a short-barrel wouldn't produce that much heat, thereby maintaining the integrity of the weapon. He probably conducted many experiments before getting it perfect. You know, it's too bad he chose the wrong fork in the road. Cochran could have been a respected scientist, contributing valuable innovations instead of wasting it all on being a crooked politician."

"Yeah." Jenna allowed a single moment to mourn the man who might have been before gleaming over her mountain of evidence.

"And there's one more thing," Hendrix added with a wink. Handing Jenna a printout, he explained, "I analyzed the GPS tracking chip in both drones. The one whose camera recorded the killing shot started its journey from the community college parking lot, flew five miles to Hamden's residence, hovered for a few minutes, and returned to the hotel where Cochran and his crew were staying. Now, I can't pinpoint the exact spots, but it probably took off through the sunroof in Cochran's car and landed on the balcony outside his hotel room. Those would be the most likely spots. It would be nice to have his physical phone, but his internet records I pulled with the warrant show that his phone number was transmitting and receiving data at the stadium during the window for the murder."

"He operated the drone, camera, and triggering device from his phone while sitting on stage, about to give his speech. That's the story the evidence tells," Jenna concluded, "and I believe we can convince a jury." Still, she'd rather have a confession.

"Hey, Ferrari?" Owens called from the office doorway. "The chief is here, and everyone's about ready. Where's Jamison?"

"Hanging out with Bennet until we're ready for him," Jenna replied. "Just one more minute. Tell Captain Myers I'm on my way."

"Sure thing."

"Hendrix, Chief Clarkson and Dr. Grayson will be in the booth with you. Don't let them make you nervous. You've got this." She pinned him with a confidence-inspiring gaze and patted his bony shoulder.

"Yes, ma'am." With a grin, the young man bounded toward the exit.

Alone for a moment, Jenna texted Randi. *'About to interview Cochran. Wish me luck!'*

'You're going to roast him!' followed by

Jenna laughed to herself, filled with love for her precious wife. *'I'll be home sometime and then Florida.'*

'I love you. See you when I do.'

"Now, for the moment of truth." Jenna straightened and strode toward the booth. She shook hands and exchanged pleasantries with Chief Clarkson, thanking and assuring him their evidence was overwhelming. Next, she greeted Dr. Grayson—*Jane*—and thanked her for her assistance.

"Don't forget what we talked about before," the psychiatrist reminded her. "If you want a confession, laying out the evidence won't secure it."

"I haven't forgotten." Jenna nodded and stepped out to meet Captain Myers in the hallway.

"Ready, Lieutenant?" He peered at her, a tinge of trepidation on his chiseled face.

Jenna held up a folder full of evidence photos and lab reports. "We've got this, sir."

"After you." Myers opened the door and ushered Jenna in. At the table, a man around Cochran's age, with just as pristine a haircut and an equally expensive suit, sat behind a closed briefcase at the congressman's right hand.

"I'm Captain Myers, and this is Lieutenant Detective Ferrari." He remained standing for the introduction before pulling out Jenna's chair and following her to sit.

"Mr. Richard Wurth, from Congressman Cochran's legal team." His accent suggested he could hail from Georgia or South Carolina, as did his trim mustache and goatee, both bearing a heavier frosting of gray than the hair on his head. When Myers extended his hand, the attorney ignored it, sliding on a pair of readers instead. "Right now, my associates are drawing up a motion to suppress to submit to Judge Vance of Roanoke County, challenging the admissibility of all so-called evidence collected from my client's home."

Myers retracted his polite gesture and shot Jenna an irritated expression. "Mr. Wurth, my officers complied with all stipulations of their legally obtained search warrant. Congressman Cochran's rights were not violated, and you can make all the motions you like."

Wurth inhaled sharply through his nose and whispered something to Cochran, accompanied by a stern expression. Cochran glowered and shot a scorching glare at Jenna.

"Furthermore," Wurth added, this time bothering to glance up at them, "I've advised my client to say nothing. So, are you charging him with a crime or not, because we'd like to go home."

Myers responded with a withering glance at Wurth and turned his focus to Cochran. "This interview is being recorded. Would you please state your name for the record?"

Cochran brooded for a moment, then straightened, shooting his nose into the air. "I am Congressman Nash Cochran, U.S. Representative for Virginia's Sixth District, and, whatever you're accusing me of, I deny it."

"Thank you," the captain responded. "You should also be aware that you have the right to remain silent, that anything you say can be used against you, and you already have your attorney present. Do you understand your rights, Mr. Cochran?"

"That's Congressman Cochran," Wurth corrected, "and we demand to know what charges you are reckless enough to bring against him."

When Myers flicked a glance at Jenna, she took it from there. "Congressman Nash Cochran, you are being formally charged with first-degree murder for the shooting of Judge Lester Hamden. ADA Altman, who is standing by, has arranged an arraignment hearing for you with Judge Williams at his earliest convenience, which, conveniently enough, will be tomorrow at 1:00 p.m. Then, your attorney, the DA's office, and Judge Williams can decide whether you will be released on bail or remanded into custody awaiting your trial. You *will* spend the night in lockup—nonnegotiable."

"I must protest!" Mr. Wurth's face reddened as his mouth turned down into an angry frown. "I will move that these preposterous charges against my client be dropped immediately. Are you people so dull-witted? Congressman Cochran couldn't have killed that man on Friday afternoon. He was on stage at a campaign rally, making a speech before thousands—and on TV! Stupid Roanoke police," he mumbled, shaking his head.

"Oh, yes, I know all about your 'unbreakable' alibi," Jenna directed toward Cochran, "only my team has broken it." She opened the folder and turned a picture to face Cochran, who sat across from her. "This is a blown-up shot, time-stamped, of you on your phone—you know, the one you dropped in the pool and had to replace—at the same time your competition, who had taken the lead in the polls, was being shot."

"He never took the lead!" Cochran bellowed. "Those polls were faulty, carried out by a liberal news media organization, and did not reflect the lead I held the entire race."

"Nash," his counsel warned, "don't say anything. Let them put on their show and I'll take care of this."

Whipping his glare toward Wurth, Cochran said, "I already told this woman I was reading and answering a text from my wife before I went onstage."

"Except you weren't." Jenna laid another piece of paper on the table. "These internet server records show you weren't texting but using app data. Even though the phone was destroyed, the company records still exist." He gave it a cursory glance and waved his hand, as if the figures on the page were inconsequential.

"Then there's the video footage of Judge Hamden being shot."

As Jenna turned on a copy downloaded to her electronic tablet, Cochran's eyes shot wide. "That's impossible! I era—I, I never took any videos of a murder. You planted that!"

"It was uploaded from the camera attached to your drone found in your garage to your cloud server," Jenna explained. "That's where my tech guy found it."

As the disturbing video played, Cochran turned to his lawyer with an anxious expression. "They can't do that, can they?"

"We're moving that all the evidence from your home be suppressed from the trial. Now, please, just be quiet."

Snapping his chin toward Jenna, Cochran declared, "That wasn't my drone or camera. Somebody must have put them in my garage to frame me."

"OK," Jenna emitted with a chuckle. "If you say so. But here is the GPS tracking data for that exact unit." She placed another page before him. "It shows the UAV began its trip from the community college parking lot, traveled to the coordinates of Judge Hamden's residence, where it hovered for a minute, then flew to the hotel where you and your entourage were staying, all conveniently at the time surrounding and during the shooting."

"Like I said, it's not mine." His scowl grew even darker as his fingers coiled into a fist on the table. "Someone must have done that on purpose to frame me."

"But this is your 3-D printer." She laid out a photo of the unit taken into evidence, along with a copy of his purchase receipt from two years ago.

He shrugged. "A lot of people own 3-D printers. So what? Did you find a gun? No, I didn't think so." He sneered at her, a smug veil covering his former apprehension as he crossed his arms over his chest.

Cocking her head at her suspect, Jenna commented, "You know, Captain Myers, we never released any information about our suspicion a 3-D-printed, plastic ghost gun had been used in the murder. Are you aware of that detail being leaked?"

"No, ma'am, Lieutenant," he confirmed with authority. "The press never learned of that detail, and nobody's shared it outside this station."

"I'm just guessing," Cochran rebutted. "Why else would you be looking at my printer? I'll bet you found lots of recipes for trinkets and toys, but none for a gun on my machine."

"Actually, no, not at first glance." Jenna flipped another sheet to face him. "The device's memory had been totally wiped. A funny thing—an IT expert can retrieve deleted information, and all those little bytes floating around? It seems they can be reassembled. Don't you remember your science, Mr. Cochran? Neither energy nor matter can be created or destroyed, only transformed or transferred. It's a fundamental principle of physics. Our specialist found every recipe you wiped, including the one for a Liberty printed handgun and the improvements you added to the design."

"I don't know what you're talking about!" Cochran shoved the pile of papers back at Jenna, curling his lip at her.

"This is all circumstantial," Mr. Wurth said dismissively, gesturing toward her folder and the flying sheets. "Anybody could have switched another printer for Cochran's."

"Anybody?" Jenna's tone and brows shot up in surprise. "Congressman, is your estate so inadequately secure that anyone off the street could have entered your home, walked downstairs to your hobby room carrying a large, expensive 3-D printer, switched it out for yours, and strolled out again undetected?" She shook her head as if in disbelief. "If so, you need vastly improved security at your place. I at least have a hefty German Shepherd to rip apart intruders."

"I had nothing to do with it," Cochran continued to deny, yet Jenna detected the glint of fear in his sea-blue eyes.

She laid out one more set of papers—photographs from Jamison's body camera and the DNA reports. "Mr. Cochran, do you have a twin?"

His insult morphed into confusion, and his arms fell from covering his chest. "No. It's public knowledge that I'm an only child."

"An only child who won first place in the Virginia State Science Fair for a robotics project when he was a child. How proud your parents must have been."

Instantly, the boy from the newspaper article emerged in the man across from her, nostalgic pride in his achievement evident. It fell as fast as it had risen, and Cochran shook his head. "Dad said it was just a toy, and I should pursue business like he did. That's where the money is, and the power of influence. That's where I could best make my mark, and he was right. Look at all I've accomplished. I'm a powerful leader of the House of Representatives. What I do makes a difference."

Jenna shrugged. "I think a guy who invents a robotic arm that can assist disabled people in living a fuller, more independent life is more important, but that's just me. This is the coffee cup you had your aide throw away at the polling place we visited. This is the DNA profile from the rim of that cup, and this is the DNA profile report from a drop of sweat swiped off the bullet recovered from Judge Hamden's body. They are identical. Furthermore, we're currently running the sample CSI Wilcox collected from you earlier this afternoon and expect it to also be an exact match. You wore gloves when you handled the bullet, which was smart," she admitted, "but you couldn't help that one drop of sweat.

Oh, and we found the half box of matching bullets in a drawer in your hobby room. I suppose you had to make a lot of practice runs, perfecting your design and technique, target practicing to ensure nothing went wrong. Most people's attempts at printing a plastic gun blow up when they fire them, but not yours. No, you made sure it would do exactly what you designed it to do. It was almost the perfect crime."

Jenna made sure to catch Cochran's eye when she regarded him in appreciation of his intellect and skill, an admiring look beaming in her gaze.

"I demand that an independent lab perform a fresh analysis on both Congressman Cochran's DNA and what your lab recovered from the slug," Wurth charged, wagging a finger toward Captain Myers. "Clearly, your people made a mistake. Now, about getting my client out of here. There is no reason for a respected U.S. Congressman to spend the night in a common *lock-up*." He uttered the word with disdain, his nose shooting into the air.

Jenna kept her focus on the perpetrator. "Congressman Cochran, in light of this mountain of evidence against you, are you still maintaining your innocence?"

"Of course, I didn't kill anybody. It's just a ridiculous accusation." His brows pulled down as far as the corners of his mouth, looking like a child who'd been scolded and sent to the corner for a timeout.

Sighing, Jenna gathered her sheets back into their folder, shook her head slowly, and rose with nonchalant ease. "I must say that I'm disappointed. Here I thought you were this brilliant scientist, shrewd strategist, a powerful man who makes things happen, who goes after what he wants and takes it, when all the while you're just a fool who can be duped and have a murder pinned on him right under his nose, just an idiot who drops his phone in the pool, a user who dumped his first wife after she paid his way through graduate school, a grifter who married his second wife for her trust fund, a little boy who never lived up to Daddy's expectations. I'll bet he asks, 'Nash, why aren't you president by now? You aren't getting any younger.'"

Cochran shot out of his chair, fury flaming his face, as he snarled and thrust a finger toward her. "You stupid bitch! I'm no such thing! You were right the first time—I *do* take what I want. I *am* a brilliant scientist and an unmatched tactician. You won't make this stick, none of it!" He sliced his flattened palm through the air. "I practiced and planned and made sure nothing went wrong. What juror will believe your pile of junk when they can see me on TV when the murder took place? You've got words and numbers on papers—I've got an unbreakable alibi!"

"Nash, sit down and shut your mouth!" screeched his attorney.

Jenna just smiled and held up her folder. "In case you didn't notice, my team already broke your alibi. I'll see you on the stand, Congressman Cochran."

"He won't be convicted," Wurth asserted. "My firm will tie up the courts for years with motions and appeals. You'd be wise to let this matter go."

"Is that so?" Captain Myers stood beside Jenna, returning a skeptical look to the lawyer. "Since the founding of this nation, well over a hundred federal officials, congressmen, and executive branch members have been found guilty of crimes in a court of law. While the majority were for financial corruption—accepting bribes, tax evasion, and the like—a few were crimes against individuals for domestic violence and sexual offenses. Mr. Cochran will have the distinction of being the first sitting U.S. congressman convicted of murdering his opponent. Lieutenant Ferrari, please bring in ADA Altman and have Sergeant Owens standing by to take our distinguished prisoner to booking."

"Yes, sir." She exited to two men's tirades as both shouted their objections simultaneously, her satisfaction radiating from the inside out.

"You played that well, Jenna." Dr. Grayson met her in the hallway. "Not a clear 'I did it,' but close enough to a confession, I think."

"Thank you, Jane," she replied, using her therapist's preferred designation. "His lawyers will try to tie it up and postpone as long as they can."

"You built a solid case," affirmed Chief Clarkson. "I understand why Captain Myers speaks so highly of you, Lieutenant Ferrari. Now, I must prepare a press statement while you ladies carry on." He tipped an imaginary hat at them and walked away.

Jane touched Jenna's arm and smiled. "You went out on a limb and caught your prize. What the courts do isn't up to us; you've done a stellar job."

"It was my team," Jenna explained. "They—"

"Follow the example of excellence set by their leader." Dr. Grayson's smile broadened into a grin. "Now, go congratulate them, and get Bennet and Ron over here. We don't want to leave poor Jerome in there alone with those two forever."

"Aye-aye, Doctor," she quipped with a salute and a suppressed grin. "And thank you."

As Jenna headed down the hall, Jane's voice rang behind her. "Session next week?"

Jenna, who could practically feel the sunbeams caressing her skin, threw back over her shoulder, "No can do. We'll be in Florida on a beach somewhere!"

28

Destin, Florida, a week later

"Look, Jenna!" Randi enthused from her beach lounge chair as she pointed at some seashell or whatever it was. She looked adorable, with one hand holding her straw hat down, sunglasses covering half her face, and long, bare legs, glistening with lotion, stretched out, making Jenna salivate.

Nash Cochran had been booked, his mug shot taken, and he spent the night in jail. As Jenna had suspected, Judge Williams granted him bail but set it at five hundred thousand dollars because of Cochran's income bracket and the compelling stack of evidence. It took a couple of days to complete all the associated paperwork, and Jenna asked Captain Myers if she could keep Hendrix. "He might be a kid, but he's a whiz and really helped make this case." Myers had agreed.

The captain had another bonus up his sleeve. Friday afternoon, a delivery van arrived, and two workers with a dolly rolled a giant box through the lobby and into the DNA lab. Jenna had been stunned speechless. "Is this what I think it is?" she had exclaimed in amazement.

"Why, Ferrari, whatever do you mean?" he deadpanned, before giving her a wink. "The chief was impressed with us, so, while he was feeling generous, I put in the request. Say hello to the RapidHIT ID System from Applied Biosystems. It's FBI-approved and top of the line. Don't say I never gave you anything."

Jenna couldn't help herself. In her excitement, forgetting to be official, she sprang up on her toes and threw her arms around her captain's neck in a big hug. Myers laughed.

"I know, I know. If we had had this unit when we started the case, we could have arrested Cochran before he made his acceptance speech, and it will prove extremely helpful going forward, so you're welcome."

Regaining her dignity and knuckling a tear from under her eye, Jenna answered, "Thank you."

Tyr had blubbered something about the captain being like Odin, her being like Thor, and the new DNA machine being the oddly-named hammer Thor used on the giants. He went on to dub Jamison as Freya and Owens as Vidar, some burly warrior-god who survives the end of the world. Jenna decided he had them all properly pegged.

With enthusiastic animation, Randi scrambled out of her low-to-the-sand chair and romped to where the surf lapped at the white, powdered sand. Some people call it 'sugar sand' because it is so soft, fine, and cool on the feet, even when the sun beats down. Gazing over the emerald waters with their gently curling, white-foam waves, listening to the rhythmic lap of the tide, feeling the twin delights of warm sun and cool breeze, relaxed Jenna more than she had remembered it could. She could lie in her reclined chair with an ice-cold beer in her hand all day long. But not Randi. She had to explore, to experience, to interact with the nature surrounding them. They had already spent an hour in the salt water, which was therapy itself, and now her wife was chasing seashells.

Not wishing to seem disinterested, Jenna had just worked her way out of her comfy seat to stand when Randi rushed over, a child's glow on her face and something wiggly in her hands.

"Look, Jenna—it's a ghost crab! Isn't it just the cutest little thing?"

Jenna blinked. In Randi's palm sat a tiny crab, no more than two inches wide, with two black eyes sticking up from its buff head, honey-colored legs, and bleached white pinchers writhing from its sandy shell. It seemed to give Jenna a curious look and waved a claw at her.

"Aren't you afraid it'll pinch you?" she asked Randi as she leaned in for a closer inspection. The little crustacean *was* cute. It exhibited personality. Who would have thought?

"Nah," Randi dismissed as she stroked the back of its shell with a gentle finger. "And even if it did, it wouldn't hurt. I'm sending it soothing vibes, so it won't be afraid of me. Do you want to hold it?"

The crab was so small and vulnerable, even if it was waving sharp pinchers at her. Jenna stretched out a finger, and its eyes followed it, like the creature was assessing if she presented a danger. Randi flattened her palm and moved her other finger away so Jenna could feel its shell. She noticed the texture, the warmth it had absorbed from the sun, and how it backed away at her touch. Randi had to thrust her other palm up to catch it so it wouldn't fall.

"I don't think it likes me," Jenna determined. She hadn't expected the disappointment she felt, as the detective wasn't accustomed to playing with small creatures. Actually, she'd never even thought about it. Her cat was one thing, but this was ... something wild and wonderful. She moved her hand away slowly and bent closer to look the crab straight in its stick-up eyes. "I won't hurt you, you know. I might not have Randi's enchanted touch, but it's not like I'm a pelican or a seagull and will eat you or something. Now, I might love crab legs, but yours are *way* too small."

Randi giggled, beaming at Jenna with such deep appreciation that the often-thrown-around word 'love' didn't seem to do it justice.

The bond Jenna sensed with her wife surpassed her wildest imaginings, and, in that moment, she felt especially blessed.

"Come with me to take it back to the water, so we can make sure a bird doesn't just scoop it up."

Who was Jenna to deny this spectacular mother of their child anything? "Alright, but don't let it pinch me," she warned teasingly.

Together they padded across the pristine sand, surrounded by locals and snowbirds alike. Children built sandcastles, teens threw a frisbee, young mothers splashed in the water with kids on their floats, young men combed the beach, checking out the women, while older couples lay on towels, held down bag chairs under umbrellas, or soaked up the sun. Brilliant yellow beams glistened off the water under an azure sky adorned with a scattering of fluffy clouds.

"Have you ever noticed that the ebb and flow of the tides are like the earth breathing?" Randi mentioned. The observation arrested Jenna, as she hadn't ever considered it. "I mean, all living things have to breathe, right? So, it makes sense that the Earth, being like a giant living organism, would need to breathe too. Think about it; our bodies are made up of billions of cells, some working in conjunction with others, some doing their own thing, a few rogue ones out to do damage. The people, plants, animals, rocks, water, air, are all parts of Earth, like our cells are parts of us. And Earth is just one tiny planet that's part of the Milky Way galaxy, which in turn is just a minuscule piece of the unending Universe. We all have to breathe—sustenance flows in, waste products exhale, the tide flows in, the tide flows out."

Jenna marveled at the things that Randi's brain conjured. "But doesn't the moon cause the tides with its gravity?" They stopped as a small wave splashed their feet in the wet sand where the gulf met the land. As it retracted, it sucked against Jenna's ankles and she glanced down in observation of the constant, never-ending phenomena.

"It does," Randi confirmed. "It's just all so intriguing, so wonderful and awe-inspiring." She looked at the sandy crab in her hand. "Like this little guy—or girl; I can't tell them apart. It's so adorable and fragile, with a unique genetic makeup, unlike any other creature on the planet, even other ghost crabs. Notice its perfect camouflage, how it blends in with the sand."

She crouched, setting the crustacean at the cusp of where the surf lapped the shore. "If it hadn't moved, I'd have never seen it. If God cares enough to create such individual variety, to so artfully craft a seemingly insignificant part of the food chain, with a face like this, with the instinct to recognize I was no threat to it and hold its claws from pinching me, a tiny creature with an abbreviated lifespan, just think how much love, care, and intention the Creator is putting into forming Jellybean. Life is a miracle."

Randi stood up, lowering her gaze to the crab. Jenna watched with her as it scurried sideways and burrowed into the wet sand. No seagull scooped it up—at least not while they stood watch. Jenna supposed the birds had to eat too. The song about the circle of life from the movie popped into her mind along with a child's sense of wonder at the complexity of the Universe and everything in it. It couldn't all merely be random; the physics and biology came together too smoothly. Whether he, she, or they cared about what happened on this planet, Randi was right about one thing—an intelligence, far surpassing man's, designed everything and brought it into being. Nothing else made sense.

"You know, you're going to have me believing in these miracles of yours if you keep being so delightfully compelling," she said. "The earth, a living being? And we're like its cells?" With an amused smile, Jenna took Randi's hand, entwining their fingers, enriched by the connection. "What *don't* you think about?"

They began a leisurely stroll, toes digging into cool, wet sand, clear water advancing over their feet, then sucking back into the gulf, its low roar a soothing white noise. Randi resecured her hat with her free hand, turning to Jenna with a dour expression.

"I don't dream up preposterous ways to murder someone under the delusion that I'll never be caught." She squeezed Jenna's hand, a triumphant smile invigorating her face. "But my stupendously brilliant detective wife foiled the perpetrator's evil plan and saved the day!"

Jenna laughed and shook her head, a gust swirling her short black hair around her face. She needed a cut. "I wish I could've saved Judge Hamden."

Randi stopped right there on the panhandle beach of a red state, caught Jenna's cheeks between her palms, and kissed her soundly. "Nobody could have known ahead of time. You are the victor, and he couldn't have been saved. Now."

Randi re-entangled their fingers and resumed the stroll. "What are we going to call Jellybean for real? Did you have any names picked out?"

Casting a worried glance at Randi, Jenna asked, "You weren't planning on Leia or Hermine, were you? Please, not Hermine!" Jenna let out in humorous horror, though the thought of such a nerdy name was the thing of nightmares.

Randi's laugh was endearing. Her cheeks appeared red, but, whether from embarrassment or the sun, Jenna wasn't sure.

"No, silly. Although some fantasy character names have been floating around, calling to me."

Jenna groaned and rolled her eyes. "What names?"

"I like Rey, from the new Star Wars," she clarified. "It's cool and different without being weird. And Elsa—what a beautiful name, what a strong woman." She snuck a peek at Jenna, who didn't balk at the name. "And I also really like Trinity—you know, the hot, badass warrior gal from the Matrix movies, not the Father, Son, and Holy Ghost. Although ..." She stopped talking as a faraway aspect captured her expression.

"And if the baby turns out to be a boy?" Jenna posed.

Snapping back to the here and now, Randi drew in her shoulders, poking her head out like a turtle and cringed. "Luke?"

Jenna burst into laughter.

"Or, or," Randi raced to offer more names. "I've always loved the name Michael. And nothing ridiculous like Gandolf or Frodo, but Lance, short for Lancelot—not the full name, or he'll be teased mercilessly. But you need to suggest some names too."

Jenna smirked playfully and bumped hips with Randi as a small V of gulls squawked overhead. "Not Renita, and I know he's the father, but two Vinces in the family are enough to keep straight. I wouldn't mind an Italian name, though. Leo—you like Leonardo da Vinci, don't you?"

"Who doesn't?" Randi laughed as if it were an absurd question. "He was only one of the most creative and brilliant minds of all time."

"And then there's Michelangelo," Jenna mentioned, "another Renaissance guy, the one who carved the David."

"I know who he is, love." Randi's tone was patronizing, but Jenna supposed she deserved it.

"Or, like you suggested, maybe first name Michael and middle name Angelo. Oh!" Jenna came to an abrupt halt, pivoting to face Randi. "Whose last name will we use?"

Randi shrugged. "Ferrari-McLeod, or McLeod-Ferrari. Either's fine with me."

Jenna stood, her toes buried in sand, while she quickly considered the options. "We don't have to decide today, but Ferrari-McLeod would put him or her closer to the front of the alphabet. I remember in school, everything was alphabetical, especially your place in lines. Better for our kid to be near the front, don't you think?"

Randi's smile turned so adoring, so magical, so captivating that it could have lured a sailor from his life at sea to remain on dry land for all eternity. "You think of the darnedest things. Not like me. Your ideas are practical, and I love you for it."

Jenna brushed her lips in a quick kiss so the natives wouldn't descend on them, thumping Bibles or issuing lectures. "Whatever we decide, it'll be wonderful. But this I'm putting my foot down about." Her expression turned commanding, and Randi's eyes widened in curiosity.

"What, sweetie?" She blinked her lids across those luscious brown eyes that Jenna could swear held all the secrets of the Universe behind them.

Trying to keep a straight face, Jenna decreed, "The kid's nickname is Jellybean."

MORE BOOKS BY EDALE LANE

Tales from Norvegr
Sigrid and Elyn: A Tale from Norvegr
https://www.amazon.com/dp/B0B5W48342
Legacy of the Valiant: A Tale from Norvegr
https://www.amazon.com/dp/B0BZK7Y655
War and Solace: A Tale from Norvegr
https://www.amazon.com/dp/B0CGP4WVYP
Jorunn, Shieldmaiden of Hárfell (prequel to The Long Winter of Miðgarðr)
https://dl.bookfunnel.com/bpowqyeg4j
The Long Winter of Miðgarðr
https://www.amazon.com/dp/B0DKP2MWD2
Viking Quest
https://www.amazon.com/dp/B097NTZVPC

The Lessons in Murder Series
Meeting over Murder
https://www.amazon.com/dp/B0B7R69R7B
Skimming around Murder
https://www.amazon.com/dp/B0B9R6FJWL
New Year in Murder
https://www.amazon.com/dp/B0BDQSPT6L
Heart of Murder

https://www.amazon.com/dp/B0BQQS57FY
Reprise in Murder
https://www.amazon.com/dp/B0C2YDKLSB
Homecoming in Murder
https://www.amazon.com/dp/B0C7M2VKSH
Queen of Murder
https://www.amazon.com/dp/B0CKRYLNSW
Cold in Murder
https://www.amazon.com/dp/B0CSXMBJLJ
Foreseen in Murder
https://www.amazon.com/dp/B0D3G5JMLP
Matrimony in Murder
https://www.amazon.com/dp/B0DDJY4JXY
Innocent of Murder
https://www.amazon.com/dp/B0DRZ2G3RM
Alibi for Murder
https://www.amazon.com/dp/B0F86FKN98

SapphicLover69
https://www.amazon.com/dp/B0DCZRW2K
Cash Target
https://www.amazon.com/dp/B0F2WXJRJK

Daring Duplicity: The Wellington Mysteries, Vol.1
https://www.amazon.com/dp/B09QDTF9YN
Perilous Passages: The Wellington Mysteries, Vol. 2
https://www.amazon.com/dp/B0B16FWN63
Daunting Dilemmas: The Wellington Mysteries, Vol. 3
https://www.amazon.com/dp/B0BMDQ8TLC

Atlantis, Land of Dreams
https://www.amazon.com/dp/B0D7TB52CG

Heart of Sherwood
https://www.amazon.com/dp/B07W4M3R5L
Walks with Spirits
https://www.amazon.com/dp/B09VBGQF27/

The Night Flyer Series
Merchants of Milan, book one
https://www.amazon.com/dp/B083H6WNKD
Secrets of Milan, book two
https://www.amazon.com/dp/B088HFM7Q5
Chaos in Milan, book three
https://www.amazon.com/dp/B08Q7H6DFX
Missing in Milan, book four
https://www.amazon.com/dp/B09CNXF1CX
Shadows over Milan, book five
https://www.amazon.com/dp/B09KF53VTZ

Visit My Website:
https://www.authoredalelane.com
Follow me on Goodreads (Don't forget to leave a quick review!)
https://www.goodreads.com/author/show/15264354.Edale_Lane
Follow me on BookBub:
https://www.bookbub.com/profile/edale-lane
Newsletter sign-up link:
https://bit.ly/3qkGn95

About the Author

Edale Lane is an Amazon Best-selling author and winner of Rainbow, Lesfic Bard, and Imaginarium Awards. Her sapphic historical fiction and mystery stories feature women leading the action and entice readers with likable characters, engaging storytelling, and vivid world-creation.

Lane holds a bachelor's degree in music education, a master's in history, and taught school for 24 years before embarking on an adventure driving an 18-wheeler over-the-road. She is a mother of two, Grammy of three, and a doggy mom. A native of Vicksburg, MS, Lane now lives her dream of being a full-time author in beautiful Chilliwack, BC, with her long-time life partner.

Enjoy free e-books and other promotional offerings while staying up to date with what Edale Lane is writing next when you sign up for her newsletter.

https://bit.ly/3qkGn95

Printed in Dunstable, United Kingdom

67239090R00118